LEGEND OF THE AMAZONS

THE

BOOK ONE

AWAKENING

JOHN G MINICHIELLI

The Awakening
Legend of the Amazons, Book One
by John G Minichielli

Contributors
John Nelson, Bookworks, LTD
Cynthia Mitchell, Editing
Cover design / interior layout, Suzanne Fyhrie Parrott

Cover image "portrait of the woman" © Dmytro Buianskyi; shutterstock.com
Back cover image "Old battle axe" © woverwolf; shutterstock.com
Illustration "wolf" © Suzanne Fyhrie Parrott

ISBN   978-0-9717767-1-5 (ebk)
        978-0-9717767-2-2 (pbk)

CONTENTS

PROLOGUE

Mattie Foster, short for Madeline, would have to be considered by the majority of the world's population as one of the most privileged people on the planet. Mattie grew up as the only child in one of the richest families, if not the richest family, in the world. She also just happened to be beautiful, intelligent, and highly educated. The unbelievably terrifying story she would soon hear from her somewhat estranged mother, Melissa Croft, would not only change her life in ways she could never have imagined, it would eventually change the course of evolution for the entire human population. But we are getting ahead of ourselves—let's begin the journey here:

Mattie leaned over her chipped oak desk and reread the last paragraph of her paper for the Journal of Evolutionary Biology. She hoped that her research on the OvaHimba tribe of northern Namibia, Africa, would put another nail into the heretical theory that genetic drift could even compete with Darwin's natural selection as the driving force of evolution. She looked up and swatted the loose strands of blond hair that had fallen over her forehead. Mattie again smiled at the framed picture on the wall of her bare-chested photo, her arms looped around two equally exposed women of the nude Dassanach tribe of Ethiopia. The photo, which had been published in another journal, had scandalized her mother and had created a further division in their already strained relationship. The fact that she had followed after her father and preferred field research to her mother's linguistic study of languages, or philology, which she had once characterized, to her mother's great displeasure, as linguistic "pillaging," didn't help to repair the relationship.

What did she expect? On every Christmas or spring break during her adolescence, Mattie would desert her New England boarding school and fly to join them at some remote and exotic location around the world. Earlier on she had become fascinated by the great diversity of people she had encountered on these trips, and even more so when later learning of their uniform genetic makeup. There is less genetic diversity among humans than any other mammal, or a 99.5 percent similarity. So Mattie naturally gravitated toward an interest in evolution. In fact she had asked for a copy of Darwin's Red Notebook—his penciled notes from his famed HMS Beagle trip to the Galapagos Islands—for her twelfth birthday. Her father had been curious, her mother skeptical—another passing fad she thought—but Mattie followed that with a request on her next birthday for a pair of Darwin finches, which she subsequently named Charles and Emma.

They had both tried to steer Mattie away from her interest in evolutionary biology, which had only been introduced in college curricula in the 1980s and wasn't, in their minds, reputable enough. But Mattie persisted, a trait that her grandfather, Connor Croft, the pharmaceutical giant, had claimed came from him. She defied both parents and went to UCLA in Los Angeles for her undergraduate degree in biology with an emphasis on evolutionary ecology and afterward enrolled in postgraduate programs at the University of Chicago. There she met and married the paleontologist Everett Foster, and she traveled the world with him for several years, doing her own research on genetic drift and other such evolutionary theories. But after a while she found her husband's interests as boring as he, and she split from Foster but retained his name. Her aging grandfather wanted her back in Miami, and so he made a huge endowment to the University of Miami for a department of evolutionary biology, with his granddaughter as its head, bestowing on her a permanent tenured professorship and unlimited funds for her research. This was smart of him because if he had just given his granddaughter the money, she would have lost half of it in her subsequent divorce, but, as set up, it was beyond the reach of her husband's pernicious lawyers.

Mattie's cell phone chimed. She picked up the iPhone and glanced at the caller ID: Dr. Joel Marcum, her mother's personal physician. She let it go to voice mail and turned off the volume, returning to her article. She did note that the message was long, but then Joel was longwinded, especially when making solicitations for her mother. Thirty minutes later the phone chimed again. This time it was her mother, Melissa. She was very ill, and the prognosis wasn't good, so Mattie took the call.

"Mattie, is that you?" the voice asked.

"Depends on what you want," she said rather coolly, still looking down at the article and catching another typo.

"I want . . . I need to speak with you now," Melissa said, her voice strained and breaking up.

"Mother. I'm rather busy and need to get this article off today.

"Madeline, I am going to die soon, and I have something urgent to discuss with you."

Her mother was prone to melodramatic flourishes, but this somehow had the ring of truth to it, or was it the raised tenor of her voice that bothered Mattie. "Mother, really, I can't possibly drive over today. I mean, it's already two o'clock and the weekday traffic will be horrendous."

"Part of what I have to say pertains to your field of interest."

Mattie shook her head. "My field of interest! You mean evolutionary biology?" She didn't wait for an answer. "You despise the subject, so how in the world could anything you have to say—"

"There's a reason for that, and it has to do with the . . . expedition I took to the Amazon in the mid-1960s, the one I've always refused to talk with you about."

This did grab Mattie's attention. She slid the magnifying glass apparatus to the side. Her mother had never mentioned this expedition to her while growing up, and it wasn't until her grandfather let it slip that he once thought he had lost Melissa for good "on that damn expedition to the Amazon Jungle," that she had even learned about it. She questioned her mother, but she merely dismissed the subject, until Mattie did some research in the family archives and discovered a photo of her mother with two explorers in an Amazon River town. She showed her mother the photo and asked for an explanation; Melissa grabbed the photo, tore it up, shoved the pieces into her pants pocket, and wouldn't say a thing about it, ever.

"So, this is a deathbed confession?"

Her mother coughed on the other end of the phone. "You can be so cold sometimes." She paused, and Mattie could hear Marcum telling her to calm herself.

"But to answer your question . . . yes, I guess you could say that."

Mattie looked out the window to the distant freeway jammed with cars, as was the Causeway to Key Biscayne. "Okay, Mother. But it'll take an hour to get there."

"Hurry, Mattie. I don't have much time." Her mother then clicked off the phone. In the past she would've called her father, or even her grandfather, to get some clarity on one of her mother's insistent entreaties. But sadly they were both gone, her father to a fall down a well in northern India ten years ago and Connor to cancer years before that. So, all she had, or at least in terms of immediate family, was her mother. Mattie placed the ten-page article back into its blue sleeve and locked it in her top desk drawer.

Fifty minutes later she pulled up to her parents' seaside estate in Key Biscayne, which had been in the family for many generations. The circular driveway was wide, and she pulled up and parked next to her mother's old Bentley. One of the servants, Edward Balsam, an old black man who had worked for them for thirty years, stepped out onto the porch.

Mattie stepped out of her BMW Z4 Roadster. She was

rather tall, 5 feet 10 inches, with green eyes and curly blond hair, wearing a white summer dress, fashionable sunglasses, and a wide-brimmed sunhat. She walked up to the house. "Hey Eddie, they keeping you busy?"

The hunched-over old man in his late 60s with close-cropped grey curly hair shook his head and looked very sad. "Ms. Melissa isn't doing well at all. Don't think she has much more time left, Mattie."

She almost answered him with a characteristic smart remark, but could see that Balsam was hurting. He had been very close to her father and took his sudden death badly. Her mother had to give him a month off with pay to get over it. They'd probably have to hospitalize him after her mother's passing. She now followed Balsam into the house, across the blue-flower-patterned marble floor, and up the long ornate staircase to the second floor. Her mother's bedroom studio now took up half the upstairs, its double doors with glass slats to the right of the stairs. The room itself had spectacular views of Biscayne Bay and the Atlantic Ocean to the East.

In the wide hallway, converted to a waiting room and medical center, was a retinue of white-clad nurses busy with their oxygen replacement canisters, IV tubes, and a pharmacy of medication bottles, some of which were in a glass-front refrigerator. The male nurses stopped and nodded to Mattie. He also acted as her mother's driver and bodyguard, and her contentious daughter was definitely someone that required a leery watch.

Dr. Marcum stepped out of the inner sanctum and closed the door behind him. He took Mattie by the arm and walked her to the other end of the hallway and out of an earshot of the domestic help, as he would no doubt call them. "Mattie, I'm glad you came. Your mother's breathing is shallow, and her heartbeat is slowing down. I would've put her on hospice care a week ago, but she wouldn't hear of it."

She looked at the man and could see his sincere concern. He had been the family physician forever. Marcum had even overseen her delivery at the hospital some forty-two years ago. "Joel, I'm sure you've done everything possible for her. You know how much my mother trusts you."

He nodded his head. "But she wants to talk to you alone, and I'm afraid to leave her side at this stage."

"You'll only be thirty feet away. I'm sure you can give me one of those electronic summoning devices." He nodded his head. "I'll keep it in my hand, and if I think she needs you, I'll call you."

Marcum let out a sigh and walked Mattie back to the doorway. He motioned to the male nurse, who stepped over and handed him the caller. "I can sit in a chair at the far end of the room and listen to music on my iPod. Won't hear a thing," the man said.

The doctor shook his head. "I suggested as much, but Ms. Melissa wants this talk private, and Gerald," he looked down at the man's suspect iPod, "don't even think about recording it remotely."

"No, Sir." He handed the caller to Marcum who passed it on to Mattie.

The doctor now opened the door and stepped inside while she followed after him. The nurse sitting by Melissa's side stood up and stepped back. "Henrietta, that'll be all for now."

The nurse left as the two of them stepped over to the bed. Her mother's eyes were closed. "Melissa, there is someone here to see you."

The old woman slowly opened her eyes. "Oh, Mattie, you came." She lifted her hand off the bed, and Mattie sat down in the nurse's chair and took her mother's brown-spotted and wrinkled hand.

"Yes, Mother. Sorry if I sounded reluctant, but I've been busy."

"It's okay. I understand, but now you're here, and we need to talk." She looked up at the doctor.

"Well," Dr. Marcum said, "I'll be just outside the door if you need me."

"Joel, I don't want anybody listening in."

"I wouldn't think of it, Ma'am." The doctor now turned and walked out the door, carefully closing it behind him.

The old woman closed her eyes as if to summon energy from her depleted reserves. Mattie waited patiently for her mother to speak, feeling a bit guilty now about her obstinate refusal to come to what appeared to be her mother's deathbed. Finally Melissa opened her eyes, but there was a distant look in them that her daughter had never seen.

"The archeologist Sterling Hawks came to me around the mid-60s with this wild tale of an unknown tribe of light-skinned women, uncontacted by Western explorers, but widely known to some of the indigenous Amazon Indian tribes of western Brazil. He had heard of them from an uncontacted tribe that he had first discovered deep in the jungle."

Mattie shook her head. "Impossible. I mean, that was fifty years ago, and surely somebody . . ."

Melissa shook her head to silence her daughter. "I was skeptical to say the least, and you can imagine Sterling's first reaction. It appears that one of their tribesmen upon hearing the legend had gone in search of them, but was never heard from again. And then, a year later, they found one morning a light-skinned male baby wrapped in leaves just outside the village. The boy, who was adopted by the tribe, was then fifteen years old, and Sterling gave him a thorough examination and concluded that he had few Indian genetic traits. This was indeed puzzling."

"Mother, really. Some white explorer screwed an Indian, and this was their excuse to explain the child, so the government wouldn't come looking for him."

"Yes, Sterling assumed as much, but then they showed him a bronze artifact, which he was able to barter for with 'magic lights,' or flashlights. They claimed it was from this Amazon women tribe, but wouldn't say how they got it. Sterling brought it back and handed me the metallurgical analysis: it was part of an axe forged thousands of years ago, and, by its bronze composition, somewhere in Mesopotamia. He even showed me a similar axe, this one complete and double-sided, on display at the National Museum of Iraq, or before it was despoiled by looters during the Gulf War."

Mattie stared back at her mother with renewed interest. The woman was one of the least imaginative people she knew, and wasn't given, unlike her daughter, to flights of fantasy. "And you're telling me this now. If it's true, do you know what this could mean for my research . . . an unknown and uncontacted tribe of light-skinned women in the Amazon rain forest? They would be a treasure trove of genetic data."

Melissa squeezed her daughter's hand. "You need to hear the whole story."

Mattie studied her mother, who until now had shown no signs of dementia. She wondered if her mind was clouded over.

"There is a very good reason why I didn't tell you and have you traipsing off into the jungle after them."

"Oh, really. I've got to hear this," Mattie said with some skepticism.

"Well, that's part of the story I have to tell you. So, settle in, and let's start from the beginning."

CHAPTER ONE

Melissa Croft continued to study the photograph of the ancient Mesopotamian axe from the National Museum of Iraq that archeologist Sterling Hawks had handed her. She was in her early thirties, blond-headed with green eyes, her skin almost China white and lacking the suntan of most other southern Floridians, even if it was still April. She had been sipping her morning coffee in her office at the University of Miami and reading the Herald article about My Fair Lady winning the Oscar for Best Picture last night. Hawks, a longtime friend of the family, had arrived unannounced.

"This is all very interesting, Sterling, but what does it have to do with me?"

"I plan on mounting an expedition to the Amazon River basin of western Brazil to seek out this tribe of Amazon women."

She leveled the aging explorer with eyes used to discerning fact from fiction. "But no one will fund such a wild goose chase so you need a secondary protocol."

Hawks ran his hand through his thin graying hair, the lines on his forehead wrinkling, his mouth twisted in an ironic smirk. "Yes, very perceptive, my dear. You can imagine National Geographic's reaction."

Melissa sneered. "Oh, God, Sterling. You didn't?" Hawks shrugged his shoulders. "What did you promise them, photos of bare-chested white Amazon women?" The mere thought of it made her titter with laughter. It also stirred something in her.

Melissa sat back in her chair, picked up her bone china cup, with its delicate rose flower design, and sipped her coffee. She stared at Hawks over its lip. What a crafty old bastard, she thought.

Instead of first going to her father's pharmaceutical company and pitching him on the possible medicinal plant finds in this area and their drug potential, he approached her, knowing full well the allure of her sexual orientation. Melissa was bisexual and in a relationship with a professor of the romance languages, who was of Scandinavian descent, although it was running its course and wouldn't last much longer. She did like those Nordic women. She could also trace her interest in women back to her childhood fascination with Greek mythology and history, which were replete with accounts of a race of warrior women. Herodotus linked them to the Scythians, a people who lived on the shores of the Black Sea in what would be modern-day Ukraine. Their Queen Hippolyta fought in the Trojan Wars. There are even sculptures in the Temple of Apollo at Bassae of Hercules fighting these Amazons. Theirs was a women-only tribe who only permitted sex with men once a year to perpetuate their race; the male offspring were either killed or sent back to their fathers, and the girls were trained to hunt and to be warriors.

"You realize, besides being utterly preposterous, your tale relates back to the Greek legends of a warrior women tribe they called Amazons, who had sex with men for procreation only and returned the male offspring to their fathers or his tribe, like what your tribe describes."

"Yes, isn't that fascinating," Hawks said. Melissa just stared back at him incredulously. "You know the Amazon River is said to have been named by the Spanish explorer Francisco de Orellana after he had a fierce battle with a tribe of women warriors."

Melissa tilted her head. "The accepted etymology is from the Portuguese Amazonas, the boat destroyer."

"See! Exactly why I need you. If I contact this tribe, you'll have to communicate with them."

Melissa couldn't help but laugh. Hawks was sounding like a snake-oil salesman. "I'm a philologist who studies ancient languages; you need a linguist, if perchance you should . . .

stumble on them."

Hawks smiled. "Ancient languages like Sumerian or its derivatives, which the inscription on the axe suggests?"

Melissa took a magnifying glass off her desk and studied the axe with its faint inscriptions. "It's definitely Sumerian cuneiform but where it was beginning to merge into Akkadian in the early Bronze Age in Mesopotamia."

She now looked up at Hawks. "The question is, how did it get to the Amazon River basin? Maybe the aforementioned Spanish explorers?" she asked, but rather weakly.

"Why would they need a four-thousand-year-old bronze axe? They had more formidable steel weapons."

Melissa's eyes narrowed. "Yes, and blankets infected with smallpox."

Hawks winced as if expecting another one of Melissa's diatribes on the subject of native decimation, but she backed off. She stood up, stepped over to her bookshelf, pulled down a book on Greek mythology, and thumbed through it. Melissa found the page with the sculpture on the frieze of the Treasury of the Athenians at Delphi showing the Greek soldiers battling Amazon women warriors. She showed it to Hawks.

"If there is even a chance in hell that there is something to this . . . wild tale, we must pursue it."

Hawks broke out in a wide grin. "So, where does that leave us?"

"Well, we need to approach my father's ethnobotanist, Adam Caruthers. Tell me. This tribe you discovered, do they have plant cures that would make suitable pharmaceuticals?"

"Yes, in fact they do, like the other recently discovered tribes in the area, but that's not the real payoff." Melissa looked back at him skeptically. "It appears that this tribe of women doesn't hunt game, or so the rumor goes, and only fishes in the high-water season."

"So they must have a potent source of plant protein?" she asked.

Hawks smiled. "Yes, but also my tribe collects the dark purple, olive-sized fruit from a local palm with a striped stem, the pataua. It tastes like olive oil, and so I brought back a sample and had it tested. Its protein content is comparable to animal protein, much higher than traditional legume sources."

"Good. I don't want to mention the woman tribe to Caruthers or my father, and just stick with the plants that your newly discovered tribe uses and leave it at that, with the idea that we may look for other tribes in the area."

"Yes, after my foray at National Geographic, I agree.

Several days later Melissa and Hawks met with Adam Caruthers at the company's greenhouse outside of town. Here Croft Pharmaceuticals were growing plants, mostly from Southeast Asia, which the local populations have used for medicinal purposes for centuries. They walked down rows of plants and then came to a wet, swampy area and stepped onto a long wooden platform that jutted out into this cultivated mangrove. Adam now reached over and lifted the spiny holly leaves of the Acanthus ilicifolius, or Sea Holly of Southeast Asia. "In Indonesia its roots are chewed and used as a cure for poisoned arrows; elsewhere the roots cure snakebites and its leaves have shown promise in the treatment of rheumatism."

Hawks reached over and touched another leaf and ran his fingers over it. Melissa stood back so as not to dirty the cuffs of her khaki trousers. Caruthers stood up and led them back to his office and laboratory located nearby. "Believe it or not, we're the first pharmaceutical company in America looking into plant cures from rain forests."

"That's surprising," Hawks said.

"It's obvious to all that there are bounties to be had, but the process of finding plants, extracting and testing for their pharmaceutical properties, is long and laborious, and of course costly."

"My father, the visionary."

"Yes, indeed. Connor 'Rushes in Where Angels Fear to Tread.' It's his motto, adapted from Alexander Pope, I believe."

Melissa laughed. "It's also the title of the E.M. Forster novel, which was required reading in my family."

They reached his office door, but Adam stopped and turned back to her. "Apparently, it sunk in, my dear, if you want to traipse off to the Amazon River basin."

They now stepped into his office with its dehumidifier humming in the background. The overhead fan twirled around and cooled down the still-humid room. Adam offered them coffee or tea, but they both declined. He leaned forward in his chair and picked up the chemical analysis of the palm fruit that Melissa had sent by messenger that morning. He turned to Hawks. "Besides its surprising protein content, what are its medicinal uses?"

"They use it for coughs and, by the symptoms they described, the relief of bronchitis and other respiratory inflammations."

"Well, cough syrup is a multimillion dollar business, which might interest Connor." Adam sat back in his chair, swiveled it around and looked out the window to the rows of plants in the greenhouse. "We've been talking about the Amazon River basin as an incredible source of medicinal plant remedies. No concrete plans to exploit this resource as of yet, but I must say a newly discovered tribe using these kinds of plant remedies would be enticing."

"Yes," Hawks added eagerly, "and you'd be the first on the ground there."

Caruthers smirked. "It's 1965, and nobody else is even considering this kind of expedition." He turned his attention to Melissa. "But what exactly is your interest in such an expedition? I mean, you're a philologist, I believe."

Melissa turned to Hawks in an already-rehearsed exchange. "Should we show him?"

Hawks nodded. "Your father is going to ask the same question. Might as well present the evidence now."

"Evidence?" Caruthers asked. "Is there some archeological discovery as well?"

Hawks now presented their case for the bronze axe, pulling out the artifact and showing it to him, as well as the photo from the Iraq Museum. "Very interesting, but again, what is your interest in it?"

"The faint inscription on the handle is cuneiform, and my expertise is in ancient languages."

"Mesopotamia, 3000 BC?" Adam asked.

"Thereabouts."

"And what the hell is it doing in the middle of Amazon basin with a tribe of Indians?" Adam asked, picking up a magnifying glass and examining the inscriptions.

"That's what we both would like to know."

Caruthers narrowed his eyebrows. "Hawks. You did probe the Indians for its source."

The archeologist smiled winningly. "By that point, I had run out of my 'magic lights,' and they wouldn't tell me."

It took Adam a moment to make the connection. "Oh, flashlights." Hawks nodded. "Well, you probably don't know, but my first love was archeology. When my mother came down with cancer, and there was no help for her, I gravitated toward botany and its possible plant cures."

Melissa now leaned forward over the glass-topped desk, her rather pointed breasts pushing the confines of her white blouse. "So, you're in?"

Adam pushed back from his desk, to keep an objective distance between himself and his boss's provocative daughter. "I'm intrigued, but of course we'll have to run all this by your father." The two of them nodded their heads. "Give me a week or so to put together a formal proposal for an expedition in search of medical pants, using Hawks's find of the medical values of the palm tree fruit oil and his analysis."

"What do you need from us?" Melissa asked.

Caruthers turned to Hawks. "Can you work up the logistics

for the expedition and some estimate as to its cost?"

"Yes. I'll model it after the last trip there. We had one more person, but I'll use the same local guides, and I can cost all of that out."

"Good. How about two weeks from now?"

Hawks shook his head. "It's mid-April, and we have to get there during the rainy season, when the rivers are high, or lose our access into the deep jungle."

"Okay. I see. The end of the week?"

"Perfect," Melissa said, standing up. "Make the appointment for Friday morning. Father usually takes the afternoon off for an extended weekend. It might put him in a more receptive mode."

"Yes. You're right. If he's free, how about ten o'clock?"

Melissa and Sterling nodded their heads, left copies of their material with Caruthers, and left the office for the drive back into town.

Connor Croft, a big man with a surprisingly fit physique for someone in his mid-sixties, read through the proposal one more time. He was a little annoyed that it wasn't sent earlier for his more careful review, but he accepted Sterling's excuse that he, or, they, as it turned out, were pressed for time. While the archeologist was a longtime friend, or associate, to be more accurate, he was also a good salesman pitching a hurriedly put-together expedition. Connor wasn't about to be flimflammed.

Connor now set down the proposal and looked at his chief botanist. "Adam, did you test this palm tree oil yourself?"

The man twisted his mouth. "Didn't have time, but Sterling's laboratory is first class, and its findings line up with other plant oils, and its protein content is more promising than most."

"Sterling, what other remedies is this tribe using?"

"These rainforest shamans have been experimenting with plant cures since before the Spanish arrived, and their shaman has a tent filled with hundreds of ointments, oils, and salves." He paused as Connor considered this cornucopia of possible products. "What interested me was, given the extreme humidity of the rain forest, that I didn't detect signs of wholesale fungal infections, or even gum disease. When I asked, he showed me the bark from a tree that they boiled and drink as a tea. I pointed to my own receding gums, and he gave me an ointment that I've been using that has been very helpful."

Croft considered this pitch. "So, you're running out of it and want to get back before your teeth start to fall out."

Sterling laughed. "Well, I'm also having it chemically analyzed to see if someone can't replicate the formula."

Connor stared back at him. "Give me a sample, and I'll have my people look into it."

"Do I get a finder's fee?" Sterling joked.

"Consider it payback for the cost of this expedition." Sterling nodded his head.

Melissa leaned forward in her chair. "So, you agree to fund it?"

Connor smiled. "I may agree to fund an expedition in search of medicinal plants, but your involvement, my dear, is rather a stretch." Melissa started to defend her position. "Yes, I read your insertion about the bronze artifact and its cuneiform language, and find its discovery, if one can classify it as such without further authentication, rather tangential to the proposal itself."

Before Melissa could respond with one of her contentious remarks and send this meeting sideways, Hawks added. "Connor, there is something very mysterious about this artifact. For one thing the tribe traded it to me for baubles. Seemed like they couldn't wait to get rid of it—that it had some kind of bad juju or something."

"That the shaman couldn't offset?" Connor said with a smirk.

"I think it points to another uncontacted tribe in the area whose origin is a mystery to them." Melissa looked over at Hawks in surprise. "There have been no white explorers this deep into the jungle, today or in the past—no one to drop a five-thousand-year-old artifact into the jungle."

Adam now added. "Such a tribe, this isolated from even other tribes in the basin, might have even more exploitable plant cures."

Connor looked over at his daughter. "Well, I see that if I don't let you go along, despite its questionable practicality, it's going to make for difficult Christmas dinners in the near future."

Melissa's beaming smile was the match of any flimflam artist. "I'll give you a two-year pass on that."

Connor Croft snorted. "Okay, but I'm not going to let you traipse off into the rain forest to research this tribe or search for any other uncontacted tribes without an anthropologist to ease the way."

Sterling asked first. "Connor, I've lived among these tribes for years without incident."

"Well, this bronze axe tells me you may be on to something very different from half-naked Indians sitting around chewing coca leaves." Melissa leaned forward to add her opinion, but her father put up his hand. "This is my condition for your participation. End of discussion."

The three would-be explorers sat back in their chairs. Finally Sterling asked, "Do you have someone in mind?"

"Yes, I do." He now gave the three of them a hard look. "You may think I just sit back and manage the business end of a multimillion dollar enterprise, but any great business requires great foresight. I look out to the marketplace fifteen to twenty-five years from now, and it's going to be filled with indigenous plant remedies. I've been exploiting the resources of the Southeast Asian rain forests and have planned to extend that to the Amazon basin and its indigenous tribes. I know from experience that it'll take an assortment of people, not just explorers, botanists, and scientists, but anthropologists who can deal with the tribal people with sensitivity."

"Whom do you have in mind?" Melissa asked, resigned to her father's condition.

"There is a guest lecturer this semester at the University of

Miami, the English anthropologist Dr. Bennett Deering. I read two of his books on his interaction with tribes in East Asia and Central and South America. I like his cultural sensitivity and respect for the rights of indigenous peoples, while knowing they might hold the hope for our own future, not only in their plant cures, but their ability to live in harmony with nature."

"Before they get plowed under for grazing land," Melissa said bitingly.

"Yes, unless their value is ascertained early on."

Sterling nodded his head. "I know of him, and I agree he's a great choice in some respects, but I've heard he's rather hardheaded and can be uncompromising."

"That doesn't sound good," Melissa added.

Connor turned to his daughter and smiled mischievously. "Just who you need to keep you safe and in line, my dear."

CHAPTER TWO

Melissa, Sterling, and Adam hurried up the steps of the auditorium at the University of Miami. They were late for Bennett Deering's talk on the Emberà People of Panama and Columbia, and had scheduled a meeting with the anthropologist after his lecture. When they found seats in the last row, Deering was just concluding his talk. The scientist, even from this distance, cut quite a handsome figure with his six-foot-tall lanky frame, dark hair, and square jaw, in a rough, manly kind of way. Melissa looked around the back rows of the filled auditorium and found moonstruck coeds swooning over the early-thirties professor and explorer.

"So Stage One of the Panama government's push to integrate the Emberà peoples into communities for greater access to social services, schools, and health clinics has been fairly successful. As I mentioned earlier, I was brought in by the government to see that this transition from rural riverbank groupings of families into villages proceeded without a disruption of cultural . . . nuances. Of course, heads of families used to autonomy now found themselves among other family heads or chieftains, and helping them form cooperative village councils was most tasking."

A hand shot up and Deering motioned for the person to stand and asked their question. A gray-haired woman in her fifties, dressed in a blue business suit and who appeared to be a professor, spoke up. "But, aren't the Marxists threatening to take control of the country?"

"After last year's riots over the continued American control of the Panama Canal, I think it's inevitable."

"But you're an American, and you would still work with them?"

Deering paused. "Pardon me, Madame, but I am a British citizen, and my concern is for the welfare of the indigenous native population. The plantation owners who run the country now have been exploiting them for centuries."

With a huff the woman edged her way down the row of seats and charged out of the auditorium. Deering took a deep breath. "Well, does anybody have a question germane to my talk?"

Several coeds raised their hands, and there was a thirty-minute question-and-answer period after which Deering concluded his lecture. Several admirers swarmed onto the stage, as Melissa and her party walked down the aisle toward this grouping. After the coeds dispersed, Hawks stepped forward. "Dr. Deering, I'm Sterling Hawks; we talked on the phone earlier today."

Deering stood there for a moment and surveyed the group. "Yes, of course. You are mounting an expedition into the Javari Valley of western Brazil."

"That is correct," Hawks said. "Is there somewhere we can talk?"

"How about the Cuban restaurant across the street? I haven't eaten dinner, and something tells me I need to fortify myself for your inquiry."

Melissa stepped forward. "I've eaten there, and their sea bass is superb."

Deering lifted his hands. "Then it's settled. Lead the way, Ms. . . ."

Melissa extended her hand. "Dr. Melissa Croft."

As they walked back down the aisle, Deering inquired, "A doctor of what, may I ask?"

"I'm a philologist."

Deering paused, a puzzled look on his face. "Who's part of an expedition to the Amazon Basin in search of its uncontacted indigenous tribes?"

"The proof of the pudding, dear sir, is in the eating," Melissa said rather obliquely.

Deering laughed. "That would be plum pudding, I would imagine."

Hawks slapped him on the back. "Right on, dear chap. It's Christmas year-round in the States."

After a rather large dinner of varied dishes and lots of Cuban Rum, the atmosphere was much more relaxed as Sterling laid out the prospectus for the expedition. Deering read it through, studied the photos of the axe, and looked up with a mischievous smile. "Are we chasing after one of the lost tribes of Israel?"

Hawks laughed. "Not quite. The axe handle and its inscription are a mystery to all. That it is authentic is beyond doubt. But this is at most of secondary interest."

Deering sat back in his chair and studied the group. "An expedition funded by a pharmaceutical company with an ethno-botanist as a key member?" Hawks nodded his head. "So you're looking for plant remedies and want an anthropologist to deal with—"

Hawks broke in, "We need to further question this tribe of mine and need someone better versed in indigenous tribal customs, and if we get . . . directions, to deal with any new uncontacted tribes."

"Whose customs vary, as you must know, from country to country, and tribe to tribe."

"That's like saying every language is unique and has no commonality between them," Melissa said.

"Not quite, but I see your point." Deering held the photo up to examine the inscription on its handle. "Cuneiform, you say, from Mesopotamia?" Melissa nodded her head slightly. "Deep in the Javari Valley where no white explorers have ever been?"

Hawks nodded tentatively.

Deering put the picture back into the folder and handed it to Hawks. "You're holding out on me, and I won't undertake an expedition this perilous without knowing . . . everything."

Melissa looked to Hawks and nodded her head. "That's

only fair, but what I'm going to tell you . . . and Dr. Caruthers . . . must be kept secret, since any premature release of this information could be disastrous, not only for our expedition but for the tribes of the area." Hawks looked at the two men, who nodded their heads.

"After spending several days with my tribe, I noticed a light-skinned boy of fifteen or so, and I asked about him. I was told the most improbable of stories: that there was a rumor of a tribe of light-skinned women living by themselves without men in the deep jungle for as long as anybody could remember. One of their young tribesmen went looking for them and never came back, and a year later this light-skinned male infant was left outside their village."

"Like the Amazon tribes of Greek Mythology did?" Deering asked.

Melissa added, "And Greek history, but there's hardly a connection to them."

Deering snorted. "To quote Arthur Conan Doyle, 'there is nothing more deceptive than an obvious fact.' The axe may indeed be real, but that does not validate your premise."

Melissa squinched her face. Hawks interceded. "Well, we're hiring you to help us deal with this tribe and other dark-skinned tribes we may find. The wild goose chase, if there is one, is on us, and you and Adam can remain in the first village."

"And report back to Connor Croft, who I hear is a most formidable opponent, that I lost his daughter in the Amazon jungle." Deering smiled and shook his head. "In for a penny, in for a pound."

Melissa smiled. "So you'll go with us?"

"We Brits didn't colonize the world by sitting home twiddling our thumbs."

"'Once more unto the breach,'" Hawks added.

Adam looked around at the three of them. "I think I'm in over my head."

When Bennett Deering returned to the slate-green bungalow, rented for him by the university for this semester's lecture series, he heated some water on the two-burner stove and fixed himself a cup of Earl Grey. Slipping off his loafers, he padded his way into the den and took a seat at his desk. He turned on its reading light and opened Hawks's formal expedition folder prepared for him in advance of their meeting. They must have figured that the allure of a newly contacted Amazon jungle tribe would be enough inducement for him to sign on. However, it was the allure of this rumored women's tribe that really sealed the deal for him. What they didn't know, and what few others were aware of, was his long-term interest in the "wild childs" of the ancient and modern world. What had always intrigued him was how human children left stranded in the jungle and seemingly adopted by animals had survived in the wild to become excellent hunters using ancient stone weapons to kill game. The difference for this women-only tribe, as opposed to other uncontacted native tribes, was the socialization process of men and women living together and building family ties from which our civilization arose.

It is true that the mythical Amazon women tribes of the ancient world lacked this same cultural element, but they were not so isolated from contact with the greater world, and traded with others for the necessities of life, as meager as they were in that age. But an actual tribe of women living in the deep Amazon jungle and shunning contact with even other primitive tribes would have a unique social dynamic that would be of interest to anthropology. Did they have a queen like Queen Penthesilea, whose Amazon tribe fought the Greeks in the Trojan War? Of course, kings and queens ruled most societies, primitive and civilized, in the ancient world. Was this an archetypal fixation or the trend all primitive tribes followed and which dominated political structures until the democratic movements of recent times? Or would these women have a collective ruling structure? And without the constant companionship of men, would they seek their sexual satisfaction from each other? This thought had Deering thumbing through the folder to the bios and pictures of each expedition member. He picked up Melissa Croft's photo and examined it. She was dressed in the kind of Capri pants made famous my actress Marilyn Monroe, a white blouse with deep v-neck, and Gucci leather sandals. This was not the photo of a demure philologist but of an adventuress.

Deering opened his desk drawer and pulled out his tattered address book. It was still early evening, and he called a contact of his at Reuters who was manning the late desk in their Miami office. "Hey, Chet. How's it going tonight? Any South American revolutions I'll read about in the morning?"

"Pretty quiet. Most such coups d'état happen during the day so they won't accidently shoot their compatriots."

"Or their CIA handlers," Deering added.

"No comment, old boy. They're probably listening in." He paused. "What can I do for you?"

"You did a profile last year of Croft Pharmaceuticals. Any background on the daughter, Melissa Croft?"

Chet Barth snickered. "Well, Bennett, if you looking to marry an heiress, I think you're out of luck."

"Not that I'm interested, but why's that?"

"Well, first of all, the old man is as strong as a horse. The only time I could interview him was jogging on the beach at six in the morning in Key Biscayne. And one hears that the daughter . . . well, might be somewhat immune to your male charms."

"How discrete of you."

"Well, I am a writer. I do remember her showing up one morning, driving past us in her BMW coup like a bat out of hell as we headed back to the house. Then standing on the front steps of their mansion, her hands on her hips, she demanded that her father's subsidiaries stop hiring child labor in Indonesia or something like that."

"Yeah, she seems like a real pistol, as the Americans say."

Chet very casually asked, "So what's your interest, Bennett?

She's an ancient language expert, nobody who can help you in the wild."

"Well, that depends 'old boy' on just how far we go."

A phone rang in the background. "Give me a second." He put Deering on hold, and a minute later, picked up the line. "Well, got to go. Something's brewing."

"So, it's going to be a hot night after all."

Chet laughed. "But not like those steamy summer nights in August." He paused. "Let me know if you need anything else."

Deering hung up the phone and turned back to the photo of Melissa Croft. "She's going to be a handful for sure." He now picked up the photo of Sterling Hawks, with his graying hair and big bushy mustache—a loose-limbed man with a rough tanned face and a wild glint in his eyes. He looked more like the modern world's picture of Allan Quatermain of King Solomon's Mines than H. Rider Haggard's description of his hero as small, wiry, and unattractive. What they did have in common, along with him, was a distaste for English cities and the homeland's dreary climate. Personally he'd rather cut his way through a snake-infested jungle than tromp across Piccadilly Circus and its open square. He had read one of Hawks's books and was impressed by the depth of his research and his reverence for the structures and artifacts he was examining. He now picked up Adam Caruthers' photo: short, squat, with wire-rimmed glasses, who appeared to be one of those henpecked American men who let their women run the show. However, the monograph included in the proposal, about tropical flora and their pharmaceutical possibilities, was excellent. He wondered, if they ever did come across a women-only tribe, how this sexually repressed man would react to a group of Amazon women keen for an annual mating ritual.

Bennett put down the folder. There were no photos of Hawks's tribe—no doubt the natives were camera shy at this point, but Hawks's research of them and their customs was illuminating. He now sat back and looked at the photo of him with a group of

Emberà tribesmen and women in western attire sitting around a camp stove and cooking Capybaras meat for dinner. Looking closely at them, they had the look of caged animals trying to adapt to their confines but longing for the deep jungle. After six months in Miami, which still had some old world charm, unlike New York and Chicago, he, too, felt like a caged animal. Civilization can erode your soul with its slow dance of manners and civility. He needed to get back to the wild and let its rhythms once again course through his veins, but looking down at the folder, he wondered at what cost to his sanity.

CHAPTER THREE

Two days later Hawks had set an appointment for all four of them with a doctor from Columbia who had immigrated to the U.S. after the civil war in 1948 and had a general practice on Beacom Blvd. in the Little Havana section of Miami. The four of them sat in plastic chairs in the hot outer office with a swirling fan as the only heat relief. They were surrounded by Columbian immigrants, mostly laborers and their families, and Melissa felt out of place.

She leaned over to Hawks and whispered. "I don't see why we couldn't get our shots from my family doctor in Key Biscayne."

"Who would've been only concerned about what infections you can get traveling in the Amazon, but not what you can give the Natives there, especially newly or uncontacted tribes, and who wouldn't prescribe for such things as traveler's diarrhea."

Melissa looked around the room self-consciously, but most of the patients only spoke Spanish and didn't understand the exchange. She now looked down at the form that she had brought from her family doctor attesting to the fact that she had had vaccinations against measles, chicken pox, mumps, rubella, and a host of other childhood diseases. She also studied the list of vaccines that were to be administered: Hepatitis A, Typhoid, Yellow Fever, and even a Tetanus-diphtheria shot.

"Really, Sterling . . . a Tetanus shot. A lot of wild dogs in the Amazon?"

"A lot of wild animals, period, my dear."

Deering leaned over and added with a smirk, "It's the Malaria pills that have a real bite. Be sure to read the label about its neuropsychiatric symptoms."

Hawks gently elbowed Deering in the side and turned back

to Melissa. "Mostly nausea and vomiting, and maybe some insomnia for the first week."

Melissa leaned back in her chair. She didn't appreciate Deering's remark. If there was a loose cannon in the group, it was the English anthropologist who hated living in his home country. Maybe some childhood demons lurking in his family tree, like most of the upper crust Brits she knew.

The nurse now called her name, and she stood up and followed the Hispanic woman into the doctor's office. Dr. Julian Molina was not what she had expected, given his waiting room of lower class patients. He was of medium height, dark hair with graying temples, wire-rimmed glasses, well groomed with sharp probing eyes. The doctor quickly read her doctor's note, and squinched his eyes at something he read.

He now looked up. "A doctor in Key Biscayne. Croft," he said with hardly any accent. "Are you the daughter of Connor Croft, the pharmaceutical owner?" She nodded her head. "So I take it that your trip to the Amazon is not for humanitarian purposes."

She studied him for a moment. "No, doctor. I'm afraid that we are going to further add to the 'White Man's Burden.' But we are bringing the natives more flashlights."

The doctor looked back with narrowed eyes and then laughed. "I can see that you are as formidable as your father, and not subject to the customary entreaties."

He now motioned for the nurse, who held out a cloth-covered tray with the required syringes, and the doctor administered the vaccinations one by one. After he finished, and the nurse taped a Band-Aid over several puncture marks, he went to his cabinet and pulled out a plastic prescription container, broke the seal, and handed Melissa a pill. "This is an anti-Malaria medication. Take this once a week from now until four weeks after your return."

"You want me to swallow the first one here?" she asked, rather annoyed.

The nurse handed her a cup of water.

"You may have heard of its initial side-effects, and I want to make sure you take your first one now."

Melissa shook her head. "Doctor. I'm not like your . . . customary patients. I don't have to be monitored."

Molina didn't back down. "Take it now, Ms. Croft, or I won't sign the vaccination release."

Melissa could see the doctor was serious. She swallowed the pill with a sip of water, and took the canister from him. The doctor stepped over to his desk and wrote out a prescription on his pad, stepped back, and handed it to her. "In case you misplace the medication on your trip."

Melissa took the prescription and slipped it into her purse. "I'm sure the tribe's medicine man can fill it."

The doctor laughed again, and as Melissa stepped over and opened the door, he added, "Enjoy your trip, Ms. Croft, 'Into' as Conrad would warn, 'the Heart of Darkness.'"

Their next stop, driving in a white Croft Pharmaceutical van, was Eagle's Army-Navy discount store in South Miami. When they pulled into the parking lot, Melissa turned around from the front seat. "Sterling, a discount store? Let's not do this on the cheap."

"Trust me; what we can buy in the States, they have it. I've seen army special forces guys shopping here."

Deering looked at him. "Really. You know them on sight?"

"Shoot with them at Lock and Load on occasion."

Melissa turned back around and looked at Caruthers in the driver's seat, shaking her head. "Guys and their guns."

While Hawks and Deering had a lot of their old gear, Melissa and Adam needed to be outfitted from top to bottom. The first stop was in the boot department. Hawks picked out a high-top laced leather boot in black. Fortunately, Melissa was tall for a woman, with larger-than-normal feet, since most of the boots were for men. "These are too heavy; what about canvass or something lighter, and in a lighter color?"

Hawks shook his head. "You need waterproof boots for the low-lying swampland we'll be traversing, and dark-colored. You don't want to catch the attention of the critters slivering around the ground as we hike."

This settled the question for her and Adam, who picked out a pair in his size. There next came several sets of quick-drying Khaki pants, shirts, and a canvas hat for her and him. Deering's expedition clothes weren't best suited for the kind of jungle they would be traveling through, and he bought a few items of clothing himself.

"What about backpacks and tents?" Melissa asked.

"And hammocks?" Deering asked.

"I have some, and whatever else we need, we'll get them in Brazil. It's a long flight, with lots of stopovers, and we don't want to get exhausted hauling things around we can get just as easily in Manaus or Tabatinga."

"I guess that's where we're also getting bug spray and knifes—in-country?" Deering asked.

"Yeah. Bug spray by the case. And I have a small cache of equipment and some weapons that my guide keeps for me in Tabatinga. I think it's best we keep a low profile by traveling without any weapons. I'm sure that if I don't already have what we will need in Tabatinga, I can get anything else we would want from my sources there."

"We'll need them?" Melissa asked.

"Mostly for bandits and drugged-out jungle cretins, but yes, I've been known to deter a robbery with a gun to someone's face."

"That's reassuring," she said with an ironic twinge.

"Yes, and loose-fitting clothes are the order of the day," Deering added.

Melissa smirked. "Does my femininity make you uncomfortable, doctor?"

"No, but having to fight off human predators just adds to the danger."

"Yes, well," Hawks interjected, to deter this line of questioning. "I think that does it for outfitting for now. We fly out in a week. I suggest everybody, especially you, Adam, work out and build up your stamina. It's going to be hot, humid, bug-infested, and very draining, and while we take a motorized canoe down the main rivers, once we turn inland on the furos, shallow channels leading off from the rivers, we paddle."

"Really," Melissa said.

Hawks smiled. "You get a pass, while you prepare lunch and dinner."

Melissa rolled her eyes. "Talk about stereotypes."

"Speaking of lunch . . . ," Adam suggested that they dine out together, but both Croft and Deering wanted to get back and tie up loose ends before they headed out.

The night before the group was scheduled to fly out, Melissa accepted, or was required to accept, an invitation to dine with her father and mother at their mansion in Key Biscayne. He had invited the entire group, but the others begged off, still behind in their last-minute preparations, or so they claimed. Melissa felt that it was at Hawks's initiation, trying to keep her and Deering apart and not to expose to their sponsor, even if it was her father, the tension between them. They had had several group meetings in which Melissa tried to assert her authority as the expedition leader, and Hawks mainly deferred to her, but Deering was adamant that once they were on the ground and in the jungle, that Hawks would take the lead. He had even threatened to walk out if she didn't agree to this stipulation, which she finally did.

They ate on the patio overlooking the Atlantic Ocean at sunset. It was still a bit cool, but the torch lanterns kept them warm. Despite that, her mother, Elizabeth, tall but thin with keen intelligent eyes, wore a sweater over her exposed shoulders. She was still opposed to Melissa going on this expedition, but after repeated entreaties, both over the phone and at lunch, Melissa refused to back out. What her mother couldn't understand was why a language expert was traipsing off to the Amazon jungle. She had voiced this particular objection over lunch the previous week:

"Mother, Sterling discovered an artifact from ancient Mesopotamia belonging to one of the tribes, which I was able to decipher, and he wants me along if anything of the same type is discovered."

Her mother scrunched her face. "Ancient Mesopotamia? My dear, somebody is taking you for a ride. And I wouldn't put it past Hawks, trying to wiggle the money out of your father for this expedition by playing to your vanity."

Elizabeth shook her head and turned to the tropical garden setting of the Jamaican Inn with its twenty-foot waterfall in the center of the room. Melissa figured her mother had picked this location for lunch in Key Biscayne so that she could feign not hearing replies that displeased her over the ambient noise.

"Well, whether you believe its authenticity or not, it could be the find of the century for Hawks and collaterally for someone in my field, and worth taking the risk."

Her mother, of course, disagreed and told tales of explorers getting lost in the Amazon and never being heard from again, or of finding parts of them mauled by jaguars. To this last warning, Melissa had blithely replied, "I'll carry a self-addressed Amazon Special Delivery box with me so they ship back my remains."

To which her mother replied, "What, what was that?"

Now sitting on the patio after dinner and drinking Courvoisier in brandy snifters, her mother, who had been civil during the meal, couldn't contain herself any longer but at least now turned her ire on her husband. "Connor, how can you just go along with this? Letting her traipse off to one of the most dangerous locales in the world. I mean, if the natives don't to kill her, the jaguars or caiman will eat her alive."

"Liz, I've told you that Hawks and Deering are reliable and experienced and will keep her safe."

"Hawks, Jesus. The man's on his last leg and can't protect himself. And Deering? I hear the man is an absolute ass."

Melissa chuckled. "Well, at least we agree about something, Mother."

Elizabeth looked back and forth between the two of them and stood up in a huff. "Reginald," she called to their butler, "I'll take my brandy in my sitting room."

She now charged off without so much as a good night. Connor looked out over the ocean, as the first star came out in the evening's twilight. He turned back to his daughter. "Queenie," he said, calling Melissa by her childhood nickname. In Greek mythology Melissa was a nymph, whom Cronus had turned into a worm for some offense, but whom Zeus later changed into a queen bee. "A mother's fear and concern are not something to be taken lightly."

Melissa closed her eyes. "I know, but what am I supposed to do, live cloistered in my academic tower? I mean, it's not like South Miami is any safer than the Amazon jungle."

He nodded his head. "But you're pleased with the preparations and feel that Hawks is on his game and that this Deering fellow, ass or not, will be helpful?"

She took a moment to compose her reply. "Sterling has definitely lost a step, and he may be grasping for one last big archeological score, but Deering is rather solid, despite being bullheaded, and I trust his judgment. I think you were right to insist on his inclusion."

"And you're not just saying that?" he asked pointedly.

Melissa laughed. "Have you ever known me to couch my opinion to assuage the concern of others?"

Connor smiled. "No, even as a child, you were sharp-tongued and to the point, which is why we had to move you from school to school, I believe."

Melissa stood up, stepped over, and kissed her father on cheek. "Don't worry, Daddy. I'm not going to get lost, eaten, or swallowed alive. I've got too much to live for, and a huge inheritance to spend at some point."

Connor snorted, "Over my dead body."

Melissa patted her father on the back and left. Driving home and looking into the clear night sky, she did allow some of her own suppressed fear to come to the surface. It was interesting; she wasn't afraid of dying, or so she told herself, but of validating Deering's apparent low estimate of her. Why would she care? He was a self-absorbed ass, but there was an emotional edge to her thoughts of him. Melissa now wished she had invited Pamela over for the night, instead of a chaste good-bye lunch at the university. It was too late for other plans. She was being picked up by the airport limousine at six o'clock in the morning, and she still had packing to do. Well, a few people had underestimated her in past, and they all had lived to regret it, as he would.

*****

Melissa had a coughing fit, and Mattie reached over and adjusted the hospital bed with the remote control, raising it slightly. The door opened, and Dr. Marcum stuck his head into the room. Melissa waved him off, and he closed the door. Mattie handed her mother the water bottle with the straw. She took several sips and handed it back to her daughter. She closed her eyes and, after a moment, opened them.

"Where were we?" Melissa asked.

"You were telling Connor about what an ass Bennett Deering was," she said with a smirk. "Which is kind of ironic, don't you think?"

Melissa shook her head. "But that was more about me and my insecurities than it was about him at the time."

Mattie stared at her mother. "Really? That's surprising. I would never have suspected as much."

A smile curled around the old woman's mouth. "Yes, one of the things I wanted to talk to you about."

Mattie looked puzzled. "You want to talk to me about your insecurities as a young woman?"

Melissa nodded her head. "What this trip and its horrendous ordeal brought to the surface was my animus complex, or how, as a modern woman of my time, I had become possessed by my masculine side."

"I'm familiar with the Jungian terminology, which is even more in vogue these days, but your reference is surprising."

"Well, when I came back from the trip, I was an absolute mess, and though I resisted, your grandfather insisted that go into therapy, which really saved me in the end."

Mattie sat back in her chair. "Okay, but what does this have to do with me?"

"Well, you're even more liberated than I was, but I see the same need to prove yourself and the same insecurities, even though you're ten years older than I was at the time."

Mattie bristled. "Well, at least I don't have . . . girlfriends, like you did."

"No, but you're also not happily matched as they say. It's been years since your divorce."

Mattie stood up. "Well, if this is the extent of your deathbed confession. I've heard enough."

"Sit down, Madeline. I haven't even scratched the surface of it."

"Okay, but let's get on with . . . the story."

CHAPTER FOUR

They boarded their Pan Am DC-8 jet airliner at eight o'clock the next morning for the six-hour flight to Caracas, Venezuela. Melissa insisted on flying first class, and so she and Hawks sat up front while Deering and Caruthers sat hunched up in coach. Adam was a bit put out by the seating arrangement, but Deering had flown too many cargo flights in and out of Central America, to not appreciate cushioned seats and a beverage service. At first Adam had tried to engage Bennett in conversation but gave up after a few unresponsive openings and took a book from his carry-on and began to read it. For his part, Deering just sat back and relaxed knowing full well the chaos that awaited them at the airport and that their next flight from Caracas to Manaus, Brazil, would be even less hospitable. It was also something of a tradition for him, on the first leg of an expedition, to sit back and quietly assess the situation before they hit the ground.

While he had traveled to the upper Amazon Valley in Peru, which was at a higher elevation and thus much cooler, he had never traversed the river at sea level through dense jungle with its teeming humidity. The jungles of East Asia and Panama were tame by comparison. Jungle expeditions of any nature were fraught with danger from the environment, its wild animals, and the local tribes in various stages of their acculturation to the ingress of the modern world into their primitive locales and psyches. He had watched this process with the Emberà people of Columbia and Panama, where the slightest upset sent some tribesmen slithering back to the archaic past and its primitivism. He could just imagine this same process with Hawks newly discovered tribe, which was part of the incentive for his joining the expedition, or at least that is what he had told himself. But he had to wonder whether it was the primitive tribe that attracted his interest or what it would further draw out of him.

Between his Stage One Emberà acculturation assignment in Panama—he had chosen not to proceed to the more pedestrian Stage Two—and his lecture series in the U.S., he had visited England and his family estate now run by his sister Margaret. She had turned their small ancestral castle into a bed-and-breakfast for tourists. He stayed one night before he fled to London but found the bleak, cold climate there even less to his liking now after a year in the hothouse of Central America. When the lecture tour was proposed in less civilized America, he jumped at the opportunity to flee the country and the tempting university offers that were coming his way. Or was it Leslie Ann Albright that he was really fleeing and her desire to resume their on-again, off-again relationship? She taught history at Oxford and was no doubt behind the teaching offers, but just one night with her and her four-course idea of a mating dance was enough civilized sex for him. He found the rough sex with native women more to his liking. Had he really gone that native, he wondered.

"Hate to interrupt, old boy," Hawks said. Bennett looked up at him, his eyes still a bit distant.

"Hey, Adam, how would you like to trade places? First class is too hoity-toity for my liking."

Caruthers practically jumped out of his seat. Quickly grabbing his carry-on, he pushed his way past Deering into the aisle and hurried along before Hawks changed his mind, or so it seemed to Deering. Sterling laughed. "I bet as a kid he was the first to grab the turkey leg at Thanksgiving dinner, afraid someone else would get it first."

Deering lifted the divide and scooted over to the window to give the rangy Hawks more leg room with his aisle seat. "No doubt," Bennett chirped.

They both settled in for a moment. "So, having second thoughts yet?"

Deering turned to him. "About us, or the expedition?"

Sterling laughed, his broad smile parting the grey hairs of a bushy mustache in need of trimming. "Right on. We are a rather ragtag group. I don't know what's going to be more trying, dealing with our tenderfoots or coaxing the tribesmen to confide in us."

"Confide?" Bennett asked.

"About the bloody axe of theirs and these Amazon women."

"So that's what we're calling them: Amazons?"

"As good a name as any, and I kind of like its historical reference, gives us more of a . . . footing."

Deering snickered, "Yeah, on one leg, with a hand tied behind our backs."

Hawks nodded his head. "Well, that's why the deep jungle is called the great unknown. If these tribes were easy to classify, some Oxford don would have a hereditary chart on them already."

Deering laughed. "I know just the person for that."

They both sat back in their seats as the plane experienced a bit of turbulence that rocked them. One of the advantages of these new jet airliners was that they could fly through rough weather faster than the prop planes. After a minute or two, it was smooth sailing again, and the stewardess resumed pushing her beverage cart down the aisle. They both got jiggers of Scotch and cups of ice. They poured their drinks and took quick sips.

"Look, Deering, I've known Melissa since she was a tot, and she's made of stern stuff. If the going gets rough, you can count on her to keep her head. It's this Caruthers chap that worries me. These American men, or the common run of them, are not very . . . sturdy, not much beneath the surface."

"Well, if you've forgotten, they bailed our ass out of the last war."

"Yeah, and then got sucker-punched into fighting the damn Commies in Southeast Asia."

"Talk about the jungle. They don't know what they've bought

into."

Hawks now turned to Deering with a paternal look. "How about letting up on Croft; she'll be all right. It's Caruthers we need to team up on."

Deering stared the man in the eyes. He didn't like getting braced in confined spaces like airplanes. You couldn't tell the fellow to screw off and then bail out like at a bar or office. He calmed himself. He was the one who had anointed Hawks as team leader; live with it, he told himself. "Okay, I'll back off, but it won't do any good. She's got a twisted thing for me."

Hawks sighed. "Yeah, I noticed that. Too much like Daddy, I'm afraid."

They both settled back in their seats, resigned to the unsettled situation of their little expedition's entourage.

By early afternoon their DC-8 approached the airport in Caracas, which was so close to the ocean Deering wondered if its runways were ever swamped by hurricane-level high tides. They landed and disembarked, quickly went through customs, and found a crowded restaurant/bar to wait out their flight to Manaus, Brazil, which didn't leave until early evening. After a quick bite to eat, Melissa and Adam went shopping. Adam wanted to find postcards and send one to his wife before they flew out that night. After they left, Sterling shook his head. "He's gone six hours, and he wants to send her a postcard."

"Better from here than Manaus or Tabatinga. Imagine that would take awhile, if it got there at all," Deering added.

"So, tell me, Bennett. No wife? No longtime girlfriend?"

"No wife, for sure. I have an on-off relationship with the aforementioned Oxford don, but it's more off these days since I left for America and wouldn't accept a teaching position at Oxford." Deering didn't like talking about his personal life with strangers, but since the two of them would be cheek by jowl for the next couple months, he figured he could loosen up a bit. "And you?"

"Divorced twice. Two kids. The boy's a civil servant moron in Manchester, but the girl, Emily, is my pride and joy. A paleontologist on a dig now in the Middle East. Iran. Speaks Farsi and a couple other languages. A real chip off the old block, as they say."

"Middle East can be tough on a woman," Deering added tentatively.

"Not for a Black Belt who carries Walther PPK in her purse."

Deering practically spit out his last sip of beer. "Just like James Bond, huh?"

"My girl could take that Connery fellow to the mat any day." Sterling saw the man's interest. "Have to invite you over to Christmas dinner one of these days."

"Well, I only learned a few judo moves during my army stint."

"Better brush up. Emily likes to beat up on guys that she likes. Her kind of foreplay."

Melissa came back and sat down. "Foreplay. Sure you guys don't want to get a room?"

Sterling laughed. "Was telling Bennett about my Emily."

Melissa nodded her head. "The paleontologist. Yes, we've met." She turned to Deering and smiled. "She'd eat you for lunch and spit you out."

Bennett didn't react. "Then I'll take her to dinner."

Sterling lifted his beer. "Touché, old boy. Touché."

On the flight from Caracas to Manaus on a moonless night, Deering didn't spot a single light as they flew over the jungle of southern Venezuela an hour out from the city and on into Brazil. While the other three slept fitfully—the Convair CV-340 was a two-engine turboprop and much louder than the DC-8's jet engines—he had taken a window seat and stared out into the dark night. Sterling's talk about his daughter and her proclivities had stirred something in him. While he found Leslie Anne too gentile, would some two-fisted woman like Emily Hawks be more his type, if there was such a thing for him? What he liked about the native women was that sex was just another natural function for them, no attachments, no expectations, just a temporary bonding of wants and needs. Did this indicate some great lack in him, or an inability to conduct an adult relationship with its give and take and compromises, he wondered? This didn't paint a pretty picture of a loner anthropologist in his early-thirties, and it gave him pause. After a while, with the lights in the cabin lowered, he fell off to sleep.

Sometime later he felt someone moving beside him and then heard a series of muffled cries. He woke up to find Melissa sleeping in the seat next to him. She had switched with Adam, probably for the aisle seat's leg room. He watched her fitful sleep with concern. No doubt a Malaria pill was causing bad dreams. Deering waved the stewardess over and got her to retrieve a blanket, which he draped over the woman. Bennett watched her, and then after a while she woke up and found him staring at her. Melissa momentarily brushed off her sleepy veneer, then discovered the blanket draped over her. She smiled. "Well, Deering, I never figured you for the paternal type."

"Don't expect cookies and milk, my dear."

Melissa smiled, then fell off to sleep again, which proved to be less turbulent than earlier.

They arrived in Manaus, the largest city in the state of Amazonas {Brazil is divided into states}, with a jarring landing that woke everybody who wasn't already awake. Deering checked his watch. It was 2:00 a.m. They deplaned, and there was hardly any custom's check. Out on the street, Sterling flagged down a cab and had the driver take his group to what passed as a decent hotel where he had booked three rooms for the night. Everybody was too tired to notice the dingy curtains and wallpaper and the cockroaches in the main lobby. Before bedding down, Stirling warned them that they had a four o'clock flight the next afternoon to Tabatinga and a late-morning supply run in the city's jungle outfit stores. In the morning, only Hawks and Sterling were up and dressed and ready to go at the appointed time. The other two members didn't answer their phones or knocks on the door, so the two men left them, ate a quick breakfast at the hotel's cafe, and headed out into the city.

They returned two hours later with two tents, four good-quality hammocks, bell-shaped mosquito nets, canvass backpacks, and a case of local insect repellent. They had the store pack the lot of it in two sturdy boxes that they could carry onto the plane, since the flight to Tabatinga would be in a puddle-jumper without a cargo hold. They found Adam in the café eating breakfast. He looked like he was badly hung over from jet lag. He had tried to rouse Melissa earlier, but said she wouldn't answer her phone or knocks on the door. They stored the two boxes in the hotel's storage room, and Hawks paid the bill. They decided to wait until noon before they had the hotel manager open Croft's door.

The late-morning sun peaking through the curtains had finally awakened her. Melissa sat up in bed, still fully clothed from yesterday's flights and sweating profusely. Once fully awake she lay back down on the bed, the wet sheets flung aside. She had had several troubling dreams, including one with vicious dogs chasing her through the streets of a shanty town that could've been in a South American city, given her present locale. Thinking back, she realized that she may have internalized Deering's snide remark at the doctor's office last week about the malaria pill's "bite," and transformed it in her dream into rabid dogs. Maybe it was sitting next to him on the flight to Manaus that triggered this association. But the last dream was what would be called a trickster dream: she was trapped in a cellar by vicious monkeys and goblins, and then she heard knocks on the door but couldn't fight her way through them to open it.

Melissa now rolled out of bed, stripped off her traveling clothes, hurried into the bathroom to relieve her bladder, and then took a long hot shower. With the water rushing down her body and pounding the cracked tile floor of the shower, she could have sworn she heard ringing bells. Melissa had taken psychology courses in college, especially after she had realized and acted on her sexual proclivity, and tended to gravitate toward Jung and away from Freudian associations with their overly sexual connotations. She knew these were animus dreams from the male side of her psyche, but also that the sound of chimes, knocks on the door, and ringing bells were alerting her to possible avenues of change and transformation. Did it take a trip into, as Dr. Molina's had warned her, "the heart of darkness" to bring these unresolved aspects of her psyche to the forefront? She hoped not. This trip was going to be testy enough with its teeming jungle and primitive tribesmen without having to deal with latent emotional conflicts at the same time. The room phone rang. Melissa jumped out of the shower, wrapped a towel around herself, and stepped back into the room. She picked up the phone.

"So, Cinderella wakes up?" Deering said on the other end of the line.

"But you're no Prince Charming, Deering. More like the wicked witch in drag."

She could hear him laughing. "Well, you need to pack, if you unpacked, and get down here. We're leaving for the airport in an hour, and the food here will be better than what we can scrounge together there."

"Your concern is noted. Give me fifteen minutes."

Twenty minutes later, Melissa dragged her duffel bag out of the elevator and left it with the bellhop who couldn't be bothered to retrieve it from the room. She walked over to the café, where the three men were finishing up lunch. She sat next to Hawks and waved the waitress over. She tried to order breakfast but was told that they had stopped serving it an hour ago, and so she got several chicken tacos with Spanish rice and black beans and a carafe of black coffee.

She turned back to her traveling companions, who were staring at her. She looked down at her clothes wondering if she had left her blouse unbuttoned. "What?"

Hawks smiled. "You look rather rumpled, my dear."

"Yeah, well that was some trip yesterday, and combined with the heat and humidity and no air conditioning, I didn't sleep well."

Hawks nodded. "The next leg is going to be even more grueling—a thousand miles in a puddle jumper. So, eat well, because you're going to need it."

Melissa looked around the table with its half-dozen empty plates. "I see you've taken your own advice."

"And be sure to use the bathroom before we leave the hotel. The airport bathrooms down here are less than sanitary," Hawks added.

To avoid Deering's stare, Melissa turned to Adam who was penning another postcard. "Writing home again, Adam?"

"They say this is my last chance."

Melissa smiled at the idea that popped into her head and looked around at the others. "Yeah, this trip sounds like a last chance for some of us."

None of the men took this well.

CHAPTER FIVE

The prop plane flight from Manaus to Tabatinga was slow and punishing; Hawks and Deering got drunk and slept most of the way, while Caruthers, who didn't seem to be bothered by boredom, read until they turned off the overhead lighting. Melissa seemed to be caught in a round of bad dreams, and the three men just left her alone. Another rough landing woke everybody up again, and they hurriedly pulled down their luggage and Hawks's two boxes of camping supplies and scurried off the plane.

They were met in the middle of the night at the airport by their Indian guide, Joao Silva, in a jeep with an overhead carryall. He was short in stature, but wiry, with a head of close-cropped black hair, and appeared to be in his mid-twenties. While Joao spoke some English, he only answered their inquiries on the drive into the city with short if polite answers. The only extended conversation was with Hawks in Portuguese. After he dropped them off at their hotel, which was even less accommodating than the one in Manaus, he drove off and left them to manage their luggage and check themselves in.

As they waited for the hotel clerk, who had to be summoned from what appeared to be a television soap opera in the back room, Deering asked Hawks, "What did Joao have to say?"

The others leaned in to hear the response. "It's been raining for the last two weeks, so the rivers and their furo offshoots should still be navigable when we get there. And there's still some unrest in the north Javari valley between his Marubo tribe and the Mayoruna or Matses."

Deering asked, "Why two names?"

"Mayoruna in the Panoan language covers several of these tribes, but the Brazilians are increasingly calling them Matses, one of the largest in the Javari region, and so that's what we river travelers use."

"So, is it just a poaching conflict?"

"No. A little more serious than that: Wife-stealing and some murderous tribal retributions a few years ago that keep things tense."

Deering turned to Melissa, who beat him to it. "Don't say it, Deering. No wives here."

He laughed while Hawks pushed him up to the desk to sign in first. The sleeping arrangements were the same: Hawks and Deering in one room, and Melissa and Caruthers each in their own. Since Connor Croft was footing the bill, the two men didn't object to them having private rooms. The next morning Hawks got everybody up early and passed out their backpacks, hammocks, and mosquito nets, since everybody needed to haul and maintain their own gear. Hawks also carried their one sleeping bag. They met in the lobby at 9:00 a.m. to be picked up by Joao, whom they were told was addressed as Jo. He was taking them across the Columbian border to Leticia for breakfast and to shop for their remaining supplies, since Tabatinga was more like an outpost than an actual city. They stepped into the jeep with Hawks and Deering up front and the other two in the more spacious backseat. The town's streets were cluttered with old Chevys and Fords and motor scooters. At the border, there was a sign in Spanish, "Entering Columbia," but no guards or passport checks.

As they drove off, Melissa asked, "Jo, why aren't there border guards?"

"No sense. People cross in boats all day. And many cars and trucks on the border road."

"What about drug smuggling?" she asked.

"Not problem, but soon, we hear, it make things bad for

everyone."

The café on the river was hardly a restaurant, or one they would classify as such, but they were served scrambled eggs with onions and peppers, black coffee, and freshly baked bread, and found it to their liking. Before they went over trip details, everybody was curious about Jo and his background. He explained that his Marubo tribe in the central Javari region had been in contact with the outsiders since the late nineteenth century. The first intruders were the Peruvian rubber tappers, followed by the Brazilian rubber barons, and the tribesmen went to work for them in exchange for goods but were badly taken advantage of and practically enslaved. His father had worked for them since he was a young man, and when the industry collapsed in the late 1930s, instead of going back to the jungle for subsistence living with the others, he joined a couple of the tappers and headed back to Tabatinga, where he stayed when they pushed on to Manaus. He married a Brazilian woman, took her last name, and Jo was born here in 1940.

"While you were growing up, did you have any contact with your tribe?" Deering asked.

"My father want me learn heritage, and we go to the Javari every summer, when I just want play with friends. He buy goods, building materials, and fix things for them. I learn Panoan language, or their . . . branch of it, and can speak with them and other tribes there mostly, but hard to talk with new ones."

Hawks added, "He also speaks Spanish, besides Portuguese and a little English."

Jo added, "Thing outsiders need know, and those from El Norte, the Indians here not like in America, not many in the tribes like there, and many villages, small, 100, 200 people most."

"I hear that the newly contacted tribe along the Rio Orinoco in Venezuela is quite large, thousands of them, or at least from the air, they appear to be," Deering added.

"Hear of them; they call 'fierce people,' not know much more."

Melissa added, "The Amazon tribes, were they killed off by disease?"

Jo nodded his head. "Even before Spanish come, Amazon Jungle here not big with people. Hard. Very hard to live there."

"So we must respect who they are, help them, and not take from them like others," Deering said.

Jo nodded his head again and looked the man in the eyes, before turning his head away, but Melissa kept her eyes on Bennett for a moment longer.

"So why don't you take out the map and let's show them the lay of the land," Hawks said.

Jo opened his beaten-up leather satchel and pulled out a rolled-up map. The group now helped the owner clear the dishes and pulled two tables together. Jo spread out the map with his Portuguese and English-equivalent names, and they placed condiment shakers on the four corners to hold it down. "This is the Javari region. On the east side the Itaquai and Jutai Rivers, and there is Kanamari tribe. They get killed and fight with rubber tappers 1950s and go deeper into jungle, south of Jutai. Many uncontacted tribes there." He paused and then pointed to the western side of the region. "First we head south on Rio Solimões, what Amazon called upstream, then west on Javari River. This is border with Peru; many small villages on the Peruvian side are Matses, then South on Curuca River— separate Matses on west, Marubo on east side—then south beyond Marubo territory into unexplored jungle."

"Unexplored? You mean none of the other tribes go there?"

Jo shook his head. "Why? They got all they need where they at. Not like white men always going where they not belong."

Melissa smiled. "Does that include us, Jo?"

He shrugged his shoulders. "You pay; I take you there. It's a . . . job."

Hawks laughed and gave Jo a pat on the back. "That's the

spirit."

Jo nodded his head, but Melissa caught a look from him that didn't bode well for their journey "into the heart of darkness," as she had been hearing lately. "Well, let's get a move on, shall we," she said standing up and helping Jo roll up his map.

They did a little shopping amongst the market stalls, gathering up rough soap bars, razor blades, sun screen lotion, tackle and fishhooks, cigarette lighters, and batteries for their flashlights. Then they crossed back into Tabatinga and drove along the river front until they reached a marina of sorts, which was actually a series of clapboard boatsheds. At the third one down, they found a thin and pretty Brazilian woman with nets and boxes of foodstuff sitting on a tree stump. Jo introduced her as his wife, Camila; she had long black hair and had prepared the expedition's initial food supply. When she spotted Sterling, she stood up and stepped over and hugged him.

"I introduced them," he said in explanation.

She now said something in Portuguese to Hawks, who nodded his head and said something back, which appeared to be reassurances.

Jo added, "She tells him to bring me back or her brothers will be waiting for him."

Deering laughed. "I hope that doesn't apply to the rest of us."

Jo translated for her, and Camila nodded her head vigorously. "'In for a penny, in for a pound,' I guess."

Another man now stepped out of the shed and walked over. Jo introduced him as Paulo, their helper on the expedition. He was a bit taller, an Indian but with more Brazilian blood. Everyone noticed that he had a machete slung from his belt and was carrying a firearm. Melissa stared at it.

Paulo said, "Protect from indios bravos."

Hawks translated. "Wild Indians." Melissa pulled out a Polaroid camera and got Jo and Hawks to stand up against the boatshed. She took two pictures and handed one to Camila. She started to put the camera into her backpack, but Jo came over and asked for it. "No bring into Indian villages; they think you take their souls with pictures."

Melissa handed it to Camila with her extra film. "You can keep it until we get back." The woman started to read the instructions on the back of the film packs.

Paulo now pulled Hawks over to the duffel bag against the wall of the boatshed. From it Hawks took out a knife and another pistol and boxes of ammunition.

To forestall any further inquiry, he told the two men to carry the foodstuff in their nets into the shed. The group followed after them and found two long canoes with outboard motors and faded canvass canopies for sun protection. They packed both of them equally with food and gear to spread the weight in case they lost one of the canoes. Jo stepped outside to say goodbye to his wife and handed her the keys to the jeep. When he returned, Hawks had put himself, Jo, and Deering in the lead canoe with Melissa and Adam in the follow-canoe operated by Paulo.

Hawks had a machete and now handed one to Deering from Paulo's duffel bag. "What about us?" Melissa asked.

"It's mostly to cut back the overhead vines as we travel down the narrow furos once we get off the main rivers, and so the follow canoe will be free of them."

They now pulled away from their mooring, motored out into the river with its many canoes and working boats, and headed south on the Rio Solimões where they soon took the left fork to Benjamin Constant, the county seat, and a much larger city than either Tabatinga or Leticia. There was a lot more activity on the river here, which had a few double-decker river boats, and the canoes stayed close together to forge their way through the fishing and tourist boats.

In the front canoe, Deering asked, "Why didn't we fly into here? Looks a lot more accommodating."

"Yes, and with more bureaucrats and police and curious Indian officials, or sertanistas—government agents of contact."

Deering nodded his head. "They hear Americana pharmaceutical, and there'll be a hundred hands to grease," Hawks added.

This is where they picked up the Rio Javari and headed northwest. Once they had left the city, the river was fairly wide with jungle on either side. Since the river was the border between Brazil and Peru, they kept to the south side and motored along. It was late morning now with the sun higher in the sky, and it was hot and humid with a little breeze and not many mosquitoes or, not yet. Hawks looked back at the second boat and could see that Melissa had already soaked through her khaki shirt, even under the canopy and that Adam was waving off some of the mosquitoes. Jo just smiled and shook his head. He did more tourist gigs than full-fledged expeditions, so he was use to dealing with the gringos, or foreigners. While it was only twelve miles or so from Benjamin Constant to Atalaia do Norte, the river was flooded over and with unusual currents, which slowed them down. When they came up on the river town, Hawks told Jo to pull into the docks and motioned for Paulo to follow after them.

As they docked, an eager boatman came down the dock to offer his assistance. He told them in Portuguese that he would watch the canoes for them if they wanted to get a bite to eat and clean up. Paulo stood up, and the guy took one look at him and the pistol strapped to his leg and realized that they weren't easy gringo pickings and begged off. Paulo agreed to watch the canoes while the rest of the group took a break.

Melissa brought a bag with her, no doubt a dry shirt, but as they walked down the dock to the white stone building with a Coca Cola sign out front, she asked, "Hope this isn't for my benefit?"

"No, we got a late start and could use some refreshment. It's better to travel in the early morning and late afternoon, and pull over under the tree cover at midday for a siesta."

Deering now asked, "How far have we come?"

He looked to Jo. "Twenty kilometers."

Hawks added, "Twelve miles."

"And how far to the Curuca River?" Deering asked.

Jo made the calculation in his head. "About eighty miles. Reach tomorrow if we push today and get early start in morning."

"Are we sleeping under the stars?" Melissa asked.

Hawks shook his head. "Yes, but there's a Matses village we'll camp a little ways from to do some trading, but once we head south on the Curuca River, it's river beaches all the way."

"But the Marubo are in conflict with them," Melissa said.

Jo added nervously, "Yes, but I look Brazilian, and we send Paulo to deal with them."

The café had fried fish and cooked vegetables, and Coca Cola, and they sat outside at the picnic table and ate. Jo stayed inside for a while, and Hawks said that some Marubo tribesmen had migrated here, and he may have found one. A while later, while the others were eating, Jo came out of the hut and took a sandwich and drink to Paulo at the canoes.

After he was out of earshot, Melissa asked, "So, Sterling, how long have you known Jo and Paulo?"

"Well, I've used Jo on several expeditions going back three or four years."

Deering shook his head. "Must've been really young back then?"

"Well, the Marubo's life expectancy, or at least in the bush, isn't much past forty years, so they grow up fast, even those who escape to the city. Must be in their genes."

"And Paulo?" Melissa asked, her concern showing.

"He's a friend of Jo's and was on our last trip, the one down the Curuca into uncharted territory. But if you're asking if I trust him?" Melissa nodded her head. "Well, these Indians get spooked easily, but Jo has a good heart and is reliable."

"And what if we have a problem with Paulo?" Melissa asked.

"Well, we've got him outnumbered three guys to one." He paused, but before he could correct himself.

"Yeah, don't count me in," Adam volunteered.

Deering smirked. "Actually, Hawks was thinking about Melissa."

"Damn you, Deering," she said. She stood up in a huff and took her change of clothes back to the latrine hut.

Hawks turned to Deering. "What did I tell, you? Cut it out, Deering, or you can make your way back from here."

Jo came back and could feel the tension in the group. "Better we shove off. The Matses village about three hours up river." When nobody moved, he asked, "What I miss?"

Hawks stood up and took Jo by the arm as they walked back the canoes. "Nothing. Just gringo craziness. You know how they get."

Jo laughed. "Wait until they see the caiman in the river."

"I just might throw Deering in if it's anytime soon."

CHAPTER SIX

They motored along for several hours and then a torrential afternoon thunderstorm, where they couldn't see fifty feet in front of them, threatened to swamp the boats. Jo had them pull over to the north bank under overhanging tree branches to wait it out, but not before it soaked through their canopies and drenched everybody. It lasted only twenty minutes but did cool off the temperature and chased away the swarms of mosquitoes that had been bothering them, or at least for now.

While they waited Adam asked, "So this is early winter with eighty degree daytime temperatures. Does it get colder at night?"

Hawks said, "In the seventies, Fahrenheit, range. The heat doesn't hold very well, unlike in the northern hemisphere. You'll see a drop in the late afternoon."

Jo added, "That is 'til get hit with friagems; then get very, very cold."

Everyone looked to Hawks. "Cold waves of Antarctic polar air sometime penetrate the upper Amazon basin, and temperatures can get below thirty degrees for a few days."

"But we didn't pack warm clothing," Melissa said.

Hawks shook his head. "It's rare, and hardly ever this early in the season, and if it comes, by then we'll be in the village and in one of their huts, or out of here." Melissa nodded her head but seemed unconvinced.

Jo said to Melissa, "You need put something over wet shirt and put hat on?"

Melissa smirked. "I make the boys uncomfortable?"

Jo shook his head. "We in wife-stealing country, best not to . . . make show of it."

Melissa looked to Hawks. "Good advice." Hawks paused and looked sharply at Deering to forestall any wisecracks. "Okay, the rain has stopped, let's get moving again."

The two canoes motored out into the river and headed west, while Melissa put on a jacket and a straw hat. Hawks had Jo pick up the pace, and after a while Melissa turned back to Paulo in the follow-canoe and asked why.

"We get late start. Hawks want get to Estirón Village by dark so we can barter."

In the front canoe, Hawks and Jo were having a much different conversation.

"I no like we stop there. These bad people; we not stop last time," Jo said.

Hawks turned back to Jo running the outboard motor, as did Deering, who was interested in the exchange. "Jo, we didn't have . . . tourists last time, or a woman."

"That what I mean. As I say, they take women. Much bad blood between us and Matses over women."

"But since they are spread across both sides of the Javari to the Curuca River, we trade something they need, word gets out, and they leave us alone now and coming back."

Jo shook his head, and Deering said, "Sounds logical to me, Jo."

"White men don't know what bad blood mean in Amazon. No one reason. Take what they need and kill you."

This alarmed Deering, who looked back at Hawks. "There is a risk either way. But these river Matses are fairly acculturated, not like their inland brothers, or the Stone-Age tribe we're heading for."

Jo looked away and sped up the canoe. With the sun low in the sky, they reached their destination by late afternoon and pulled over to a clearing on the river bank. For last few miles they had seen Indians looking out from the high bush along the river, alerted, no doubt, by the sound of their motors. They pulled the canoes out of the river and up the incline, given the rising water later. Jo and Hawks quickly erected two tents and began to tie the hammocks to trees.

"Why the tents if we're sleeping outside in hammocks?" Melissa asked.

"In case it rains," Hawks said over his shoulder and went back to work. If it came to that, Melissa was to sleep in one tent with Adam while Deering shared the other with Hawks. Jo and Paulo would sleep in the canoes for protection, but it was obvious that Jo would be on alert all night. Now on shore, they were also swarmed by gnats, and Hawks lit the bug sticks that kept them at bay.

Jo and Hawks started a fire, and once it was going, the men huddled. "Paulo, take one of the extra machetes we brought. Go to the village and trade for a large chicken, some potatoes, beans, and bananas."

Deering added, "Is it safe for Paulo to go into the village alone?"

Melissa smirked, "You volunteering, Deering?"

Paulo shook his head. "Not good. White men in the Javari are missionaries, loggers, or miners. All slavers. Better I go alone."

"Do you speak the language?"

"No, but nobody does. I show them machete; they get the idea."

Deering turned to Hawks. "Sterling, I think you should follow at a distance with a pistol."

Melissa nodded her head. "For once I agree with Deering."

Hawks was going to protest but could see it was a unanimous decision. "Let's make it quick, Paulo. I'm getting hungry."

The men were gone for thirty minutes and came back carrying a live chicken and bags of foodstuff. Everybody was curious as to how it went, but Hawks wanted to start dinner preparations. "I'll kill and skin the chicken. Boil some water and cook the beans and potatoes, or start them, and I'll be back in ten minutes."

While Melissa was helping with the food preparation, she

said, "Why don't we just use the food Jo's wife prepared?"

Paulo said, "Once we head down the Curuca and get past Jo's Marubo tribe, we either live off the land or eat what's been prepared."

"That is until we reach our tribe?" she asked.

"Even then—you might not like the offerings or think it sanitary."

Hawks came back with a properly skinned chicken. Everyone figured he had learned the trade over the years living in the bush. He took out a metal skewer he had packed for the occasion. Melissa had taken off her now-wet outer garment and hung it on branches to dry, and Hawks told her to at least change the blouse, that the jungle had eyes. They ate; the chicken and sweet potatoes were good, but the beans were undercooked. Hawks regaled the troop with tales of campfire meals cooked and eaten in the bush around the world. What interested them most were the wild animals he had eaten. Hawks said that zebra and Cape buffalo were some of the best African meats, but nothing compared to marinated crocodile.

Deering laughed. "So the guns aren't just for wild Indians and bandits?"

"Right on, old boy. I'm thinking we'll bag a croc going down the Curuca in a day or two, and you'll see what it tastes like."

Adam said nervously. "I guess it's we eat them or they eat us."

"It's not that bad. They do keep to themselves, and the motor sounds scare them away.

Afterward they all went to their hammocks, while Jo and Paulo spread mosquito nets over them.

"What about the two of them?" Melissa asked.

Hawks said, "They don't have any sugar in their blood, so they leave them alone."

Jo and Paul now went over and lay down in their respective canoes, but everyone doubted if Jo would sleep a wink in Matses territory.

In the morning, Jo reported little or no contact overnight.

He had heard a few Indians in the bush watching them, but after he had brandished his pistol, they had scattered.

"So they were intent on harm?" Melissa asked.

"I think they want more machetes, best trade-off ever."

"With that in mind, let's shove off," Hawks said.

Adam peeped, "No breakfast?"

Hawks reached into a cellophane bag and pulled out a leftover chicken leg and threw it to Adam. "That should do you for now."

Though it wasn't very far to the Curuca River, the Javari was very circuitous at this point, and all the twists and turns slowed them down. By mid-afternoon they had made good progress, and since it was overcast and the sun wasn't too hot, they decided to push on. Along the shore, squirrel monkeys chattered away and jumped from branch to branch following their slow progress down the river. From within the jungle they could also hear the screech of howler monkeys, which sounded ungodly. Jo was driving this decision not to stop and siesta as much as Hawks, since he wanted to get out of Matses's territory and into his own native lands as soon as possible. They barely made the Curuca by nightfall and had to camp along its river bank. At this point, a few miles south and away from the Javari, Jo did feel safer. Tomorrow they would pull into a Marubo village and hopefully spend some time there before they pushed on.

The isolation of this spot for the night revealed how far they were from civilization. The weather cleared, and the night sky was spectacular, but the sounds of the jungle, especially the howler monkeys, and the absence of other human beings, even the wary Matses, was sobering. Around the fire that night, after one of Camilla's prepared meals, the edginess between Melissa and Deering seem to melt as everybody looked to each other for comfort and support. Deering even volunteered to watch the canoes so Jo and Paulo could get a good night's sleep. They appreciated the gesture, but they told him that in the jungle, whether in a tent or hut, they slept with one eye open. It was best that Deering sleep well since tomorrow his skills may be called upon at the Marubo village.

They fell asleep to the added sounds of chirping frogs. The jungle woke up with first light, and pretty soon the lively daytime animal sounds, especially the bird caws, awakened their group. Hawks had made a fire, and they had some hot chocolate that was part of the food stores before they broke down their camp and shoved off. By mid-morning, on a river that was lighter than the Javari, with its white clay foundation, they were motoring into a Marubo village.

Deering had a word with Jo before he acted as go-between. "Don't ask to barter; say this goodwill mission, in your words, and offer them gifts."

Jo turned to Hawks who nodded his head. "We'll give them some metal fishhooks and plastic fishing line and a pound bag of rice."

Deering looked at him, and Hawks responded, "You never go to an Indian village without food."

Jo moved to the bow as Hawks ran the outboard motor, and he stood there as the sound of their motors brought everybody in the village down to the riverfront. Jo greeted the assembly and made his introduction in Marubo. He had visited here with his father as a teenager, but it wasn't his home village yet. Despite his Western attire—jeans, T-shirt and baseball hat—he was still recognized as one of them. He was waved off the boat, and a group of men took him into the village to meet with the elders.

This was their first real meeting as a group with the native Indians of the area, which was a little astonishing for them. All of the women, from young girls to old women, were bare-chested with straw skirts of sorts. Some of the young women had white bark strings running from their noses to their ears, and the men were heavily tattooed on their bodies and faces and had shell earrings or drooping bones through their noses and a kind of g-string for their genitals. They lacked some of the elaborate facial ornamentation of other local tribes with their jaguar whiskers, due to the tribe's earlier exposure to missionaries, who had dissuaded them from such tribal excess. The Marubo, who had first come into contact with outsiders a hundred years ago, had been isolated in recent years after the collapse of much of the white man's industry in the region. They had relations with some neighboring tribes, like the Matis and Kulina Pano who occupied land to the east of them and were in bloody conflict with the Matses. So a group of white men just popping in on them was unexpected and not entirely welcomed, or so it seemed at first.

After some negotiations or reassurances, Jo came back and said that they were welcomed to the village for a short visit. Hawks brought out the metal hooks and fishing line and handed it to one of the men and handed the bag of rice to a woman. Another woman now stepped forward with animal pelts, which Jo waved off until Melissa stepped over and took one. She reminded him of the cooler nights coming as winter progressed, and so he graciously accepted this trade on their behalf. After the exchange, they ate a meal but first had to trek up the hill to their molocas, their palm-covered shelters located on hilltops to keep them dry from river flooding. Some of the other tribes in the area had their shelters on stilts for the same reason.

They ate cooked fish and wild boar, raw vegetables and fruits, and the Acai berry, which was new to them but would become popular in the West in the future. Jo was now questioned by one of the elders, and he gave the Marubo a long recitation. He explained that he was tracing his lineage from his mother's side. When he concluded, he was peppered with questions, which he answered and drew smiles and nods from the tribe. After a while Deering asked what the exchange was about.

"I tell them about White Man's ways, and they find them . . . funny, or the young ones who not around during last contact."

Adam asked. "Can I talk with their shaman about his medicine cures?"

Hawks shook his head. "This is a first meeting; best not to

press our luck. We'll stop by on the way back and see if the opportunity presents itself."

But as the lunch dragged on, another focus of interest was Melissa and her brassiere. The women were fascinated by it, and after lunch she followed them to a hut where she removed it and let the women try it on. Hawks explained to the others what was going on with the women, which he had seen numerous times in Africa with white women on safaris. He also added that all of their outsider contact had been with men. Deering said that he hoped she didn't hand it over to the women in exchange for more pelts. Eventually Melissa and her entourage reappeared, and she was fully contained and ready to push off. She was smiling and chuckling to herself but was unprepared to share with the group.

Out on the river and down the stream a bit, Melissa finally broke out laughing. Jo slowed down the front canoe so Paulo could come abreast of them, but Melissa couldn't stop laughing. Finally, Hawks told her to share it with the others.

"They wanted me to take a husband. Of course this was all in pantomime, but I got the idea that their men had . . . okay, dicks, the size of wild boars and would give me many babies."

The others laughed, and Hawks had to admit that was a new one on him. Deering restrained himself, and they then went back to their single-file canoe arrangement with smiles on their faces. The river was even more twisting than the Javari at its worse, and they made slow progress the rest of the afternoon. They were hit with another thunderstorm and took refuge under overhanging trees again. By now it was late afternoon, and the spot that they had come upon was actually quite suitable for a campsite, and looking at the dark sky, Hawks decided to make camp here. It looked like it would rain all night, and he didn't want to get caught out on the river and have to look for sites through a deluge. They pulled the canoes farther into the jungle and used the machetes to cut back more of the undergrowth to widen the clearing, afraid that the river might rise during the night. Just in case, they tethered the canoes to sturdy trees with rope through metal bow loops made for that reason. They pitched their tents on a higher incline for drainage.

It rained hard the entire night, but Hawks had purchased waterproof and tight zip-up tents, and so they folded up their hammocks and they stayed inside the tents to keep dry. Jo and Paulo accepted offers to sleep in the tents with them. In the morning they found that their campsite was flooded, and the canoes were floating in water. It was fortunate that Hawks had tethered them to trees. It was too wet to make a fire, and while Jo wanted to wait until the water in the river was lower, Hawks decided to shove off. They'd look for high ground down river and pull over for an early lunch. It took nearly an hour for everybody to break down the tents and pack their gear in the canoes and head out.

Jo was going cautiously slow and staying in the middle of the river since the high water level was covering up normal shore debris. In the follow-canoe, Adam asked Paulo, "I thought winter was the dry season."

Melissa answered him, "It's like the last big snow in March."

Adam nodded his head, but then their canoe hit an underwater boulder that tipped the canoe onto its side, and the three of them and their gear were tossed into the fast-moving current of the river.

CHAPTER SEVEN

The water splash immediately caught Jo's attention. He yelled for Hawks to take the motor, while he and Deering did shallow dives into the river. Deering caught up with Melissa who was totally submerged, while Jo grabbed Adam, and they made it to shore. Jo kept looking for Paulo, but he didn't come to the surface, and by the time they had reached dry land, it was too late to go swimming for him. Jo called out to Hawks, who was gathering up some of the food stores and plastic gasoline containers, to search for their guide. Hawks was also able to retrieve Adam's specimen kit of vials and bottles of alcohol, which he had put in a floatation bag for this very reason.

Hawks turned the canoe around and went downstream some ways, but could not find him. If Paulo had hit his head on a boulder and gone unconscious, his body would have floated to the surface, but with this rain-fed current and with Hawks looking to salvage the supplies, he could have floated past him on the other side of the river. Finally, after twenty minutes, Hawks brought the canoe around and headed for shore. Jo and Bennett helped him pull it up to high ground. They took out blankets and handed them to a shivering Melissa and Adam.

"No sign of him?" Deering asked.

"If his body didn't float to the surface that means—" Hawks said.

"Caiman get a man, they keep underwater, kill him and eat later."

"Jesus," Melissa said. "Do you think that's what happened?"

Hawks said, "Paulo is a good swimmer. He's been swamped

before; it's the only thing that makes sense."

While they were talking, Jo had started a fire and stepped over to the canoe to retrieve a pot to boil water. In minutes, the four wet survivors were drinking hot cocoa, and everybody sat down around the fire to gather their thoughts. Finally Melissa spoke up, "Bennett, thanks for the rescue." Adam looked to Jo and nodded his head.

"Well, if I had known there were caimans in the river, I might've thought twice about jumping in."

Melissa smiled but added, "No, I don't think you would have . . . that is, thought twice about it."

Deering quickly turned to Hawks. "So, where does this leave us?"

Hawks took a deep breath and waited a moment to reply. "Well, I was able to recover two of the gasoline containers, which should be enough to get us there and back with the extra load, since we may have to paddle through the furos, if the water recedes farther."

"Will the canoe hold two more people?" Adams asked.

"Well, most of the foodstuff is in waterproof plastic jars— Camilla is a veteran of these trips—so we can just drape them over the side in their nets to make more room," Hawks said.

Deering looked around at the others. "So, you want to go on?"

Hawks actually looked startled. "Of course."

Deering stared back wearily. "Come on, Deering, you've been on expeditions that have lost men."

"Land expeditions, but what happens if you lose our one remaining canoe?"

Everybody gave this a moment's thought. "We'd be screwed," Melissa said.

Deering turned to her. "So you agree. We should turn back?"

Melissa didn't immediately reply, and Jo added, "We can go to Marubo village, rest, and then go back to Tabatinga."

Adam added, "If I can spend some time with their medicine

man and bring back some cures, maybe Connor will fund a bigger expedition next summer."

Melissa was still thinking it over. Finally, Deering added, "Come on, Croft. The idea of a lost tribe of white Amazon women is rather preposterous to begin with."

Jo looked startled. "White women tribe?"

Hawks turned to him. "It's a long story."

Deering pressed on. "I say we put it to a vote." He looked around the group. Finally, Adam piped up. "I'm with Deering. This is way too dangerous."

When Melissa still held back, the two men turned to Jo. "I do what Mister Hawks wants."

Finally, Melissa added, "We push on. Too many people in our group already know about this . . . legend. If we return now, it will get out, and the lower Curuca River basin will be swamped before we can get back."

Hawks added, "Okay, now that that's settled, let's push on."

*****

"Jesus, Mother. What were you thinking?" Mattie asked.

Melissa took another sip of water from her container. "I wasn't thinking, I guess, or my fixation was thinking for me."

Mattie laughed. "So, knowing they would be 'bare-chested' after your last tribal encounter, you sure it was your 'fixation' talking?"

"Don't be crude, Madeline."

"No, Bennett was right. It was a harebrained idea, and when the dangers of the expedition became apparent—"

"The animus, or my masculine side, as I was to learn later, can be tyrannical, and, so, in its grip, I 'pushed on,' like Hawks encouraged us."

"It had to be more than that," Mattie said after a moment.

Melissa nodded her head. "As my therapist told me later, my denied feminine was never the enchantress, but more the devouring 'witch' aspect, and it could sense, or even smell, its counterpart in this legend, and I needed to confront this aspect of myself."

Mattie sat back in her chair and gave her mother a long look. "Witch aspect?" She shook her head. "Connor always said you were a little crazy."

Melissa coughed, and then nodded her head toward the bay windows. "Coming from a man who would shoot skeet with a shotgun off that very balcony."

"Okay, I can see that this hits a sore spot, so let's just go on." Mattie paused. "But you're right. It's a . . . fascinating tale."

"I'm hoping it'll be instructional as well my dear."

"You can hope all you want, Mother, just tell me more."

*****

It took them two hours to repack their one remaining canoe, store the extra foodstuff in nets, which they flung over the side, and continue their trip down the river. After about two miles, Jo saw it first and nodded to Hawks, who looked to his left—it was the eaten remains of Paulo. Fortunately, at that point, the others were looking to their right as they passed overhanging trees where a flock of colorful miner birds was perched. They passed several small Marubo villages on either side of the river, where the Indians, alerted by the sound of their outboard, came to the riverfront to watch them pass. Hawks glanced at Jo, who shook his head, and they just motored on. At some point hours downstream, Hawks asked if everybody wanted to pull over and eat lunch, but nobody had an appetite at this point, and Melissa went through the food cache and passed around dry fruit that Camilla had packed.

By late afternoon they had reached the juncture where the Rio Curuca turned into the Rio Pardo, and the Curuca split off and went south with a river width and flow that was much the same. Hawks decided to pull the canoe over at this point to camp, since the jungle was more lush and inviting here, and tomorrow they would reach and turn down the much narrower

Rio Arrojo. From that the point the passage would be more difficult, though it wasn't far from there to their destination. He could sense the letdown in the group from the loss of their guide and from the divided group decision to push on with the expedition.

Dinner that night was the most somber of their meals so far. It was obvious by his absence that Paulo had been the live-wire of the group who either kept everybody entertained or pressed them for stories. Finally, after they had eaten their meal but before they had repacked what remained and put away the containers, Jo asked, "Tell me about white women tribe."

Hawks said, "Remember, the white-skinned native boy at the camp last time?"

"Yes. But you talk him and elders, and I not there."

"They claimed that one of their native boys went off into the jungle on his own and never came back, and then a year later this white-skinned baby was placed outside their village."

Jo thought about this. "Must be white-skinned mother, you say?"

"Yes, that's the idea."

"Before then I not come this far south on Rio Curuca and Arrojo, but they say Indians here smoke . . . dream-making stuff."

Hawks smiled. "Well, the boy was no dream, nor was the axe I trade them for."

"You go look for white Indians?" Hawks nodded his head. "I go with you."

Melissa snorted. "You just want to see the bare-chested white women."

Everybody else laughed, but Jo was completely serious with his reply. "Breasts I see plenty, but white natives. I like see them. We take some back?"

It was Hawks turned to laugh. "Now wouldn't that be a kicker."

Melissa had an intense dream that night after all the talk

about bare-chested white women. She and her girlfriend Pamela were making love on the beach, her mouth half filled with sand and Pam's sweet juices. She had apparently masturbated in her sleep with the accompanying sounds, which Adam apparently heard in his nearby hammock, because the next morning Adam asked what the sleeping arrangement would be at the village. Melissa blushed, and the others figured out the cause of his inquiry.

This would be the last day of their trip downstream, and Hawks said they should arrive at the village by late afternoon. This got everybody moving more quickly that morning, and they ate breakfast and were packed and off in the canoe earlier than usual. It was another clear day, and the hope was that the winter's dry season had finally taken effect and that they wouldn't be hit with any afternoon thunderstorms. They rode downstream for about two hours when they came to the juncture with the Rio Arrojo, where Jo steered the canoe left for about a quarter mile into much darker waters and then south into the Arrojo—there was a loop heading north that apparently came back around to this same spot. What was interesting was that the riverfront, like that of the Curuca River, was of lighter clay but the water was much darker.

This river was not as circuitous, although it had several ring loops they hadn't encountered on the other rivers they had traveled. After three hours, they came to another fork that headed southwest a bit, and the river thinned out further and was more circuitous. Here the branches from both sides of the river occasionally met in the center, but they only rode down their offshoot branch of the river for a couple miles before they turned into a much smaller furo. The water was still high enough here to navigate it with the motor running; there were two other turnoffs into even smaller furos, but soon Jo pulled over to a clearing that had a definite path leading into the jungle.

"Okay, we're here, or a half-mile or so from their village," Hawks said. "Let's pull the canoe up a hundred yards or so, and make camp."

Melissa asked. "We're not going straight to the village?"

"We're not; I'm going to head there and tell them I'm back and that I've brought visitors."

"So, you'll then come back and get us?" Adam asked tentatively.

"Oh, I'll be back, but whether they're ready or willing to meet with the rest of you, outside of Jo, who they know, is another question."

"Well, let's hope that changes, or this is a waste," Deering added half-heartedly.

Hawks didn't feel like he had to explain himself. He packed a backpack with gifts that he had prepared for them—flashlights and batteries, metal utensils, and a few other sundry things.

Deering asked, "No food?"

Hawks shook his head. We'll have to show them how to cook rice before I give them some." He now turned to Jo. "Take out a machete and strap it to your leg. Make a show of it, so that any Indians spying on the group from the jungle won't think you're easy pickings, as I believe the Yanks call it."

"Well, that sounds unfriendly," Melissa added.

"Like with the Marubo, these tribes aren't used to white people just dropping in on them."

As Hawks headed out, he turned back at the last moment and told them, "Don't worry, it's just polite to show up alone and get reacquainted first."

After Hawks had been gone for nearly two hours, and the sun was low in the sky, Deering told Jo to break out the tents and make a campsite. Melissa gave him a look. "I don't think we're spending the night at the Tribal Inn, so let's set it up here before it gets dark and start cooking some food."

"Yeah, I'm getting hungry," Adam said rather nervously.

They pitched their tents, started a fire, and when Hawks hadn't come back within the hour, they ate dinner. It was nearly dark when Sterling returned with a wizened old native with short gray hair and a loose wiry body. Everybody stood up to greet him.

Hawks introduced him. "This is Alem, or the name I've given him. He is an elder and their medicine man, and he's here to welcome us."

Nobody knew how to greet a wild Indian, and so they followed Deering's lead and just bowed their heads at Alem. He bowed back to each of them, and they understood that this was some kind of universal greeting. Deering offered him a cup of cocoa, which he accepted, took a sip, and nodded his head in delight and finished it off.

Hawks told them, "For tonight, we'll stay here, but tomorrow we are welcomed to come to their village. We will be assigned huts, but are also expected to work for our keep in terms of food gathering, cooking, cleanup, and whatnot."

Alem nodded his head as an acknowledgment of Hawk's statement. He turned to walk back down the path. By now it was dark, and Deering reached into his backpack and took out a flashlight and turned it on. He clucked his tongue, and Alem turned back to the group. Deering handed him the light. He graciously accepted it, clicked it off, as he had no doubt been shown how, and walked back up the path in the dark.

Hawks explained. "The guy can see in the dark, and he knows this path like the back of his hand."

"Not waste batteries," Jo added.

"Yes, they had gone through all that I left with them last time."

Hawks sat down and everybody took a seat around the fire.

"So, how did it go?" Melissa asked.

"They were glad to see me. I had told them I was coming back, but they don't track time like we do, and for them it was like only a couple months since I left."

"And white men showing up at the doorstep?" Deering asked.

"I indicated that each of you were good at something and can help the tribe. As an example, I went to Alem's hut, took out some herbs, and indicated that one of us had knowledge about them. And that Melissa could work with their 'talk.'"

"Yes, I can also help him with their cultivation of plants and herbs," Adam said with a smile, feeling better about their "first contact."

Melissa added, "I had planned to do a language primer, but it's a longtime process."

Deering nodded his head. "It's important that we show that we are givers, not takers at any level. Even though they haven't been contacted by other white men or outsiders, they run into other tribes on hunting forays and have no doubt heard the stories."

Hawks added, "And in regard to the Amazon women tribe and our intent to seek them out, let's let that go for now. We'll get into the rhythm of their daily lives and once they're more comfortable with us, we can venture the topic."

Deering nodded his head. "Excellent advice, Sterling. I agree. Don't overstep our bounds with them until they are ready to go there."

"There is one other thing that I've kept from you." He now turned to Melissa. "This is a Stone-Age tribe, and whatever the cultural anthropologists say, it is patriarchal to its core and it values women over resources, or how many wives you have, how many you've stolen from other tribes. And an unattached white female will cause problems, which Alem pointed out."

Melissa locked her jaw. "What are you telling me Hawks?"

"That, as of now, you and Bennett are man and wife, which they can respect. This will protect you somewhat, but Bennett . . ." He paused and turned to Deering. "You have to be a strong male; you show any weakness, and these men will pounce on Melissa like cats on mice."

Deering shook his head. "That's not what I've found working with other indigenous tribes."

"Other somewhat acculturated tribes, Deering. Again these people are from the Stone Age, and I'm telling you the dynamics are sexual not cultural. Look, I waited to spring this on you because I know it's going to be a strain, but it was the only way to get you both here."

Deering now glared back at Hawks. "Okay, tell us about this other agenda of yours, now that we're being forthright." Hawks smiled. "I mean, there are no ruins here for archeologists to snoop out, no ancient hidden civilizations like the Mayan or Aztecs waiting to be discovered."

Hawks smiled. "There are indications that there was a pre-Columbian civilization in the Amazon basin."

Deering sneered, "You're not buying into the old Spanish conquistadors search for El Dorado, or their tales of huge cities and interconnected highways?"

"No, that was nonsense because there are no stone quarries to build from like in the Andes and Central America. I am talking about thatched-hut cities and cleared dirt roads, whose populations were totally wiped out by disease, like 90 percent of the natives, and what you see are their remnants."

"And this lost tribe of women could've been part of that, the fierce Amazon women tribe who allegedly fought Francisco de Orellana and gave their name to the river?" Melissa asked. "And who then escaped farther into the jungle and escaped the spread of their disease?"

"Yes, my dear. That's my thinking."

Deering shook his head. "Hawks, he fought a male Indian tribe whose dress and facial adornments reminded the Europeans of women, but weren't actually women warriors."

"That's how some historians dismiss de Orellana's claim."

Everyone gave this some thought. Deering finally turned to Melissa. "Look, I see Hawks' point in regard to us living together for your protection, so let's just make it work with a minimal amount of discomfort."

"The discomfort, Deering, will be all yours, I can assure you." Melissa stood up and started to tie her hammock to two nearby trees as the others followed suit.

Jo turned to Hawks. "I wonder how you do that. Cause big problem if she go in alone."

Hawks nodded his head. "Still. We need to keep an eye on her. Tribesmen poaching her could spoil everything I tried to build here."

CHAPTER EIGHT

Later, lying in his hammock and getting a glimpse of the night sky through the thin overhead branches of their riverside camp, Deering thought about what Hawks had said about the sexual dynamics of this Stone-Age tribe. He had minored in biology in college, and so he wasn't as locked into the prevailing anthropological perspective that culture, not basic human drives, was the social organizing principle of primitive tribes in the past or in these uncontacted tribes today. He had always had a sneaky suspicion that his teachers and the esteemed authorities in the field, few of whom had any actual field experience, were projecting their own idealized view of "primitives" from the social dynamics that arose in the past from ancient civilizations far removed from the jungle or mountains from which their ancestors arose.

Earlier this year a professor in the biology department at the University of Miami, where he was lecturing for a semester, had passed him last year's copy of the Journal of Theoretical Biology. In it an English biologist, William D. Hamilton, proposed a theory he called "inclusive fitness" about how kinship relationships were the nuclear bond or social cohesion in primitive societies. This challenged the prevailing thinking in cultural anthropological circles—he could imagine his teachers at Oxford going apoplectic over this theory—as it reduced their high and mighty concepts to biological drives. He was not, nor professed to be, a Darwinian advocate, while admiring the man and his breakthrough theories, since in the field he could see his theory of natural selection at work. But, for now, he sided with colleagues about culture over biology, but this experience would certainly test that bias.

In the morning, Hawks pulled a bucket out of the canoe, which everybody thought was for bailing out water in rough weather, but then he removed a fine-mesh cloth that served as a balloon-shaped sluice with tiny holes in it.

"This is our shower. You tie this cloth filter to a branch, someone takes a bucket of river water and pours it through, and the person underneath takes a shower."

"Why don't we just jump in the river?" Melissa asked, and appeared rather put-off by this whole two-person bathing concept, being the only woman.

"There are tiny parasitic fish that will swim up any exposed orifice and cause intestinal problems, to say the least. We'll leave one of the tents here with the bucket and sluice and periodically we can come down here to bathe. So, if anybody wants to take a shower now, here's your chance."

"We can't do this in the village?" Melissa protested.

"Believe me. The concept of body odor and cleanliness is beyond them. There is a nearby stream, but not with much privacy, and we don't want to . . . expose you."

Melissa sighed.

Hawks handed Deering the bucket and added, "Look, the two of you better get used to living together as a couple."

Deering took the bucket and carried it down to the river and filled it. In the meantime, Hawks led Melissa into the jungle to provide her with some privacy. "You can leave on your underwear, but then it'll get wet," Hawks told her.

Deering returned and saw Melissa standing under the sluice half-naked. "I'll close my eyes," he offered in mock gallantry.

"Oh, screw it." Melissa stripped off her undergarments, carefully hanging them on the nearby tree branches, while Deering poured this bucket of water and then several others through the sluice for her to soap up and bathe. Adam was next, but after he finished nobody else seemed interested. Melissa now grabbed the bucket and turned to Deering.

"Deering, if you expect to sleep in the same hut with me, you're going to bathe."

He started to protest, but one look from Hawks sent him into the jungle while Melissa took the bucket down to the river. After Deering was finished, they brought the bucket and sluice back to the camp, and Hawks emptied the sluice onto a flat rock and found three of the tiny parasitic fish.

"What did I tell you?" Hawks asked.

"Jesus," Melissa cursed.

By this time Hawks and Adam had broken down the camp and filled the backpacks with what they would need, and everybody grabbed their backpack and they headed out to the village.

After about fifteen minutes of slow jungle-path hiking, they came up on Alem who was sitting on a boulder apparently patiently waiting for them. They figured he had been there for a while, but Hawks answered their questioning looks, "He's a medicine man and can . . . see at a distance." Deering had to force himself not to snort at this concept. Alem slid off the boulder and stepped over to the troop. He looked at Melissa and then to Hawks who pointed at Deering. Alem grabbed Melissa by the arm and placed her next to Deering in their line and then put their hands together. They were a bit confused.

"He wants you to hold hands as you walk into the village to assert Deering's rights to you."

Melissa made a face but didn't reply, and forced herself to take Deering's hand. "I am glad that you washed this morning, my dear," he added with a sneer.

"Well, it didn't disguise your foulness, Bennett."

Alem watched this dynamic and nodded to Hawks. Apparently marital discord was the foundation of primitive marriages as well. Alem now turned and led them down the path to the village. As they approached, Deering had expected to see high walls of leafy plants with few access points for protection, but Hawks quickly corrected that expectation.

"This is a thatched maloca or tribal village. Since they are so far south and away from other tribes who would attack them, they live close to the river furos and are fairly exposed. Most uncontacted tribes north of here live in the jungle's rugged interior between rivers to avoid any contact with outsiders and poaching tribes."

The group moved closer to the village as Hawks added, with a hand on Deering's arm, "Which doesn't mean they're friendly to outsiders, especially white men."

At the perimeter of the village, Alem put up his arm, and Hawks told them to wait there. The two of them stepped through the opening between the tall bushes and disappeared inside. Five minutes later Alem stepped out, took Adam by the arm and walked him inside. Deering and Melissa started to follow, but he put up his hand like a traffic cop. They stopped and would wait for him to retrieve them. Fifteen minutes later, Alem stepped out, pointed to their hands, which they were not holding but which they quickly clasped together again, and they followed him through the opening into the village.

Inside, they were met by a row of fierce-looking tribesmen, with red-dyed tattoos and thin cords for their male members, who upon seeing Melissa crowded around her and started to inspect her, touching every part of her body, especially her breasts. Hawks told her to be totally nonresistant and let them conduct their inspection. They also smelled her hair, her face, one of them put a nose in her crotch—she was glad she had changed into long pants. Deering kept hold of her hand, even though they tried to push him aside. Finally after ten minutes, one of the tribesmen tried to yank her out of Deering's grasp and take her away. Hawks nodded, and Deering stepped between Melissa and the man, who was either the chief or one of the tribal leaders.

Deering pointed his finger at the woman's chest and then pointed to him. Everyone understood his meaning. The tribesman stepped right up to him, nose to nose, and spat in his face. Deering spat back at him. The chief stepped back a foot, and Deering was afraid they would come to blows, but the man smiled, grabbed Deering's crotch, and said something to the others. He took it as a compliment to his masculinity. They now started their inspection of him. At one point one of the men tried to slip off Deering's camping shorts, no doubt to inspect his genitals, but he resisted and the tribesman desisted. They emptied his pockets, which Hawks had told him to stuff with souvenirs—which they confiscated—and seemed pleased with their bounty. The chief turned to Hawks and nodded his head, and Alem stepped forward and showed them to their separate huts.

Hawks had already mentioned that unlike the long houses of the Matses, Matis, and Marubos, where as many as one hundred people live together, they had small huts like the Korubos. Deering and Melissa were now ushered into their hut. They quickly unpacked their backpacks and began to string up their hammocks on opposite sides of the small space. Neither spoke to the other about what had just transpired. Melissa was somewhat shell shocked by her rough handling and the attempt by the chief to claim her as his wife or concubine, or whatever they called it here. Finally, after the hammocks were set up and their personal items laid out for easy access, Melissa turned to Deering.

"Bennett, I know this was part of the ritual going in, but thanks for standing up to them. I don't know what I would've done if the chief had taken me away."

He stopped fiddling with his stuff and looked back at her. "I'm sure you would have expressed your displeasure . . . forcibly."

"Which might have just been a form of foreplay to him."

"Well, I hope you return the favor if any of the local maidens make a move on me."

Melissa laughed. "You sure about that?"

Hawks now stuck his head through the grass hanging that posed as a door. Seeing that the two of them were cordially talking to each other, he stepped inside. "Good show, old boy.

The chief definitely got the message. In fact he was so impressed that he wanted to give you one of his wives."

Melissa snickered, "You ought to look her over; she might be a good catch."

Deering rolled his eyes. "I hope you handled my decline rather diplomatically, Hawks?"

"Well, what you have to understand is that he was just trying to add to your stature in the village. The more wives, the more respect you receive from others."

"Is this going to be an ongoing problem?" he asked.

"Let's hope not. I indicated that in our culture men only took one wife."

This made Melissa very curious. "How did you communicate something that complex to him with only a basic grasp of the language?"

"I used sign language, touched my heart with one hand, and pointed to the heavens with the other."

"Brilliant, Sterling. A marriage made by the Gods. That should keep them at bay for a while."

"Well, the next test is going to be the feast they're preparing for us. They started cooking a wild boar."

"Test?" Deering asked.

"They eat with their hands and pass around bowls of foodstuff that you dip your hand in, scoop out a portion, and eat it. Totally unsanitary, but if you beg off, it's a sign of disrespect and things could get dicey."

"Well, don't want to force the issue, but I'd like to start working with Alem to try to understand their language." Hawks nodded his head. "Does Jo know it at all?"

"We were here last time for a month, and while it's not exactly a Panoan language group or subgroup, we both figured out a few things."

"Good. Maybe I'll start with him. Where's his hut?" Melissa asked.

Hawks shook his head. "You can't go by yourself to any man's hut, not even Alem's, unless his wife comes to you and takes you there, or it will be seen as a sexual overture and will lead to . . . complications."

"Really?" Melissa threw her hands up the air.

Deering added, "From what I've seen already, at this stage of their acculturation, or lack of it, Hamilton and the biologists seem to be right on about the sexual dynamics of these primitive tribes. So, for any interaction with another male, I need to be there with you, or the man's wife invites you."

"And Jo?"

"I assume I can play the wife part in this case and ask him to our hut."

"Yes, I think that'll work," Hawks said.

Adam now stuck his head into the hut. "Am I missing something?"

Hawks pulled him inside. He turned to Deering. "Step outside and make a show of your presence, with all these males in your wife's hut."

"My wife's hut?"

"Yes, the homes belong to the first wife. If the male breaks up with her, he goes to the hut of his new first wife."

"First wife?" Adam asked.

Hawks patted him on the back. "Yes, they all take a number, his choice, and have a place. We should be so lucky."

"And he brings his other wives with him?" Melissa asked.

"Yes, there's no jealousy in this regard. The more the merrier."

Melissa laughed. "Bennett, I think you better start taking notes. There's a book waiting to be written about this contact."

"Speaking of books, when can I start working with the medicine man?" Adam asked.

"First," Hawks said, "Melissa needs to work with Alem to get a hang of their language."

"Speaking of which," Deering said, "why don't I escort the two of you out of my wife's hut, and I'll go get Jo so we can start that process."

Melissa turned to Hawks as the three men stepped toward the grass door. "Do I need a gun to protect myself, or something?"

Deering answered her. "There's a machete in my backpack if that'll make you more comfortable."

Outside Hawks and Adam headed for their hut. Deering stood in front of theirs for five minutes while people went about their business with one eye on him. Finally, he walked down to Jo's hut. There were two young women sitting outside. He stepped between them but stopped short as he heard the unmistakable sounds of lovemaking activity from inside. Boy, that was quick of him, Deering thought, but then Jo had spent time here. He must've acquired a second wife. He wondered if Camilla knew about her. He also wondered if the two girls outside were his number three and four wives.

Deering went back to his "wife's" hut. When he stepped inside, Melissa asked. "Where's Jo?"

"Well, it seems that he is...getting to know old acquaintances."

Melissa almost dropped the clothing she was holding and sorting through. "You're kidding. He's having sex with someone?"

"Yes, and there were two other girls apparently waiting for more of the same."

"Jesus," Melissa said, and Deering smiled. "Well, don't get any ideas, Bennett. Our 'marriage,' if that's what you can call it, is make-believe."

"I understand. But these thatched huts have thin walls, and at some point we'll have to . . . pantomime doing it or at least make sexual intercourse sounds."

Melissa jumped into her hammock, started pumping her hips and moaned and groaned until her pretended climax.

"Very good, my dear."

Melissa leaned over the edge of the hammock. "Don't call me 'dear,' dear."

CHAPTER NINE

In the morning, Melissa, with Jo's help, began her work with Alem to construct a basic vocabulary of their language. The tribe's language was unique but bore similarities, given their geographic location, to some Panoan languages such as the Marubo's. They first started in Alem's hut as she pointed to an object and heard Alem speak its name. Jo had a much better ear for the sound of their language and would repeat the word to her phonetically, and she would write down its English equivalent as syllables or morphemes—a freestanding word or just part of one. Alem seemed to enjoy the process and treated it like a game, especially when she pointed to his body parts like his nose, eyes, and ears to which he replied with broad similes. After a couple hours, they had exhausted the items in his hut, and they stepped outside and walked around the village, where she would point out items like a hut or a girl or a canoe, and he would give them their names. They then went onto animals and plants, and even the sky and the sun—without seeing it and only by interpreting her sign language he gave her the name of the moon as well. After she had a rudimentary vocabulary of things in their world, she would move on to actions and their verbs, like throwing a stone.

By the third day, Jo was getting bored or was anxious to get back to his "wives," or so Melissa thought. But before he left her alone with Alem, she went over the existing vocabulary and vocalized the sounds to determine the exact number of phonemes or units of sound in these words. She discovered that the language appeared to have some twelve consonant phonemes and four vowel phonemes, if the diphthongs were sounded together with the vowels, in contrast to English's forty-four phonemes. While she wasn't a linguist but a philologist of ancient languages, she could tell that this was a very sparse and simple language, but it wasn't until she tried to establish an elementary grammar later in the week, that she realized just how simple it was. Their language had no person, tense (other than the present), number, or gender. They seemed to live strictly in the present; their history was only as long as they had a memory of it, with no strict concept of time or its passage. She asked Alem, or as best as she could, if he remembered when he first met Hawks, and he told her, or she interpreted him as saying, "I see him today." Further inquiry in this direction was fruitless. At first she thought this was due to the immediacies of their struggle for survival, but without a stored food supply, the tribesmen often went hungry; they ate only when they could hunt or fish for available food.

After the first few days of gathering information, Melissa took her work to Deering, who had taken a course in anthropological linguistics. He helped her write an orthography, or a preliminary alphabet, based on her phoneme research with Alem. Anthropologists, and even missionaries are used to converting a spoken language to a written one, like the Hawaiian missionaries, had done in the mid-nineteenth century. Of course, this would take years to fill out, but they were getting a grasp of the basic structure and would soon be able to communicate with them better using this vocabulary and hand signs. The fact that their language had no tense, person, or number, made it easier than with a more complex system. But language is based on culture and its underlying precepts, and theirs was rather "foreign" to a sophisticated Westerner.

"What you have to understand, Croft, is that this is a borderline Paleolithic society, which we haven't seen in the West in ten thousand years."

"Yes, I get that, but the immediacy of everything, the almost total lack of abstraction, or how everything is based on personal experience, with no real history beyond their own memory, is rather . . . unsettling."

Deering smiled. "We've become such mental creatures that it's indeed shocking to our sensibilities, but as you'll notice, there's absolutely no stress in their personal relationships, no taboos on sex or just about anything else. They may die young, and I would imagine that's due to a lack of proper nutrition, but not to cancer or high blood pressure."

"They're lucky the missionaries haven't gotten to them yet."

"Yeah, tell me. They say they want to save the Indians' souls, but what they really want is to wipe out their rather pristine . . . state of being and pass along their own brand of madness."

"Spoken like a true atheist, or is it pantheism you ascribed to?"

Deering smiled. "Well, what I've noticed looking into their eyes is this deep connection to the natural world around them. There's a spark—an aliveness—there that you don't find in the acculturated tribes I've been around, and never among white men."

Melissa looked at him sitting cross-legged on his hammock. "Quite a contrast to Merry Old England."

"Now you know my secret. I'm a wild spirit at heart."

Melissa nodded her head. "Well, maybe not with this tribe, but you should go native, Deering, get a wife or two or three and live among them."

He smiled. "Well, the thought has crossed my mind, but the situation hasn't presented itself."

Melissa stared back at him. "You're serious?"

Deering didn't answer her. "Well, we better hit the sack, as you Americans say, because we have a long day among the primitives tomorrow."

He reached over and snuffed out the candle, leaving the hut in total darkness.

While Melissa was working with Alem and then Deering to

construct a basic vocabulary of their language, Adam was going out every day with Alem's shaman apprentice, Eno, or the name like Alem's that Hawks had bestowed on him since his native name was incomprehensible to them. They left early every morning and headed into the jungle to gather plants. Since they couldn't communicate with each other, they used sign language or pantomime. Eno would point out a plant or bush and rub a part of his body that it affected; Adam got the idea. But Eno was not collecting enough of each "voucher specimen" for Adam's further use, and he counted off with his fingers the larger number he required. The Indian smiled and agreeably added them to his collection bag. Adam was at first concerned that they were stuffing everything into the same bag, but he figured that Eno would separate them out back at the camp.

What was not foreign to Adam was the taste test that Eno had him do. All of the plants that he collected had a bitter taste to them. This was a sign of the alkaloid content of the plant, which was one of the toxic chemicals that plants produce as a natural defense to bugs and animals. It's also what gives coffee its boost and drugs like cocaine and heroin their rush. It has been the clue for medicine men and botanists from ancient times to the modern era, from deserts to jungles, that the plant has therapeutic value. Adam recalled a teacher's introduction to this subject in college using quinine, with its stringent bitter taste, in the bark of the cinchona tree, as an example. It was used by South American Indians for centuries in a powder form to cure malarial and other fevers. The tree was supposedly named after the Countess Chinchon, the wife of the then Peruvian viceroy, who was cured of malaria by a remedy using the powder.

After three days, they had collected enough herbs, bark, and sap for both the shaman's and Adam's use. The following day they met with Melissa and Alem to sort out names for herbs and what they cured. One of the first herbs had a triangular leaf. Alem examined it and then clutched his crotch and started to pump it. Melissa thought it might be for male erection or performance, but this was much too complex an idea for them to communicate at this level of her grasp of their language. Adam went and fetched Jo, who listened to Alem's explanation and got a gist of it.

"It for sex disease, I believe."

Adam's eyes lit up. The jackpot. He quickly sketched the leaf in his notebook and added a brief notation about its cure. Eno then separated out several large leaves, which Adam placed in a plastic specimen jar. Alem pronounced the name of the herb, and Melissa was able to give Adam its phonetic breakdown and a word to write in his book and on the jar's label. Next came an arrowhead-shaped leaf they used for headaches, then the sap of a tree that staunched the flow of blood in a wound, and the naming and identification process ensued. This went on for two hours with various remedies, most of which Alem could just point to a part of his body as Eno had, and they understood the ailment and cure with a little back-and-forth between them. But it was the root of the next herb that excited Adam the most. It took them some time to understand its use with their limited vocabulary. Finally Jo figured out it had to do with sugar in the blood and lowering it.

Adam asked, "How did they arrive at that conclusion?"

Melissa asked Alem, and Jo had to help with the translation, but finally he said, "They taste the person's urine before and after."

Adam laughed. "I guess that would do it, but I'd hate to ask a stateside doctor to use that diagnostic methodology."

He now took particular care with his would-be cure for diabetes. Before they had finished with the collection bag of herbs, Alem said enough for today. All this, and he pointed to his head, mental work—or they translated the gesture as such—had tired him out. They wouldn't resume their sorting and naming "work" until the end of the week. But that was fine with Adam; he had to now properly preserve his specimens for chemical analysis later. Usually an ethnobotanist would collect a kilogram or two pounds of dried and fresh plant material for further analysis, but Adam had realized from the start of the expedition, despite Connor Croft's funding, that this wasn't strictly an ethnobotanist exploration for possible drugs. He would have to be satisfied with a half-dozen specimens of each herb or bark specimen.

So, now with Eno and several tribesmen looking on, he carefully added alcohol to each of the specimen jars to preserve the herb's active chemical compounds. Hawks walked by and saw the alcohol bottles and told Adam not to let any of the natives take a sip, or they would raid his stores for sure, even his precious specimen jars. He now called Jo over to help "police" the process.

"These natives don't drink intoxicants?" Adam asked.

"They make an alcoholic beverage from the root of the commonly called cassava plant, an edible tuber, and from which they make their flour, but it's not nearly as potent as what you're using."

"Okay. I'll be careful."

Hawks watched him for a while. "You're not drying them out?"

"No, this is not to preserve pretty floral specimens for glass cases in a college library, but to analyze their chemical properties."

"Well, I know you're anxious to collect a lot, just realize our space limitations, and that of your flotation case, which, incidentally, was a brilliant idea."

"Thanks, Sterling. I've never been in the field before, but I read about river expeditions losing their specimens in tip-overs and took the precaution."

Now that they had settled into the life of the village, Melissa broke out a bag of rice and boiled some for dinner the next night. Quickly the women crowded around and watched her. She added more rice, and after she had boiled it, put small portions of the cooked rice on a plate and passed it around the group. They ate it with their fingers and seemed to like it. Two of the women went back to their huts and brought back some bread made from cassava and fresh vegetables. They sat down around the fire and ate. Melissa now knew to bring her vocabulary book with her everywhere she went in the village, and they asked where this "rice" grows so they could gather more.

Melissa waved to Jo and one of his "wives," and he helped her translate that it didn't grow wild in the forest, but had to be cultivated or grown. This apparently was the first time they had heard of this concept. Melissa asked where they got the tuber roots for their flour, and they said they went out into the forest and pulled up the roots of the woody shrub when they needed more. That night Melissa, accompanied by her "husband" Bennett, went to the hut that Adam shared with Hawks.

They had eaten some of Camilla's prepared food that night, and Melissa told them about her dinner with the village women and the rice she had cooked for them.

"I mean the whole concept of cultivating plants for food is totally new to them."

"But the other tribes here do it, why don't they?" Adam asked.

Hawks said, "They are, for all intentional purposes, an uncontacted tribe. Not part of some larger tribe where cultural information is passed along. They have lived in this remote part of the jungle for . . . ages."

"But they knew about the white babies being left outside of other tribal villages."

"The men are hunters and go far afield for their prey sometimes. They come in wary contact with others, and may exchange 'rumors,' but they don't sit down around a fire and compare hunting or food gathering tips."

"Well, the women at least felt open to learning how to cultivate this shrub whose tuber they use for flour."

Deering added, "This may all be well-meaning on our part, but so are the missionaries who push Jesus down their throats and wreak havoc on the culture of other Indian tribes."

They all considered this insight, which made Melissa bristle. "So we just leave the 'noble savages' like they are?"

Hawks quickly added, "This is different, Bennett. We're not trying to change or alter them, but help them deal with their food shortages."

Deering nodded his head. "But cultivation requires constant and steady work, especially in a rainy climate where flooding can wipe out a crop overnight. It will change them as it has changed other such societies."

Hawks said, "Wait a second." He parted the grass door and came back five minutes later with Jo, who was still buttoning up his shirt to everybody's amusement. Hawks now asked him how cultivating plants by his tribe had helped or hurt their development.

Jo realized he was being invited into serious white-man discussion, and he gave it due consideration. Finally, he added, "Before rubber-tappers and Jesus people come, my father say tribe see that we eat . . . all plants and kill all the animals jungle area and move to other, is not . . . good. So we move near to river to fish—fish never run out—and we plant food. This is what others do too."

Deering looked to Hawks. "So, if this is a natural evolution, as it has been elsewhere, why haven't they thought of it yet?"

Adam added, "Maybe they don't have enough protein in their diet."

This drew a round of chuckles from the others. Finally, Hawks said, "Tomorrow, Melissa and I will talk with the so-called chief about it. Deering, you and Adam should join us."

"Okay, but I'm still not sure this is such a good idea," Deering said.

"We'll let them decide."

CHAPTER TEN

Before the group stopped by to "talk" with the chief or headsman, they met in Hawks's hut the next morning. Deering needed to share with them some of the difficulties inherent in their cultivation plan. "Everybody thinks, because of the Amazon's endlessly thick forests, that the soil here is rich with nutrients, but it's very poor, and once you clear a large splotch of it, it takes a very long time to grow back."

"You're kidding," Melissa said, shaking her head. "All this lush vegetation from poor soil?" They both looked to Adam.

He nodded his head. "The nutrients are in the plants and trees, and because it's a close ecosystem, it draws its mineral nutrients from fallen leaves and decomposing plants."

Hawks asked, "So we don't ask them to clear a field, but create a garden amidst the undergrowth where some sunlight enters and plant a couple rows of this cassava there?"

"Yes, this is what I would recommend," Adam said.

They all looked to Melissa. "Okay, but trying to explain this to them with my limited vocabulary is going to be a stretch."

"Fortunately, once it's planted, it won't take much cultivation with all this rain, and since it grows wild here anyway," Adam said.

Melissa still looked daunted. "Why don't we ask Jo to join us?" Hawks asked. She nodded, and Deering went looking for him.

Since the idea of scheduling a meeting at an appointed time was alien to their whole culture, the group decided just to show up at Uni's hut—what she had Alem extract from his long Indian name—and hope for an audience.

They arrived at his hut and stood outside for ten minutes before he made an appearance in a suitable tribal outfit with his headband (corona) and a leafy waist belt. This seemed to separate him from the other mostly naked warriors as a man of distinction. Since the group was too large for his small hut, Uni waved them over to the common area with its tree-stump chairs and wood-plank table. Hearing the commotion, Alem had stepped out of his hut and was waved over to the "meeting" by the headsman.

They exchanged what passed for pleasantries. Uni asked how, "They like village," or that was how it was translated, which Melissa shared, and they all nodded their heads.

Melissa told him, "Life is slow and natural." This took several go-rounds with Alem and Jo, but he seemed to get the gist of the idea.

He then turned to Melissa and asked, "Husband make happy?"

Once Alem and Jo helped with the translation, she told him, "Yes. Me happy with husband." She then reached over and stroked Deering's arm, and everybody got the message.

Melissa then launched into her talk about cultivating the cassava plant, which turned out to be a much more trying endeavor than they had assumed. After several back and forth exchanges, Melissa stood, picked up a long stick, and started making two rows of grooves in the nearby dirt. Uni and Alem stood to watch what she was doing. After she finished, she pantomimed planting small plants, the rain water coming down, and then after that did an upward motion with her hands to indicate the plant's growth. Finally she dug up an imagined bush, cut off its roots, took them over to the table, and pretended to mash the roots.

Uni and Alem and now half the village were all very amused by Melissa's pantomime show. Uni and Alem sat back down and had a long exchange. Melissa and Jo tried to follow but, without the sentence structure of subject, verb, and object that formed the basis of their own language, the group got lost in the jumble of words and gestures where inflections were just as important as the words themselves.

Uni now turned to Melissa and again with Alem and Jo's help, he said, "You want take small bush, grow and make big bush, so women not go far from village to get."

Melissa smiled from ear to ear and nodded her head.

"This is good," Uni said, stood up, and turned to walk back to his hut.

Alem added, "He say . . . good thing. Not lose wives to four-leggeds."

Deering asked, "So the women aren't being poached by other tribes?"

Melissa translated, and Alem told them. "They not come back. Animals eat them. Other tribes far away."

Alem now called over two of the women looking on and had an exchange with them. They looked back at Melissa and Adam several times, and afterward came over and told them, or as best as she could figure out, "We look for bush place." They now turned and headed for the path into the forest. Melissa handed Deering her notebook, and they followed after them. Since the women weren't clued into what was really needed, Adam kept looking from side to side until he spotted what appeared to be a natural grove—a row of trees on either side with a wide area of undergrowth between them. He had Melissa stop the women, and they followed him into the wooded area on the right side of the path. It was almost a ravine, and since the trees were separated enough, some sunlight filtered through the overhead canopy. The women looked at the groove and back at Adam with a puzzled expression. Adam figured out the reason for their confusion. He now started pulling up some of the plants and smoothed out a spot for them to get the idea. It wasn't exactly an "aha" moment, but they walked over and started pulling up the plants and undergrowth and throwing them aside to create a clearing.

In the village the men had watched Melissa and Adam leave for the forest following the two tribeswomen down the path. Jo started to pull away, but Hawks grabbed his arm and pulled him back into the circle. Sterling told Jo to ask Alem if they could talk with him and Uni about serious matters.

"I not know the language well. You need Ms. Melissa."

Hawks shook his head as Deering stepped over. "Bennett will help you. He's been working with Melissa on an alphabet." Deering now handed Melissa's notebook to Jo.

He turned to Alem and tried to pass along Hawks' request. Deering added a word or two, and Alem then had an exchange with Uni who started to walk back to his hut and waved them on. There were four tree-stump chairs outside, which the four older men took, leaving Jo to sit on the ground between them and act as an interpreter. Uni had called to one of his wives who brought out small wooden bowls filled with what they assumed was Masato, the alcoholic beverage made from cassava. Hawks warned the men to drink slowly because it could be mildly intoxicating.

Uni started off by telling them he had heard of "growing plant idea, but not know how do it." He thanked them for the help, and said he "open to ideas," or that is how Jo translated it. Hawks, who had a light backpack slung over his shoulder, now removed the bronze axe. Both Alem and Uni were a bit startled. Uni now reached over and ran his hand over it like it was a sacred object.

"You want give back?" he asked Hawks.

Hawks smiled. "No. But when we exchanged gifts, you not clear about when tribe . . . find it."

After Jo's translation resulted in a puzzled look on Uni's face, Deering added a word and put a different emphasis on another, and Alem seemed to get it and translated it for Uni.

They had a long exchange, which again was hard to follow given how everything flowed together, but Deering leaned over to Hawks and said, "Uni is not sure, I think, about telling you, or as Melissa's been telling us, their concept of time and the past is different from ours."

Hawks nodded and now took a machete out of his backpack and laid it on the ground between them. This definitely got their attention and led to another exchange. Finally Uni turned to him. "My father say it come from women tribe."

Deering said, "Keep your requests related to his father, or make it personal."

"So, your father say, it belong to women tribe?"

This took several back-and-forth exchanges before Uni said, "We take it. Use until break."

"Break?" Hawks asked.

After a bit of translation, Uni stood up and stepped back into his hut. He came out with what appeared to be the other part of the bronze axe. He handed it to Hawks. He could see why they thought it was broken—it had a complicated groove and lock mechanism—and he was able to align the new piece and click it into place to create a double-sided axe. He held it up, "The legendary double-sided axe of the ancient Amazon women!"

Everybody's face lit up, but Uni and Alem didn't see the significance of this find. Jo said something, and the two men seem to understand. Uni now picked up the machete, and placing it next to the blunt-edge double-sided axe for comparison, he smiled at Alem, as if to say "good trade."

Then Hawks added, "We want go to women's village."

As soon as Jo and Deering translated it for them, Uni stood up and threw the machete to the ground.

Hawks handed the axe to Deering and started pushing his hands up and down in the universal gesture to calm down. Uni finally sat down. He now had a long exchange with Alem, who told them, in so many words, that the jungle beast Luison, or how Jo translated it—probably using a term from the Marubo language since the legend of the werewolf-like creature was widespread in the Amazon—the beast considered the women his property. He asked to hear more about Luison, and Alem said it was a jealous beast and "eat men who have sex with its women." Uni now picked up the machete, stood and walked back into his hut. The meeting was over. They walked Alem back to his hut, and Hawks asked why Uni was so . . . angry about the women tribe.

Alem said, or again in so many words, "As boy, father brother look for them and not return."

"Well that explains that," Deering added.

At his hut, Alem looked at Hawks and Deering and could probably sense that they wanted more information about the white women. He turned to Jo and said something before he stepped into his hut.

As they walked back, Jo said, "He say speak to Light-skin about them. I call him Ika. They in his blood."

"He is assuming Ika's bloodline is by genetic transfer from the women tribe—as though they were one side of his lineage?" Deering asked.

Jo didn't quite follow the complexity of this exchange, and so Hawks gave him a simple version. Finally Jo nodded his head, "Come family line, seven son has Luison curse."

Jo now shuffled off, leaving the two of them to mull over this legend. "Come inside, Bennett. Let's strategize."

Inside Hawks gave him a cup of rain water, which he had captured with several half-gallon plastic containers set out in the back of his hut but away from any spillover from its roof.

"So, we speak to the boy?" Hawks asked.

"Well, I've seen him around the village, and he's no boy. Looks to be sixteen at least, if not older, but that's chronological. These tribesmen grow up fast in the jungle. And he's probably undergone his rite of passage."

"Yeah, I've seen that in African tribes where they fashion wicker mitts containing stinging ants that the boys have to keep on and endure the bites for fifteen minutes or so. Supposedly it protects the boys from future illness."

"That's a new one on me," Deering said with twisted-mouth aversion.

Hawks nodded his head. "But that's good. It means he's his own man and can make up his mind."

"Jo tells me that he already has two wives, and is very . . . popular with the native girls."

"Did you catch the 'eat men who have sex with them' line about this Luison?" Deering asked. Hawks nodded his head. "Men aren't jealous of chaste women, and there's a reason men, given that none return from their search, continue to look for them."

"Well, let's ask . . . Ika, but bring Melissa into it."

"To translate?" Deering asked suspiciously.

"Why of course. What else would I mean?"

Later that afternoon Melissa was brought up to date on their plan, after spending the day helping to clear the garden site and looking for cassava plants whose stems they would cut off and plant. Both Adam and Melissa wanted to take showers, especially Melissa, before welcoming guests to dinner. They headed back to the riverside tent with Hawks, while Deering had a talk with Jo and Alem to get a better handle on Ika, the light-skinned native boy, before they talked.

When Deering got back to the hut, Melissa had returned and changed into a fresh pair of jungle shorts and a rather tight-fitting blouse. He found this curious but wasn't about to say anything to her about it. She prepared some rice, cassava, and a few Portuguese dishes from their diminished food stores from Camila. After they set out a woven-grass table and tree-stump chairs behind their hut, Hawks, Jo, and Ika showed up. Adam had dinner with the women planters. There were introductions, and Ika was very tentative and a bit shy around these outsiders at first, despite the reassurances from fellow native Jo about these "crooked head" people, or what the Marubo called the white men. After they talked with him about growing up in the village, the subject of their get-together was finally broached. Ika said, "Jo say you want find white women tribe."

He looked around the group, and Hawks answered him, "Yes, we want to find them."

"Why?" he asked.

"Why do others seek them out?" Hawks replied.

After Melissa's translation, he said, "Men want women." He paused, then turned back to her. "Why woman want them?"

Melissa turned to Deering. "How do we explain science to him?"

Deering jumped up and stepped back into the hut. He came out carrying an anthropological Guide to the Amazon with lots of pictures. He handed it to Ika, who was amazed by the pictures, even if he couldn't read the words. Finally he held it up and spoke to Melissa. "You make pictures of them?" Before she could reply, he added, "They not like that. You steal souls."

Melissa slowly explained, "We not take pictures. We talk to them, hear about their life, like we ask about life in village, and write story about them."

"Why?" he asked, like a true man of instincts with little concern for knowledge.

Deering added, "We understand them. We help them like we help your village to grow plants and write down words to speak with other people like us."

He thought about this, then pointed to one of the Portuguese dishes, and Melissa gave him another serving of the food. While he was eating and hopefully considering their implied offer to take them there, Hawks told everyone to go on with their meals and after-dinner talk. They left Ika alone for now. After he finished the dish, he stood and walked into the jungle.

"Is this their form of 'walkabout,'?" Melissa asked.

"That, my dear, is a little ethnocentric," Deering said. She gave him a look. "I have to stick up for my Australian cousins."

Hawks added, "He's just relieving himself. I assume you've

discovered that the jungle is an open latrine."

Melissa laughed. "Tell me. Step off the jungle path we took this morning, and you risked . . . stepping into it."

Five minutes later, Ika returned and took his seat and drank some of the rain water in his cup. "I like see them—know rivers—take us to them."

"You are not scared of the jealous beast—Luison?" Deering asked?

"Dream of many beautiful women."

"Natural selection in its purest form," said Melissa.

"What about leaving next week?" Hawks asked.

Ika looked at him confused. Hawks saw his mistake. He put up both hands and counted off seven fingers. "Seven sun days."

Ika said, "Leave soon. River water get low and dry out small rivers to get there. I speak to Uni and Alem. Tell them I go. But go three sun days. No rain, river waters low. Get to village, stay three sun days, come back, or no more river to ride."

Everyone nodded their heads in agreement. They talked a bit more about what to take and what they would find on the way in terms of food, and Ika asked if they knew how to use a bow and arrow to shoot game. Hawks assured them that they had other ways to kill animals. Finally, just before he was set to go, Ika turned to Melissa and asked something that she didn't translate but turned red-faced.

After Jo took Ika back to his hut to apparently swap wives for the night, Hawks asked Melissa, "What was that about? Did he proposition you?"

She laughed. "No. He wanted to know why I covered up my breasts."

Deering smirked. "That's a good question, my dear."

"To keep jerks like you from gawking at me, my dear."

CHAPTER ELEVEN

Leaving on their expedition was not as easy as they had first assumed. Uni was not pleased about Ika taking the "white people" in search of this tribe of women, since nobody he could remember who had ever sought them out had returned. He could not prevent him from going, since Ika had come of age, but he didn't like it. Also, they now understood that these outsiders had things to teach them that were useful, like cultivating the cassava and learning how to "make talk" with other outsiders. Hawks just wanted to leave, but Deering said they needed to placate the headsmen, especially if they would need this tribe on their return trip. Finally it came down to them "smoothing out" Uni's ruffled feathers to help him save face with the tribe. The group met outside the chief's hut again, but this time with Ika.

Uni questioned Ika. "Why you want go?" Melissa translated as best she could.

"Want beautiful strange women for me."

Uni and Alem exchanged a few words. They didn't require a course in evolutionary biology to understand how powerful his reason was, and it appeared that with just a few words Ika had made his case. Alem, as the tribe's medicine man, gave his blessing. But Uni now turned to Melissa and asked her, "Why woman go village?"

Deering almost snickered, and Hawks gave him a severe look.

Melissa had figured that this question would come up given that the only enticement was for men seeking sexual congress with the Amazon women. She now pulled out the ancient axe handle and showed Uni the writing along the edge. "This old white man language. I, like I do with Alem and your talk, translate language and want to know what they speak."

Alem and Jo both helped to translate her explanation. Uni shook his head and said something to Alem that made them both laugh.

Melissa turned to Jo, and he said, "They think white people soft in head."

Deering took the initiative and slapped his head with the heel of his hand. Everybody laughed, and this cut through the tension. Finally Uni nodded his head, and Alem told them, "If boy go and not come back. We lose good man."

Deering asked, "What's he getting at?"

Hawks smirked. "He wants compensation, even if he can't stop Ika from going."

Uni and Alem exchanged words, and then the chief looked at Melissa. It was obvious to everyone what was on his mind—the compensation he was seeking.

Jo was following the conversation. "Give him gun."

"Are you crazy? It's our last pistol. We lost the other in the canoe tip-over," Hawks said insistently.

Jo and Ika had an exchange of words—apparently Jo was more fluent in their language than he had let on. It appeared he was telling Ika about the pistol and what it could do. Ika looked alarmed and said something.

Jo now turned to Hawks. "He not go to white women village with this thing. It bring out Luison's jealousy."

Hawks shook his head. "I'm not going out into the jungle without my pistol."

Jo and Ika had another exchange. "Ika say he not take you there if you not give up."

Melissa finally added. "Jesus, Hawks. Give them the damn weapon. You can fight the women warriors with your axe."

"It's not the women but the jaguars I'm afraid of."

Finally Alem asked Ika and Jo about this discussion, and he translated it for Uni, who was very interested in this "weapon."

"Let's see?" he asked, or Melissa translated as such.

Deering added. "Don't show him how it works and don't leave him any bullets."

"You think I'm daft?" Hawks said irritably.

He removed the pistol from his backpack and handed it over to Uni, while telling Melissa to make it clear to him that he wanted it returned on their way back. Uni and Alem, and now some of the warriors who had drifted over, were fascinated by the pistol. Melissa spoke to Uni and Alem, and they gave her their assurances, but Uni quickly took it back to his hut.

As they were walking back, Hawks told the group. "That's the last I've seen of that."

"Well, on second thought, maybe you should've just thrown it into the river to appease Ika instead of introducing this tribe to weapons," Deering added dejectedly.

Hawks sneered, "Well, Jo may have saved the day, because it was either the pistol or trading your wife's sexual favors."

"What?" Melissa interrupted.

"You heard me. It's the only other 'compensation' they understand."

Before Melissa could answer him, Deering added, "Well, maybe that would have been preferable to changing the whole dynamic of their culture."

"Go to hell, Deering," Melissa said.

"Well, my dear, it was screw you or screw them, and you know where I stand." He now broke off from them and walked away in a huff.

"He'll get over it," Hawks said. "And even if they don't give it back, it'll just be another relic like the bronze ax to them."

Melissa shook her head and broke off from him, walking over to the women preparing food for their dinner.

Jo stepped over. "She get what Uni want?"

Hawks snickered. "His look was fairly obvious."

Jo added, "On way back, we leave Ika at river and go to Marubo village, or Ms. Melissa be trouble for all."

Hawks slapped Jo on the back. "Right on." They now went

back to his hut to continue their trip preparations.

It rained the next day, and Adam and Melissa worked with the two native women gatherers and showed them how to properly irrigate their cassava plot of plants to prevent them from getting washed away with the last of these downpours. They now had two rows of some thirty plants, or pieces of the brush stems stuck in the ground. The women seemed to get the idea that the full bush would grow from these stems, but it was a leap for them. They had, of course, seen small plants in the jungle grow into full-blown bushes, but they would overlook the seedlings they found not making the connection between them and the later plant. They did ask if they could do this with other plants, and the two scientists assured them they could. They were pleased that they had apparently set this tribe onto the Neolithic path to farming; they only wished that they had brought some corn with them, which had proven to be the staple crop for so many other indigenous tribes in Central and South America.

The tension between Deering and Melissa intensified after their meeting with his carnal-bargaining quips, and he spent the remaining nights in the village in Hawks's hut. Melissa was reminded of the danger of sleeping alone, and Hawks gave her one of the remaining machetes. The night before they had planned to leave, the whole village was awakened in the middle of the night with the sound of Melissa crying out in the night. Hawks and Deering raced to her hut only to find a tribesman making a mad dash into the forest. They burst in on Melissa holding a bloody machete.

"Jesus, I hope you didn't kill anybody," Deering blurted out.

"No, I just nicked him and scared him away. But, if you stay any longer, we'll see what happens."

Deering stared back at her in amazement and then started to laugh. "Okay, Lizzie Borden, as I believe you Americans would say."

Deering and Hawks stepped out of the hut, and Hawks, as best he could, told the gathered villagers that nobody was hurt. By now Jo had arrived on the scene followed by a half-naked girl. The women in the crowd were talking amongst themselves. Jo told Deering that some of the women wanted to make an amends and were offering themselves to him. Hawks warned him to be diplomatic about his turndown, "If that was his choice," he said as a snickering aside.

Deering told Jo to tell them that he was honored by their offer, but his wife did have big knife, which he pantomimed. The women all laughed, and the crowd broke up. Uni came over and patted him on the back, as if to commiserate about "wife problems."

The next morning there was a send-off from the village, with entreaties from Ika's wives who didn't want him to go in search of the women who were protected from men by the evil spirit, Luison. But the tribesmen did help carry provisions down to the river. The addition of another body in the canoe was offset by the lack of prepared foods and other items they left behind at the village. Ika also insisted that they take a tree-branch paddle to supplement the smooth one they brought, since once they left the main river and followed the tributaries and then the furos, which were quickly drying up, they couldn't use the outboard motor whose rotors, or "swirly things," would get entwined with the water plants.

They traveled south on the Rio Arrojo, which was getting narrower and narrower. It was right before they reached the first tributary that a Bufeo Colorado, or pink river dolphin jumped out in front of them down river. Ika got very excited and said something to Jo, who translated it as, "He say them bad luck. Evil ahead."

Hawks told Melissa to tell him that, since Ika has indicated that they're turning off the main river at this next fork, that boto, as they are called in some regions, is telling them only that the river ahead is dangerous.

Jo helped with the translation which Ika seemed to accept. At the fork, Jo stopped the boat so Hawks could tie a blue ribbon on a low hanging branch. Ika asked why he was wasting "pretty string," or its equivalent, on the tree. Jo tentatively explained that it was in case they had to find their way back without him. Hawks closely watched his reaction, but instead of being frightened, Ika said, "If I stay with white women?"

Jo said that was what they were thinking.

Ika now said that they ride much farther down to make camp, or boto turn into man and come after woman at night to make babies.

When this was translated, Hawks said it was part of the Bufeo Colorado myth, and Melissa replied that she would sleep with the machete again, just in case Ika got any ideas that he thought he could blame on Boto.

The next fork was only a couple hundred yards down the tributary, and they once again stopped to tie the ribbon. Ika told them to take out plenty of strings, because the many "little rivers" were coming. The back and forth travel along the tributaries and then the furos slowed them down, especially when they had turned off the outboard and paddled their way down the furos. In late afternoon, they made an early camp at a river beach with a clear overhead view of the sky. When asked why Ika had picked this place, he told them that the stars guide him. Deering found this interesting, but when he pressed Ika for more information, the boy was at loss to explain. The scientist thought he was holding back and said as much to Hawks that night around the fire after dinner.

"Bennett, you're not dealing with a logical process here. He's pure instinct and may get his orientation in the world like birds and animals from the earth's magnetic field."

"Really, Sterling," he said, but restrained himself. "Okay, I'll give you that . . . possibility, but we're not crossing the ocean, and the position of the stars won't change from river to river in the jungle."

Hawks smiled. "Maybe they're speaking to him."

Deering snickered, but Melissa, who had been following the conversation, added, "Well, the Mayans were great astronomers and knew about the galactic center."

Deering took a deep breath. "And they thought Hunab Ku, their supreme creator, resided there at the center of creation in their mythology."

"Who was depicted by a spiral emanating from the galactic center, like the spiral arms of the galaxy itself, as science discovered much later."

Hawks interjected, "Deering, these natives don't objectively view nature from the outside like us; they are subjectively part of the warp and woof of it all."

"Okay, but keep leaving your trail of breadcrumbs because I don't think any of us will be able to 'talk' our way back home."

When Adam took out a machete later and chopped down a small tree to add wood to the fire, Ika looked upset and told Jo to tell white man to leave offering to the jungle spirits for the tree. He agreed and left a half-eaten piece of fruit, which apparently wasn't a proper offering, as gauged by Ika's expression. That night while sleeping in their hammocks under the stars, they were awakened by an eerie whistling sound. Jo said that it was El Tunchi, the evil jungle spirit expressing his anger of those who disrespect his domain.

When the whistle became louder and was now at a higher pitch, Adam tried to answer it with his own whistle, Jo jumped out of his hammock, ran over, and put a hand over the man's mouth. The eerie jungle whistle suddenly stopped.

Adam pushed Jo's hand away. "Hey, I was just having some fun with it."

When Jo stepped back to his hammock, Hawks told the group, "The myth claims that those who respond to his call will meet a horrible death."

"That's if the boa constrictors or the jaguars don't get me first."

Jo yelled at him, "Don't say, it bring to us."

Needlessly to say the group had a restless sleep and didn't get back on the river until midmorning. They paddled another day on the furos, and everybody was amazed by how Ika seemed to know the route. Hawks had been watching him and thought that he had finally figured it out. "He's heading East at each juncture, or where the sun rises, and later in the day the opposite of where it sets in the West."

"Well, that's helpful to know," Deering added.

Later that afternoon, they came upon a huge ancient tree that grew in two directions from its trunk. The skull of a jaguar sat in the middle. Ika got out of the canoe as if to check his bearings, or intuitively sense the territory. He indicated that this was the boundary of the forbidden zone where the women tribe resided and were under the protection of Luison. He now pointed to a smaller furo next to the tree, which they paddled up a hundred yards until they came upon an open area that turned into a mid-sized shallow lake in the rainy season. They could have motored across the lake, but Ika told Jo to paddle along its edges. When they came across a clearly identifiable path that exited the lake, Ika told them to pull the canoe up on land and they would walk from here. Hawks securely tethered the canoe to a nearby tree, but left most of it in the lake's stagnant waters so that it would stay afloat as the lake receded.

Hawks asked how far the village was. Jo translated, and Ika said "Not know. But spirits say close."

Deering commented that it was strange for a tribe that was rumored to be defenseless to have the entrance to the village so easily identifiable.

Hawks decided to camp at the lake's edge. They immediately started to gather lake water and boiled it to replenish their fresh water supplies. Since they had made camp earlier than usual, he also had them break out the fishing lines and hooks, and the group walked back to a spot where he said the fishing would be better given the lake's receding waters. Hopefully they would catch enough to eat for dinner and fry the extra for their visit to the village.

Ika joined the fishing crew and brought a spear with him. Deering asked how he could spear fish in this muddy water. Jo talked with him and he said that the spear was for the pirarucu, or red fish, which Jo was more than familiar with. They were a freshwater catfish that could grow as long as ten feet and weigh four hundred pounds. The natives used spears to fish for them, given their size and the fact that they had to come up for air often. He said that the lower waters of the dry season were the best time to fish for them, since they couldn't dive deep into the river after getting air.

While Ika headed down the shore keeping an eye out for the pirarucu, the others fished for smaller variety of catfish, and Jo had one of them bait their hook with fruit for the tambaqui or pacu, which was a fruit- and seed-eating fish. Jo said it was one of the tastier freshwater fish in the Amazon.

The group did catch a variety of catfish, and Ika regaled them at dinner, through Jo's rough translation, of how a "red fish" got away from him. Jo then told them the myth of Pirarucu, about a cruel young warrior who killed many villagers without just cause when the chief was away. He also spoke back to the Gods who were displeased with him. Tupa, the head God, made the goddess of rain release a thunderstorm while the warrior was fishing one day. He was struck by lightning and was thrown into the river where he was changed into the fish named after him.

This was an amusing story, one of many Amazon myths, but that night while they slept in their hammocks, the eerie whistling of El Tunchi resumed, and kept them up half the night and did not bode well for their anticipated meeting tomorrow with the Amazon women tribe.

CHAPTER TWELVE

Melissa paused in the retelling of her story and closed her eyes. Mattie, who had taken out a notepad, since her mother wouldn't allow her to tape the session, finished with her last notation.

She looked up. "That must've been an eerie night."

Melissa waited a moment before she opened her eyes, which seemed glazed over. "I have never been a superstitious woman. For me, or at least until then, everything could be explained by science, or the science to explain it had not yet been discovered."

"I know how you feel. Traipsing through Africa and having a number of witch doctors hex me, you could come to realize . . . to paraphrase Shakespeare, 'There are more things in Heaven and Earth than are dreamt of in our philosophy.'"

Melissa smiled. "Not all of your education was wasted."

Mattie was angered by this slight to her profession, but didn't answer her ailing mother with a biting retort. "So, all the talk of evil spirits and horrible deaths must've given you pause."

Melissa closed her eyes and appeared to actually shiver. Mattie reached over and pulled the blanket farther up her mother's body.

"I mean, people don't realize that once you go off the beaten path, the so-called rules break down and chaos lurks around every turn."

Melissa opened her eyes. "Nicely put, my dear. And, yes, after three weeks in the jungle, and especially after our time with the—we later came to call them the 'Uni Tribe'—your . . . orientation to the world and its possibilities can become unraveled a bit."

"So your expectations of what you would find at this village were more . . . uncertain?"

"Well, the legends of the Amazon Women did enter into the picture. I mean, they could be fierce women warriors with drawn spears, or even cannibals, which was in the news in those days after reports from New Guinea of explorers and missionaries going missing."

"And again, there were the reports of their sexual allure, which is what had drawn the Native men to their apparent death."

"Yes, there was that." Melissa paused. "I guess, thinking back on it, I was hoping for something more pristine, or untouched by civilization—yes, I know, the myth of the noble savage—but I sensed that they weren't savages or primitives, but something nobler than that."

Mattie leaned forward. "So, I guess you won't get ahead of your story and just tell me what you found?"

"Like those in our expedition, a gradual introduction is better to set the stage for what was to come."

Again, her mother shivered, which only peaked Mattie's interest.

*****

The next morning the group broke camp, but this time they pulled the heavy canoe halfway out of the water and doubled the tethered rope to the tree. They now packed all their gear and headed off. They decided that Melissa and blond-headed Ika would lead the group into the village, hoping they would be less threatening to these women. Given her exposure, Melissa was a bit on edge, worried that the women might be warlike and attack them, but soon her fears were somewhat allayed. Walking down the path, they came upon what appeared to be wooded dikes with sun-baked clay fillers between the wooden branches, and on the other side were long ditches running away from the dikes.

Hawks stepped over and examined the dikes. "No doubt for

lake flooding at the peak of the rainy season."

Deering was impressed. "That's amazing, and these are irrigation ditches?"

"They appear to be."

"Guess I won't need to teach them how to farm," Adam said.

That opinion was confirmed when two hundred yards later, they came upon a cultivated plot of wheat and barley off to the right of the path.

They could hardly believe their eyes. Everyone stepped into the field to touch the stalks and rub the kernels between their fingers.

They all looked to Hawks for answers. "Don't expect me to explain it. I've been exploring the Amazon for thirty years, and I've never heard of any tribes farming wheat. I mean, where would they get the seeds to start with? No missionaries or white explorers have come this far."

"Well," Melissa started, "a white-skinned group of women didn't just pop up here. They migrated, and from what little we've seen, from a civilization in advance of the local tribes."

"Migrated," Deering added. "There aren't exactly roadways here in the jungle."

Melissa narrowed her eyes. "Of course there are, Deering. We call them rivers."

"Okay, let's move it along shall we?" Hawks intervened.

Around the next corner on the somewhat cleared and wider path, they came upon two women dressed in animal skins and pulling a wheeled cart stacked with stalks of wheat toward what appeared to be a round wooden granary. They stopped in their tracks and stared back at the group in utter amazement for a moment, before they released the cart's wooden handles and scampered down the path toward what appeared to be the village in the distance, from the plumes of smoke rising above the tree canopy.

"So much for our surprise entrance," Deering said.

"Well, we were never going to just walk into their village

unannounced."

"Besides being rather unprotected," Adam added.

"Yeah, I do miss my pistol about now," Hawks complained, glancing over at Melissa.

They walked along and came to an arched entranceway, but what drew everybody's interest was a clay tablet hanging affixed to the leafy wall. Hawks stepped over to examine it. "I'll be damned. It's a star-map of the sky with what appears to be Venus rising as the morning star."

Melissa had now stepped up to a doorpost with a ring-headed top. "This looks vaguely familiar from the mythology of Mesopotamia and its cults, but I can't quite place it."

"Mesopotamia?" Adam asked.

Melissa turned to the group. "Well, we do have the bronze axe with Sumerian cuneiform."

But before they could discuss this further, a group of white-skinned women stepped through an opening in the row of bushes. This wasn't exactly a welcoming committee, but neither were they armed with spears or bows and arrows. The two parties stood in tense silence across from each other for a long moment, until one of the women spoke to the others and they all stepped over to Ika. She tried to speak to him, but he didn't understand the language. Finally, the other women pointed to his hair, his high cheekbones, and then his finely shaped nose, and Hawks saw the similarity with the women.

The group of women now ushered Ika into the village and waved for the outsiders to follow after them. Inside there was an open circular space surrounded by a group of thatched huts, which looked sturdier and better constructed than the huts in the native villages they had last visited. But what caught their attention was the crumbling sun-baked clay-brick structure off to the side of an open area. It was covered by a high thatched roof, no doubt as rain protection, which did not appear to be part of the original structure. Hawks and Deering stepped closer for a better look.

"It's an ancient temple of sorts," Hawks finally said.

When Deering reached over to pick up one of stray bricks, a woman put a hand on his arm to stop him. She said something in their strange dialect, but he got the idea: sacred and off-limits.

Melissa now waved the two men over to a common area with a stone fireplace and a wood-planked table with a top of hardened tree resin for water protection. The women greeting them began to spread out food—a few fish dishes, some raw vegetables, and baked bread—plus clay bowls of water for them to drink. While most of the other women went about their duties—the two women they had initially scared on the path had since returned to their cart—several of these greeters ate with them, including what appeared to be the Amazon Women's go-between, who was acting as their host.

In the open sunlight they were now able to study the women more closely. They were of mixed ages, and the white-skinned label was somewhat of a misnomer: there were some women with darker skin but who were by no means of native Indian descent. The high cheekbones and delicate facial features of most of the women here were more in line with the blond women of Northern and Eastern Europe.

Deering finally said what the others were thinking. "You dress most of them in modern attire, and they would pass for Germans or Russians."

"As long as you don't talk to them," Adam said.

Melissa added, "No, I've spent time in southern Ukraine and Georgia along the Caucasian Mountains. They look like the blond village women from there."

Hawks snorted, "You mean the area of the ancient Scythians who lived on the Black Sea, and were the home of the Amazon Women of ancient lore."

Deering shook his head in amazement. "But that was 2,500 years ago!"

"Actually, more like 3,000 years ago, at the time of the Trojan Wars."

Adam had sat back and was listening to this exchange. "Then how the hell did they get to the Amazon River basin toting a 3,000-year-old bronze axe from Mesopotamia?"

The women had stopped to stare at them, no doubt amazed by their strange language and gestures. Melissa looked at them with reassurances and then turned back to the group. "Well, that's what we're here to find out."

They continued to eat, but what was obvious to Melissa was the effect these half-naked light-skinned women were having on the men in the group. While their animal skins and grass underskirts kept them fairly covered, what peeked through was even more alluring, she thought, than if they were as bare-chested as the native women in the villages. But then she had to gauge her own reaction and found herself as attracted to these wild, beautiful woman as the men in the group. This might be a problem for all of them. She also wondered how they managed their sexual drives between their sporadic coupling with the native men who found their way here.

Hawks finally stated the obvious. "Look, we're here for a short visit to examine their artifacts, maybe make some headway with their language, but we can't comingle with them, no matter how enticing they may seem."

Deering seconded the notion. "Yes, I doubt, given the legend, they have sexual taboos, but there's a reason rumors say nobody returns from their search for them."

This was a sobering reminder, and the others nodded their heads, but Jo didn't comment, and, of course, Ika didn't understand the language. After lunch, their host took the group on a tour of the village and the surrounding area. And despite the legend, they were taken aback not to find any men or male children in the village at all. There were several young girls between the ages of three and twelve, and young women, but no boys.

Hawks immediately pointed this out, and Deering asked, "How do they protect themselves from neighboring tribes?"

"Well, they are fairly isolated this far down the river, but their rather civil reception of outsiders and any lack of weaponry or its use is surprising."

"What about the natives who don't return?" Adam asked.

Jo added, "It's the jungle beast Luison who eats them and keeps the others away."

Hawks smiled indulgently. "The outlying tribes could have any number of reasons to explain it, including attacks by animals, or maybe there are tribes nearby, who commingle with them periodically and protect them from outsiders."

"I doubt that," Melissa said.

"And why? Woman's intuition?" Deering chided.

"They have a look of women who only . . . commingle out of necessity."

By this point they had been led to the edge of the village and were amazed to find a mill stone near the granary with markings similar to those on the bronze axe, no doubt another remnant of this past civilization. It wasn't particularly large or heavy, and it could be moved by cart or canoe. The huts were also a revelation. The thatched roofs were made from hollow water reeds that grew along the river banks and furos and were naturally waterproof, but it was the wood-branch joists that were cut and fitted and sealed by tree resin that attested to their sturdy appearance and craftsmanship.

Hawks was impressed. "I've never seen anything quite like this, outside of England or northern Europe where thatched roofs are still widely used in the countryside."

They also noticed the clay goddess effigies in the village, little shrines evenly placed around the circular common area. Throughout the afternoon, they noticed the women periodically touching or bowing to them, and/or leaving offerings.

Deering was the first to note it. "They must have some kind of goddess religion, maybe even connected to Venus, which Hawk pointed out on the clay tablet at the village entrance."

"Well, many ancient people treated the stars and planets like

Gods and Goddesses," Melissa added.

"Yes, but none of these Amazon tribes are as oriented to the stars as the ancient Mayans were," Hawks said. "There is definitely something strange about these women, their European look, their advanced cultivation methods, and now this."

"But we need to investigate, and the language, as with the last tribe, is going to be the big barrier," Deering added.

"Well, boys, fortunately you brought along a philologist of ancient languages."

"So you think you can quickly figure it out?" Deering asked.

Melissa rolled her eyes. "Maybe in three months, I could make some progress, but not three days."

Jo was trying to follow this conversation. "We go back three sun days?"

Hawks nodded his head. "That is the plan. Ika say waters go back soon. We not dare stay longer."

Ika asked Jo about this exchange. Jo appeared to give him a short summary. He apparently didn't like the plan and walked away.

"Is he going to be a problem?" Deering asked.

"Well, old boy, that's why we left the . . . breadcrumbs."

Their host now showed them to the less elaborate huts that seemed to be reserved for guests, as no belongings of the women were kept in them. She seemed insistent that Melissa have her own small hut, while the three white men share another, and Ika and Jo a third.

After these arrangements were made, and everybody sorted out and put their gear in their assigned huts and strung up their hammocks, they all decided to take an afternoon nap to be wide awake for the evening meal. Their host had indicated in pantomime that it would be their welcoming dinner and celebration. Hawks gave her what remained of the fish they had caught yesterday for the feast, which was welcomed. What exactly the celebration entailed, they were not sure, but the men seemed keyed up by the prospects of a lively get-together with all of these alluring women.

CHAPTER THIRTEEN

The group was awakened sometime later and taken to the common area where a round table on short legs sat covered with food items and a row of empty clay bowls. The elder women of the village sat in a wide circle around the table. The group had decided to call their host Ikagi, which Jo had suggested—a word from the Yabaana language—but denoting no closer connection between her and Ika. The woman now took the group out to the circle and motioned for them to fill their bowls first.

Melissa laughed. "It's a stationary version of the Lazy Susan."

They now stepped forward and served themselves, then took a seat in the circle, but waited for the women to do likewise before eating. This turned out to be the custom, as the other women sat down and also waited for the others to fill their bowls. When everybody was seated, the women set their bowls on the ground in front of them, raised their arms, palms up to the sky, and chanted a prayer, of thanksgiving, no doubt. Their group did the same, though they could not sing along with them.

After the thank you to the God or Gods, they all ate, and, when seeing others return for second helpings, Adam and Bennett did as well. The women talked amongst themselves, often nodding in the newcomers' direction with smiles, or what some of the men no doubt took as leering glances. Melissa had sat next to Adam in the circle and saw that he was smiling back at the women.

"You know, Adam, we're just a curiosity to them. Their smiles are not invitations."

"Of course. I'm just trying to be polite," he hurriedly replied.

Melissa smiled to herself, but noticed that she was getting as much attention as the men—maybe it was the knee-length shorts she had changed into. She now wondered what had prompted this change, and had to admit to herself that she was as aroused as the men, but wondered if these women, who obviously made babies with men, were as interested in other forms of sexuality, not that she would press the issue.

They had started their dinner celebration, or so it turned out to be, in early evening, and by now, the sun had set. Soon the women collected the empty bowls and removed the leftover food servings from the table, which was then carried off as well. A small fire was started in the center of the circle. After these preparations, the women returned and sat back down in the circle. All of them were now looking up into the sky with what appeared to be great anticipation.

The twilight slowly grew until the first faint stars appeared in the night sky, and then after a while the planet Venus rose in the western sky. Again the women raised their arms with their palms out apparently in a gesture to welcome their Goddess. The women started swaying and chanting, and soon the younger women were on their feet dancing alone or with each other in some kind of devotional ecstasy. After a while, their wild gyrations shed their animal skins leaving only their grass underskirts, but their bare-chested dancing was very sensual and definitely affected not only the men but Melissa and the other Amazon women as well.

Hawks had to call out to his group. "Okay, guys, if you can't take it, shut your eyes, but don't anybody think of joining them, or this could degenerate very quickly into something we are trying to avoid."

Melissa watched Bennett and Adam's response, but if any in their main group was ready to join the party, surprisingly enough it was the henpecked Adam Caruthers. Fortunately, a cloud cover soon blotted out their sighting of Venus, and the women slowly came back to "their senses," as it were. The celebration broke up, and Ikagi ushered them back toward their huts. Hawks looked around, but both Jo and Ika had slipped off into the jungle, no doubt to soon be joined by some of the young dancers.

Melissa noticed their absence as well. "Should we go after them?" she asked Hawks and Deering.

Deering surprisingly replied, "In this sexually charged atmosphere?" "That could be dangerous to life and limb."

Hawks practically had to drag Adam back to their hut to keep him from following one of the alluring women.

The next afternoon, after Ika and Jo had returned to their hut to sleep off their apparent nocturnal orgy, one of the younger women stumbled back to the village with a deep cut on her arm. A woman, who appeared to be their medicine "woman," took her back to her hut. Adam followed after them and pantomimed that he would like to see how she treated the wound. This was all right with the woman, and she motioned Adam inside. The medicine woman first cleaned the wound with water and then applied a moldy-like plant substance, which Adam figured was their form of penicillin. He expected her to then bandage the wound with some kind of leaf or cloth dressing, but she then applied a gooey substance that smelled particularly bad. She let this set for twenty minutes or so, while she allowed Adam to examine the substance. It had a very strong alkaloid smell, like most curative healing plants, but what amazed him was that when she washed off the substance, the wound had already started to form a scab. This was remarkably fast.

He tried to pantomime asking what went into the gooey healing balm, but she either could not understand his request or was not inclined to share her secrets. He assumed, given their civil reception in the village, it was the former of the two. Adam bowed his head in thanks and immediately went in search of Melissa, who was conducting a preliminary language analysis with Ikagi. Apparently they had been at it for a while and were ready to take a break when Adam stuck his head in the doorway. Ikagi and Adam exchanged bowed greetings, and she stepped outside.

"What's up, Adam? You look particularly excited. Did one of the women 'invite' you to 'lunch.'"

"Come on, Melissa. How about dropping that. So I got excited by their dancing ritual, what man wouldn't. But I've got something more important to discuss."

"Okay. I'm listening."

Adam told her about the girl with the wound and the plant substance the medicine woman used to start the amazingly quick scabbing process. He finished with, "I need to speak with her."

Melissa laughed. "On our next visit, maybe. But it'll take me three months here, or six months back home, to figure out this language." Adam looked disappointed. "Get a sample and analyze it when you get back."

"Well, that's easier said than done. It's much quicker to work from the plant itself, or the combination of plants, which I suspect in this case, than trying to do a chemical analysis of a complex healing remedy."

Melissa thought about his dilemma for a moment. "Go back to her with a couple plants you've pulled from the forest. Point to the substance and pantomime which of these are plants she uses. No doubt they won't be either, and then you can wave her out of her hut and suggest you go into the forest together, and hopefully she'll point out the plants."

Adam looked back at her in amazement. "That's brilliant."

"Actually, Adam, it's rather elementary, but you're so excited by your discovery, it's clouded your mind."

He laughed. "Yeah, like the dancing half-naked woman obscured my appreciation for their Venus ritual."

Melissa patted him on the back as she walked him out of her hut and sent him on his way. She looked around the village as the women worked on and realized that nobody had watched

Adam's comings and goings, unlike the sexual overtones of every male/female exchange in the other tribal village. This thought reinforced the fact that these were not tribal women and that despite their alluring physicality, they were on a whole other level of sophistication or civilization. She wished she could stay for three or four months and really explore their mythology and origins, not to mention crack their language to aide in this research.

Fortunately over the next two days, while the dinners were still collective get-togethers with prayers of thanksgiving, there were no dancing celebrations with its charged sexual atmosphere. Hawks had a talk with Jo and Ika about their philandering, and while Jo was somewhat amiable to reason at this point, Ika seemed to ignore the dire warnings about coupling with these women. Afterward Hawks brought his concerns to Deering.

"I wonder if these women are blood-related?" Hawks asked.

"Well, they may have different fathers, but some may be off-spring of the same mother." Hawks nodded his head. "So you're concerned that if any of them have a child with Ika, it will have genetic defects?"

Hawks snorted. "Yeah, not that it would faze them, but I guess that's the least of our concerns."

"So you have concerns," Deering asked. Hawks nodded. "Personally, I find our reception rather disquieting. I mean, yes we're men and potential baby-makers, as the tribesmen call it, but these women are defenseless from attack by warring tribes, or from us for that matter. And yet we were readily welcomed, regardless of Ika's presence."

Hawks was going to point out the obvious, but Deering quickly added, "Yes, I know this village is far afield from the other tribes, but they know about the Amazon Women. You would think some 'wife-hunters' would seek them out in hunting parties and take them away by force."

"Well, there is the legend of the jungle beast Luison, which Jo keeps pointing out, that seems to keep most of the, shall we say, 'less adventurous' men away,' Hawks reminded him. "Don't forget Uni's reaction to our request to seek them out."

"Like plants in the jungle that ward off predators with poison leaves or what not, these tribes have their own protective myths because they're all still very primitive and superstitious. We just heard Ika's stories of the pink dolphins that turn into sexual predators at night, or El Tunchi, the evil jungle spirit."

"Deering, like I said before, these natives are part of the natural world around them; it's alive to them and filled with evil or benign intent."

"You don't really believe this legend of Luison?"

"No, not any more than I believe in the Abominable Snowman, but as far back as the tribesmen can remember, men who've gone looking for these Amazon women have not come back, and these are well-equipped and instinctively good hunters who don't normally get killed off by wild animals."

"Okay, if we believe the tribes' stories that none of the men ever do come back, that leaves only two other viable alternatives to the jungle beast myth," Deering said.

"These women may be killing the visiting men, but right now I can't imagine these passive and religiously oriented women killing off their lovers, so maybe the men are being killed by an animal or pack of animals that inhabits just this area."

"Why do they kill the visiting men and not the women?"

"We don't know if they kill only the men and not the women, we have only been here a few days. Maybe the women have developed some kind of defense against the animals that the men haven't learned about yet. In either case, if men are being killed in this village, there should be remnants of their presence left around here someplace."

"Well, if that's the case, they wouldn't leave the men and their belongings on the 'side of the road,' so let's look for evidence of their presence or their graves."

The next day, Hawks and Deering, with Jo as a guide, searched the surrounding jungle but did not find any past evidence of visiting men or their graves. They did, however, find signs of jaguars and other big cats hunting in the area. "But where do they bury their own?" Deering finally asked.

"Some tribes leave the dead out for animals to eat, like some Native Americans, to satiate the local animals so they won't come looking for them," Hawks added.

Deering shook his head. "I can see some of these Stone-Age tribes doing that, but this society is too sophisticated and far in advance of the Neanderthals who even buried their dead."

"Well, if they did kill off intruders, the double-sided axe would be a perfect weapon, like it was for the Amazon women of ancient lore."

"So why give it up?" Deering asked.

"Maybe we should show it to Ikagi and asked if it looks familiar," Hawks said. "Might be pressing the issue, but we don't have much time before we need to shove off."

"Really? We just got here," Deering said, feeling he had just scratched the surface of his anthropological inquiry.

"Well, like Ika said before he became enthralled with the young girls, the waters are quickly receding, and we can't stay long, or we'll lose our waterway."

The two of them talked with Melissa that night and figured the best time to show Ikagi the axe was during one of her language sessions. So the next day, after they had finished working together and Ikagi was ready to leave, Melissa indicated that the men wanted to ask her something.

Ikagi eagerly nodded her head and smiled. Melissa assumed that the only question men asked of these women were for sexual favors. She stuck her head out of the door, and Hawks and Deering stepped inside. There was a short table where they were working, and after initial bowed greetings, Hawks took out the ancient double-sided bronze axe and laid it on the table.

Everybody closely watch Ikagi's reaction. She was puzzled at first, and then she examined it closer and almost gasped. She now bowed her head. This was no doubt a sacred object to her ancestors. She looked to Hawks with a big question hanging in the air.

"Melissa, try to tell her we got it from one of the tribes where they had dropped off a white baby."

"That's far too complex at once. Let's take this step by step."

She now did a pantomime, adding a few words that she had already assimilated, showing that it came from a tribe up the river. This took several back and forth exchanges, but Ikagi seemed to grasp the idea.

Next Melissa pointed to Ikagi's white skin, made the sign for a infant by closing her arms into a cradle shape and rocking it back and forth. It took a moment before Ikagi grasped that it was from Ika's tribe. She nodded her head and gave them a big smile.

"Can you ask her what they used the axe for, since it appears that they don't hunt animals, and the skins they wear must come from dead animal they find in the jungle."

Melissa took a deep breath. She now picked up a bowl and used her finger to pantomime eating with her fingers from it. She next took out a belt and wrapped it around her waist, as if to hold up her shorts. Several other demonstrations of object "use" followed, and a gleam of awareness passed over the woman's eyes.

Melissa now picked up the axe and pointed to the bowl and belt and her sandals. Ikagi pointed at the axe and used her hands in a vigorous pushing-back-the-air pantomime, which they took to be a long, long time ago. Ikagi then took the axe and walked around the inside of the hut in a crouched position and pantomimed sneaking up on an unsuspecting animal, and she then drove the axe down.

She now returned to her seat and placed the axe on the table. They were all amazed by her pantomime and got the idea: a long time ago their ancestors used it to kill animals for food and skins.

Melissa received questioning looks from the two men. "That's all for today. Save any further inquiries for another time."

Hawks agreed. He bowed his head in respect, picked up the axe, and wrapped it in its chamois cloth, and they stepped outside.

"That was a rather remarkable exchange," Deering said. "Very smart of her."

"What we civilized men don't realize is that all modern Homo sapiens have the same brain capacity, it's just a question of how it's being used or not used."

"Like the Pyramid of Giza in Egypt. I've yet to hear a reasonable explanation for its construction," Deering added.

As they walked around the village, Hawks finally articulated the question hanging in the air between them. "But that begs the question of why they stopped hunting and what has become their protein substitute, or at least in the dry season when they can't fish."

"Something we'll probably not figure out in the next couple days."

Hawks patted his fellow explorer on the back. "In time, dear chap. In time."

CHAPTER FOURTEEN

The next morning the group had a get-together in Hawks's hut—or everybody but Ika, who could not be found. They had to decide when they were going to head back. Hawks was the first to call for a delay.

"But you said a few days ago that the waters were receding, and we'd lose our waterway if we don't return soon," Deering voiced.

"Well, that was rather hypothetical on my part. I still think we have some time and should take advantage of this rare opportunity while we can."

"I agree. I'm making better progress than I had anticipated with Ikagi and their language," Melissa said.

"And I need to find someone who knows something of their history and their trek here," Deering said.

Jo added, "We go down to lake. See how far it go back."

Hawks laughed. "Of course. That's only sensible." He stood up with Jo, as did Deering.

"I'm going with you. Want to see for myself," Deering added.

As they walked out of the hut, Hawks put a hand on Deering's arm. "Don't worry, Bennett, I won't let us get stranded here."

They walked back to the lake and could see that the entry furo was still flowing with water. The banks of the second to last furo they had come in on were widening slightly but still very navigable by canoe."

Hawks turned to Jo. "How long before little river dry up?"

Jo stepped onto a higher position for a clearer look. He stood there for five minutes looking around. "Six sun days, or five, no rain."

"And the lake furo?"

"Soon, but last rain help."

"And if it doesn't rain again, what about the lake?" Deering asked Hawks, who shrugged his shoulders.

"Hawks?"

"We push the canoe through the mud to get to the remaining lake."

Deering summated their prospects. "So we've got a little less than a week, maybe a little more, depending on if it rains again, or we'll be stranded until the wet season."

"Appears right. So let's make the most of it."

After sharing their findings with Melissa and Adam, they agreed to stay five more days, but head out after that. By now Ika had returned to the village, and Jo told him when they would be leaving. Again he did not seem pleased with their decision and walked out muttering to himself.

Melissa was just as distressed by their departure plans. She was making progress with Ikagi during their language sessions and felt that within a month she would be able to at least communicate with her, other than their current pantomime "talk." But these exchanges weren't all study, or at least language study. Melissa accompanied her around the village and watched her interaction with the other women, and participated, as much as she could, in some of their household and village maintenance tasks. This allowed her to observe them up close. There was nothing rushed or frantic about any of their work. They seemed to live and be in the moment more than she had ever recognized in herself or other "civilized" people of her culture. Yes, the natives of the Uni tribe did not dwell on the past or the future, but they were also driven by deep sexual identity needs that she wasn't finding with these women. Their conduct was what she might have imagined among the oracles of Delphi in ancient Greece, or what she had read about of the sacred temple women of ancient Egypt. There was, in fact, an absence of any decidedly male or aggressive traits in them. It was all very "yin," to borrow the Chinese term, and from her study of psychology, every person had both a male and female side, but the yang aspect seemed lacking here, or under expressed. She had seen this among gay "femme" women, as opposed to their butch counterparts, but had never seen a whole society composed of them.

Before coming here she had wondered, if she did find a tribe consisting of only women, what their sexual orientation would be, outside of their periodic coupling with the native men who ventured here. She soon found out that they were definitely very physical and familiar with each other. While harvesting wheat stocks the next day, she saw two of the women touching each other's breasts, and kissing each other, as they worked. She expected this to progress on its natural course, but when it didn't, Melissa realized it was just their way of expressing their natural affection. At one point, one of the women touched her breast and became curious about her bra. She called the other woman over, and she let them examine it. Finally Melissa removed her shirt and took off her bra, and as she stood there bare-chested, the women fondled her breasts and then lightly kissed her on the lips before going back to work. Melissa put her shirt back on without her bra and decided to dispense with it from then out.

Back in the village she watched them and was curious to find that when any of the men in their group was present, they did not carry on in this manner. That afternoon, while Adam was off in the woods with the medicine women gathering plants, Melissa told Hawks and Deering to make themselves scarce, that she wanted to conduct a sociological experiment. This was fine with them. They had planned to further recon the surrounding jungle for any signs of habitation, graves, or remnants, as Hawks speculated, of any past civilization or other signs that might reveal more about this strange and unique tribe of women. After the men had gone, and while Melissa participated in some village cleanup chores, the women working alongside of her began to physically express their affection for each other, and then with her. At one point, one of the women put her hand down Melissa's pants and fingered her vagina lightly while kissing her, and then removed her hand and went about her chores. At this point Melissa was very turned on, but did not want to overtly respond to this overture, since it wasn't really behavior fitting a professional researcher; and anyway, it didn't seem to be a sexual advance but only another form of affection.

Melissa excused herself and went back to her hut. She now lay down in her hammock, slid off her shorts, and began to masturbate. Suddenly the grass door was pushed aside, and Ikagi stepped in with an expression of concern on her face. Seeing Melissa making love to herself, Ikagi stepped over, removed her hand, and fingered her until she came in a shuttering orgasm. At this point Melissa was ready to return the sexual favor, but Ikagi just leaned over, kissed her lightly on the lips, and walked out of the hut. She was flabbergasted. Melissa was so used to a give-and-take in sexual exchanges, but realized that this was her own cultural conditioning. These women weren't driven by the kind of sexual needs that warped so much of modern relationships. It was just a natural expression of affection, but she couldn't dismiss the lack of a male element. Afterward, and while she was still curious, Melissa went to Jo's hut and asked him to come out. They walked around the village, and she questioned him about his relationship with the girls of the tribe.

At first Jo was uncertain about the nature of this inquiry. "Not good?" he asked.

Melissa smiled. "No. Good. But would like to know if girls are . . . passive when you make love to them."

This question took several exchanges for him to figure out her intent. "No. They strong, want be on top, bite my lips and other . . . things."

So, Melissa thought to herself, they are more aggressive with males, or that's how their male sexual aspect is expressed. This was very interesting; among the lesbians that she knew, the butch women were almost always butch and masculine, and femmes the opposite, but then it was the 1960s and this was still "closet behavior," and purely anecdotal. But she wondered if there was a difference between the younger and more mature women in regards to their sexual expression. That night she found out. After she had retired and was almost asleep, there was a knock on her door and then it opened up. One of the older girls, whom she had seen with Jo, came over, stripped out of her animal skins, and slid into the hammock with Melissa. She realized that Jo had misinterpreted her earlier inquiry as some kind of sexual interest on her part, but there was a theory to be tested. She allowed the girl to make the first move, but she merely kissed her breasts, her lips, and diddled her a bit but nothing climactic. Melissa, while turned on, decided to be passive and see what would develop. After a while the girl fell asleep next to her, and they slept together through the night. When Melissa woke up in the morning, she was gone. Her question answered: it was only with men that they became sexually aggressive.

The next morning Melissa went looking for Deering who was alone in his hut; Hawks had gone back out to reconn the surroundings, rather disappointed that he wasn't finding any signs of a past, advanced civilization nearby. Melissa stepped inside the hut, realizing the nature of the male/female relationships in this village wasn't as rigid as in the Uni tribe.

"Bennett. There's something I want to talk with you about. Can we take a walk?"

"Sure." Deering stepped outside, sat down on a nearby tree-stump chair, and laced up his boots. He now noticed that she wasn't wearing her bra. "Lead the way."

"Let's head out to the lake. I don't want Sterling or Adam to hear what I have to say, or not yet."

They arrived at the lake, which by now was noticeably receding and was surrounded by a few feet of muddy banks. There were, however, several dry areas on the elevated land ring around the lake that they could sit on.

"Let me preface this by saying my inquiry is strictly academic, and given its sexual . . . content, not meant otherwise."

Deering snickered, "I am properly forewarned."

"Yesterday, while out in the field collecting wheat stalks, and then later in the village, after I sent you and Sterling packing, the women began to express their affection for each other, and then with me, in a very sexual way."

Deering gave her a leering grin. "And you have a problem with that?"

"Okay, I'm bi-sexual, and open to sexual contact with women, but there is something very strange about how it's expressed among them."

This wiped the grin off his face. "In what way?"

"Out in the field, after I removed my bra, the women fondled my breast and kissed me, and then just went back to work."

"I see, and you thought it was, as it is in our society, sexual foreplay?"

"Exactly. And then, in the village, it progressed even further—them touching each other's genitals, including mine, and then later in my tent, Ikagi . . . accommodated me, we'll say, but again none of this was foreplay that led to any kind of coupling."

Deering nodded his head. "When I was back in London prior to my lecture series in America, I had lunch with an old college roommate, Derreck Ward, a primatologist who had just come back from Wamba in the Congo. He was telling me about the bonobo, what some call the pygmy chimpanzee but are really a completely different species. They got separated from chimpanzees when the Congo River formed some million years ago and have evolved differently."

"That's interesting. In what way?"

"Well, they're not as aggressive as chimps and seem to resolve conflict with sex and are rather peace-loving, or so it seems. What is most interesting is that they've been seen kissing each other and having oral sex, which until now only human primates were known to do, and the female bonobos are constantly rubbing their clitorises against each other. Ward says like every couple of hours you see this."

"Wow," Melissa said in shock. "Haven't seen that, but the women's constant touching could be something similar."

"You can't make comparisons between us and them, but what it suggests is that this tribe of women were separated from our common ancestors centuries ago, and may have evolved different behaviors."

"What about the female bonobos' relationship with the males of their tribe?"

"The mothers appear to keep a close bond with their male children, but while they have face-to-face genital sex with males, they don't form family units otherwise."

"And what's their status within the tribe?" Melissa asked.

"The females seem to rule the roost in their society, or that's the preliminary assessment," Deering added. "Realize this was Ward's first excursion there, and none of this has been reported."

"I asked Jo about his sexual contact with the girls here, and he said they were aggressive and wanted the . . . top position."

"So they're passively affectionate with other women, but aggressive with men?"

"Yes, that's my point, and I'm not sure what this entails."

"But you think it has some psychological import?"

"Well, I've been . . . around a fair amount of sexual play with women, and the femmes and the butches usually stay true to their orientation, but—"

"But, when the opposite or repressed side comes out, it doesn't bode well?" Deering asked.

"Yes, that's what I'm getting at, and it's rather unsettling."

"You know, in our society sex has become such a head trip for everyone that it's hard for us to . . . appreciate its natural instinctive function. I mean, I've been in African villages, way off the beaten path and not yet fully acculturated by white missionaries or government officials, and have seen women bending over in the field to tend their plants and a man coming up behind them and having sex with them, with neither thinking much of it, and afterward they just went about their business."

"I've read tales of the Polynesian islanders acting in a similar promiscuous manner, but that's not exactly my concern."

Deering nodded his head. "I understand, and while I may not be as well read about the Jungian anima/animus complex, I think you may be over-thinking the situation."

"And you've not seen or read about something like this before?"

"Well, Melissa, I've never come upon an all-women tribe or society, or ever read about one."

"You mean, outside of the mythical Amazon Women of ancient lore?"

Deering nodded his head. "You may have a point there. If this tribe is, in the wildest stretch of the imagination, a remnant of the Amazon Women warriors Francisco de Orellana fought, though I still stick to my opinion that it was a male tribe dressed like women, then one wonders what happened or how their masculine or aggressive side was transformed."

Deering slipped off his seat, "Let me talk with Sterling about this, since you seem disinclined." Melissa nodded her head. "But let me ask, did Jo say these girls were overly aggressive, or even violent?"

"No. You can talk with him as well, but it didn't seem untoward, more like our role playing, if that's what you're asking."

They now walked back to the village, and Melissa found Ikagi sitting patiently outside her hut, ready for another language session. They split off, and Deering headed down another path to the river or furo to get away from the village and think about Melissa's concerns. He had to admit to himself, one of the reasons he had come on this expedition was his curiosity about such a women-only tribe and their social, political, and sexual mores, and how they would differ from a standard male/

female tribe in other indigenous settings. As he recalled from the legend, the Amazon Women tribe, or the ancient Scythians, were ruled by Queen Penthesilea who fought Achilles at Troy and was killed by him. This helped spread the legend, which fascinated the ancient Greeks. Since Greece was a patriarchal society and women were secondary citizens, the sexual allure of women who could fight them as equals may have contributed to their notoriety down through the ages. But from what he had seen, there was no hierarchical social or political breakdown in this tribe. And while Ikagi was their go-between with the outsiders, he had seen other women take the lead in other areas.

There were a few young girls in the tribe, but there didn't seem to be any family orientation, or a mother, per se, and they were looked after and instructed by all the women, which would be another similarity with the bonobos as Ward described them. He watched and noticed that they spent the night in different huts, depending, it seemed, on who they were working with on any particular day. This lack of hierarchical structure or a queen/kingship model, which predominated primitive tribes and even western society up until the nineteenth century, was most unusual. The sexual orientation that Melissa described seemed indicative of a kind of religious sisterhood, but something more instinctively primal. What was most unusual, in any society, at any level that he had visited or studied, was that their sexual orientation was not driven by a strong sexual drive, like with most humans, but had evolved along more peaceful lines, or so it seemed. He agreed with Melissa that human beings had both a male and female side, and the repression of one at the expense of another was always troubling in the long run. He now headed back and would talk with Sterling about it.

CHAPTER FIFTEEN

Adam had followed Melissa's advice and gone out into the jungle and picked several medicinal plants, or those with an alkaloid smell to them, and brought them to the medicine women, whom he was calling Medi. He showed her the plants and pointed to the healing salve she had used on the girl with the cut, which had scabbed over very quickly. She waved her hand to indicate a negative response, took one of the plants and pointed to another ointment bowl along her tree-planked shelve of sorts. Medi then pointed to her abdomen to indicate it was used for stomach upsets. Adam now notated that on his pad of paper, tore off the sheet, wrapped it around the plant with a rubber band, and put it in his backpack. He now pointed to the other plant, and Medi waved him off again and pointed to her mouth and then to her abdomen, indicating that it wasn't medicinal but used for food.

It was early in the day, and so Medi picked up her plant-gathering bag, placed some food items and a water bag in Adam's backpack, grabbed a pointed stick—for animal protection, or so he assumed—and led him out of the hut. Adam and the others had been amazed that the natives in the Uni tribe and the women here went barefooted all the time. While the village itself was fairly cleared and maintained, going off into the jungle barefooted was entirely different. The jungle floor, even the cutback trails, was a crisscross of rough tree roots and plants— many of them with thorns or leaves with pointed edges. Adam followed her as they headed down a trail at the north end of the village into the jungle. Soon, Medi stopped and showed Adam how she harvested medicinal plants: starting at the outer edge of the root system, she used her fingers to remove the dirt and carefully pull up the plant with its roots intact. She then, just as carefully, placed the plant sideways in her bag, and they walked on. At one point, Medi pointed to a plant on Adam's side of the trail for him to remove while she tended to one a few yards off the path into the jungle.

They continued to work in this manner for three hours and must have walked a half-mile from the village. With the sun now high overhead and the heat and humidity rather daunting, Medi headed off the trail with Adam following her. She now found a rather clear space, started pulling off low-lying fronds from some of the palm trees, and laid them on the jungle floor. She then took a sip from her water bag and shared the bag with Adam, and then laid down on the floor and patted to the space next to her for Adam to lay down. He wasn't sure if this was a midday siesta or something else, but he was tired by now and lay down. Soon Medi had fallen off to sleep, and Adam figured this was naptime and nothing else and did the same.

When he awoke sometime later, Medi had prepared a light lunch of sorts from some food they had brought and some fresh fruit and raw vegetables, which she had picked while he slept. They ate their lunch in silence; afterward, Medi stepped over to the edge of the clearing, lifted her skirt, defecated and urinated and then wiped herself with nearby leaves. When Adam saw what she was doing, he turned his head and stepped into the jungle on the other side of the clearing to urinate. They now gathered up the uneaten food and fruit, which Adam put in his backpack, and headed back. They stopped several times to gather plants that she had apparently overlooked on their outward trip, and arrived back at the village in late afternoon. They were both tired, and Adam pointed to Medi's plant bag and pantomimed taking notes, and then waved his hands to indicate later. She smiled, and they parted ways at her hut.

When Adam returned to his hut, he found Sterling, Bennett, and Melissa engaged in conversation. "Maybe, Melissa," Sterling was saying, "they need more time to 'take it to the next level,' as you say."

"You're missing the point, Sterling. I've been around a lot of lesbians, and this is not characteristic behavior."

"Maybe not in Miami or New York, but Melissa," Hawks added, "this is the middle of the Amazon jungle, with an all-women tribe that's been isolated from anybody else for God knows how long. Don't expect them to act the same way."

Deering nodded his head. "I told her something similar. They've evolved different behaviors." He now told him about Ward's bonobo observations.

Hawks smirked, "Well, our ancestors must've of come from the other side of the Congo River."

Melissa shook head in frustration. "Psychology tells us that humans everywhere have basic instinctive drives and needs. Just look at the Uni tribe and their sexual hegemony."

This point put both Sterling and Bennett back on their heels. Finally Adam asked what this dispute was about, and Melissa gave him an update of what she was encountering with the women of the tribe. Now noticing his perspiration-drenched clothing, Sterling asked, "What have you been up to."

He told them about his medicinal plant-harvesting venture with the medicine woman, and added, "Well, I might have something to add to the discussion." Everyone turned to him. "After a morning of picking plants, Medi, the name I've given her, laid out a bed of palm leaves and invited me to take a nap with her.

This certainly got everybody's attention. "Anything else happen?" Bennett asked.

"No, it was all very . . . I guess, sisterly is the word."

Hawks nodded his head and turned to Melissa. "That should put your concerns to rest."

Melissa shook her head. "No. It could be a nocturnal thing. Just be cautious about any nighttime invitations, Adam."

Jo now stuck his head into the hut, didn't find what he was

apparently looking for, and tried to leave. "What or who are you looking for?" Sterling asked.

"Had big fight, Ika. He go off mad. Not find him in village."

"What was the fight about?" Hawks asked.

"He not want go back. Stay here dry season."

Hawks and Deering exchanged looks. Hawks added, "We know that, but he will cool off." Jo didn't seem convinced. "But while you're here, we have questions to ask you."

Jo was again asked about the nature of his sexual contact with the girls of the village, and how that compared to his experience with the girls of the Uni tribe. "Very different. They like me . . . on top."

This got a round of snickers from everybody, which deflated the tension between Melissa and the others. They finally wrapped it up with the men being put on alert about any nocturnal "invitations" from the village women. Melissa left the men in their hut and headed back to hers. One of Ika's "girlfriends" was waiting there. She wondered, given the topic of her recent conversation, what this visit entailed. The girl pointed to her skin, then dangled a finger from her crotch to indicate a male. She was looking for Ika. Melissa knew enough of their language to gather that he was very mad, and she was afraid he might harm himself. She accompanied the girl as they searched the village and surrounding jungle for him, but he was nowhere to be found.

It was now early evening, and the women were preparing dinner, which Melissa and Adam helped with. Hawks and Jo questioned the girls known to be intimate with Ika about his whereabouts, but they either did not know or would not confide in them. They, too, searched the surrounding area but didn't find him. Soon they returned to the village for dinner and nothing else was made of Ika's absence in the village.

The next morning Jo woke up both Hawks and Deering early. "Canoe gone," he told them in a panic.

The men hurriedly dressed and followed Jo back to the lake

where the canoe had been securely tethered to a tree. It appeared that the rope had been unraveled, not cut, and the paddles were also gone.

Hawks said, "He must've paddled it out across the lake and hidden it in one of a hundred possible overhanging tree alcoves, or down one of the furos feeding off it."

Jo now looked at the jungle floor around where the boat had been tethered and pointed out the footprints to Hawks. He knelt down and examined them. "Only one set footprints: a man's. He do alone."

Hawks looked to Deering and Jo. "Looks like we need to circle the lake and look for the canoe while we can."

Jo looked doubtful. "Thick jungle round lake; trees grow close for water and animals come to drink."

Hawks shook his head in frustration and looked at the two of them accusingly. "And me without my pistol." It took him only a moment to formulate a plan. "We'll cut down some branches, make sharp-ended spears, and collect the seeds from the oil-rich nuts of the Andiroba tree, soak some clothes in it and wrap it around the spears to light if any animals approach."

Deering just stared back at him his mouth agape. "I'm glad we brought you along," he finally said.

"You think."

It took them until early afternoon to make their spears, shred their cloth, and collect and pulp out the oil from the seeds of the four-cornered brown woody nuts. Properly armed, the three of them—they couldn't convince Adam to join the search—went looking for the canoe. Since they only had one machete left—the other had disappeared and they suspected Ika of stealing it—they had to stay together and chop their way through the thick jungle. The lake shore was very thick with jungle growth and by late afternoon they had covered only a very small section of it. They all knew it would take many days to do a thorough search of the shoreline and decided to head back to the village since animals were known to approach water sources in the early evening before sunset. In the village, Hawks told Jo to find and retrieve Adam and Melissa and bring them back to his hut.

When everybody had gathered, Hawks told them about the missing canoe. "And you couldn't circle the lake in one afternoon?" Melissa asked in disbelief.

"Not while doing a proper search. The jungle is very thick around the lake with hundreds of hiding areas for a canoe. We were only able to cover a small section of the shoreline today. We'll continue the search tomorrow."

"It could take weeks or months to find it," Melissa said.

"We'll find it . . . unless he broke it apart," Deering added.

"Then we'd really be stuck," Adam whimpered.

Hawks shook his head. "No. He wants to go back too, just wants more time here with the women."

"Melissa turned to Jo. "How long before the furos and the lake dry up?"

Jo thought for a moment. "Four days little river furo, more for lake," he told them.

"Then we better beat the bush tomorrow," Melissa said and looked to Adam. "That's everybody."

"Let's ask Ikagi and some of the others if they'll help us look," Hawks said.

They stepped outside while Melissa went in search of Ikagi. She came back sometime later and reported that Ikagi and the other women had begged off. "Given that Ika may be one of them, you'd think otherwise," Deering added.

"Again, Bennett, we can't apply our kind of logic to their motivations. They live in an entirely different world, even if we co-habit its physical domain with them."

Deering laughed. "Maybe we should check with your astrologer, Hawks."

Sterling snickered. "Yeah, that rumor would get me drummed out of the British Archeological Society."

The next morning at first light they formed two groups: Jo led Melissa and Adam to where they had left off yesterday, and with their only machete they inched their way exhaustingly around the lake's shoreline. Each group had spears and a lighter. Hawks and Deering, without a machete, made their way as best they could in the other direction, starting from the beginning point of the first search. By late afternoon, after making little progress, the two groups returned to the village, neither having found any trace of the missing canoe.

"It's too big for him to have pulled too far into the jungle."

"He may have taken it down one of the lake furos," Hawks said.

"So we're stuck?" Melissa asked.

"He'll come back, but it may be after the little river dries up, and we can't canoe out."

This left everybody rather frustrated. That night after dinner, the group gathered together in Hawks hut again.

"So we're here for the dry season?" Melissa asked.

"We can continue to hunt for Ika, and if we find him, maybe we can get him to tell us where he hid the canoe before the water recedes to the point where we are stuck," Hawks added.

"But he knows the score and probably won't reveal himself until it's too late to canoe out," Deering added, rather dejectedly.

Melissa tried to strike an optimistic note and turned to Jo. "Let's keep an eye out for the girls he's been with, maybe we can follow one of them back to where he's hiding in the jungle."

That was the plan that Melissa, Jo, and Adam followed for the next couple of days, but the girls seemed to be on to them and were hard to keep track of. Meanwhile Hawks and Deering kept an eye on the level of the lake furos and the little river, while they scoured the nearby jungle for any signs of Ika's campsite. They didn't find either.

"Do you think the women are hiding him or sneaking him into their huts after dark? Hawks asked.

"No, they seem strangely disinclined to interfere either way."

"You think they want us to stay, and aren't being helpful? Hawks asked.

"As I said, they seem neutral about it all, and I'm not sure what that portents."

Hawks slapped him on the back. "Inscrutable is the term that many have applied to the native mind."

"But that's just it. They aren't native, they aren't primitives, but yet they seem caught up in some kind of group mindset, even if we can't communicate with all of them."

The next day the early-morning quiet was pierced by a shrill outcry. Hawks and Deering quickly dressed and stepped out of their hut. Jo was out of breath and sitting on a tree stump shaking. They ran over and tried to get him to talk, but he was too upset. Melissa joined them and had the wherewithal to bring out a bowl of water, and to rub his arms and back to quiet him down.

Finally he told them. "Jungle beast eat Ika."

Melissa put a hand to her mouth. "Oh my God."

"Take us there," Hawks told him, then turned to Melissa. "You stay here." Melissa nodded her head, as the women of the village gathered, and she told Ikagi about the boy's death, and Ikagi shared it with the others, who seemed knowingly distraught by it.

Jo added, "Bring machete." Hawks went back and retrieved it along with a roll of canvas from their stores in the hut.

They headed cautiously down a path that led to one of the smaller river furos. Before they reached the furo, they found signs of a struggle. A blood trail led them to the mostly eaten remains of Ika. Both Hawks and Deering had seen the results of animal attacks in the jungle, but never carnage to this extent. The boy's body was not only eaten but torn apart with great force. They knelt down to examine it while Jo stood back at some distance.

"Could a jaguar do this much damage?" Deering asked.

"While jaguars aren't as large as lions and some tigers, they have the strongest bite force of any of the big cats," Hawks said.

Deering nodded his head. "But still, they can only grab a

victim by their jaws and swing them about."

Jo stepped over. "Luison have hands. He pull apart body."

Hawks didn't reply. He stepped over to the tree next to the body, which had blood stains and percussion indentations. He now turned to Jo and clenched his fingers like a jaw and swung his hand back and forth as if hitting the body against the tree. "Hitting tree with body caused limbs to shred like this."

Jo shook his head. "No. It jungle beast."

He was so distraught that it appeared he was going into shock. Deering sat him down against another tree and gave him his canteen to sip from. He now turned back to Hawks. "As you said, their world, or their perception of it, is different from ours."

"Right on, old boy." He now unfurled the canvas. "Help me place the remains on the canvas. We'll take it down to the furo and dump it in the water."

"Why not just bury it here off the path?"

"I'd rather the aquatic vultures devour it than feed this jaguar anymore human remains."

After they had finished dumping the body and washing off the canvass, they walked Jo back to the village. Hawks had Melissa put him to bed, and then she joined the others in his cabin.

"So, it was a jaguar?" Adam asked tentatively.

Hawks stared at the man's timid question. "It sure the hell wasn't any mythical jungle beast, if that's what you're asking."

"That's your scientific assessment?" Melissa asked.

"I've seen plenty of mauled human remains here and in Africa, and I don't see anything different."

Melissa looked at Deering. "What about you?"

Hawks narrowed his eyes, but Deering just shook off his attempt to silence him. "Of course, I'm not as conversant with such animal attacks, but the way the body was pulled apart disturbs me." He raised a finger as Hawks was going to repeat his jaw-swinging theory. "Seems like it would take more than just a set of teeth to scatter remains around like that."

Hawks snorted. "You're thinking there is some truth to this jealous beast hogwash?"

"No, not particularly. But superstition and mythical tales usually have some basis in reality. I think we need to be open-minded."

"As opposed to some of us closed-minded educated morons."

Melissa needed to step between the two of them. "Okay. We're all upset. Can we ratchet it down a bit?" The two men nodded their heads. "So, without Ika to tell us where he hid the canoe, we're stuck here," Melissa said.

Hawks nodded his head. "We'll keep looking, but it's doubtful we'll find the canoe in time to leave."

Melissa seemed more resigned than the others. "Okay, so we adapt, learn how to survive here like they have—and for centuries it appears—but don't lose hope of finding the canoe and eventually making our way out."

The two men nodded their heads.

CHAPTER SIXTEEN

"Jesus, mother. You were really stuck now. How come you didn't see this coming? Mattie asked.

"We knew Ika wanted to stay on, but I think we, or at least I, ascribed to him our own mindset and expected him to be a . . . team player, I guess you could say."

"Despite Hawk's warning about Ika's star navigation on the way there, how his or the native mind saw things differently, and your knowledge of tribal men's risk-seeking, instinctive drive to mate with women at all costs. You said yourself that Ika was the perfect evolutionary example of nature's role in perpetuating the species."

Melissa pointed to her water jar, and Mattie filled it and passed it over to her mother. "Well, this trip was my first contact with primitive natives, or those with Ika's instincts, and it wasn't until the next day, when he was found dead, that it really sunk in that we were stranded there, and by then we were all in shock."

"But you believed like Hawks did that a jaguar had mauled him to death?"

"The way Deering described it, the poor boy was torn limb from limb."

Mattie shook her head. "Don't tell me you bought into this Luison legend?"

"As I said, we were in shock—or I was—and while we made our excuses, it was all rather hard to . . . rationalize."

"Are you saying there was more to it?" Mattie asked, leaning closer.

Melissa produced a painful smirk, but like any good storyteller, she wasn't about to jump forward in her story.

"I'm saying that we were in the middle of the Amazon, with a defenseless tribe of white women who were not poached upon by warring natives, in possession of three-thousand-year-old Mesopotamian artifacts . . . at that point it seemed like anything was possible."

Mattie sat back in her chair. "You had really gone off the deep end."

"Not yet, at least that's how we tried to position our minds, and we did our best to gather ourselves and push on, but deep down something had broken in us, some hallowed civilized core had been breached, whether we knew it or not, and we were . . . adrift in an another world beyond our control."

"Yeah, I know that feeling, the jungle will do that to you . . . but still," Mattie added.

"I can't imagine you have ever felt what we were feeling."

*****

After their talk with Melissa and Adam, Deering followed Hawks as he tramped back down the trail to the scene of the animal attack. When Deering caught up with him, he was examining the ground. The floor of the jungle was matted over with leaves and vines, and it was hard to find foot or animal prints, unlike the sandy bank of the lake where the canoe had been tied. He finally stood up.

"I'm not finding any jaguar prints or, for that matter, any human prints either."

"Are you questioning the nature of this attack?" Deering asked evenhandedly.

"I was hoping to find a trail that led back into the jungle."

"You're not thinking of tracking the jaguar without a pistol?" Deering asked in alarm.

"The natives have tracked and killed them for centuries with bows and arrows and spears."

"But you're not one of them, and you can't even find any tracks."

"In thick jungle, you don't follow tracks but broken branches, trampled underbrush," Hawks pondered. "I wonder if it was a black jaguar, not the more common yellow-spotted type."

"And if it were?" Deering asked.

"There is a whole mythology about them. The Mayans, Aztecs, and Incas worshipped them in one form or another and built temples to them."

"So are you saying this myth of Luison is actually about a black jaguar?" Deering ventured.

"Could be. It would explain how the natives project humanlike qualities onto it, but, again, the name jaguar was given to these big cats by Native Americans, and it means 'he who kills with one blow.'"

Deering snorted, "And not 'he who pulls body apart.'"

"Exactly. So, this is strange behavior for them."

At the village, they walked over to Jo's hut when Melissa stepped outside.

"We've got another problem," she said. They both shook their heads in resignation. "Jo's sick."

They followed her back into his hut and Medi was administering to him. "What's wrong? Is he still in shock?" Deering asked.

Melissa had an exchange with Medi, then turned back to the men. "Medi says that jungle stole his spirit."

Hawks and Deering just looked at her in disbelief. Finally Adam clarified the situation. "He's got jungle fever."

Hawks nodded his head, but Deering was still flustered by this prognosis. The group stepped outside.

"How did he get it, and we didn't?" Deering asked.

"I've seen this with natives in Africa and here in the Amazon," Hawks added. "They see something frightening, or something that confirms their worst nightmares, and they not only go into shock, their immune system breaks down and leaves them open to all manner of bugs."

Deering thought for a moment. "So, you're saying it's

psychosomatic?"

"No, it's more than that. He probably does have the fever."

"Is it contagious?" Melissa asked.

"Not to us. Remember, we've had all the shots, and even if it didn't cover every little Amazon bug, it gives us a greater blanket of immunity."

Deering turned to Hawks. "But it means we can't track down the jaguar."

"No, you're right. Can't do that without him and his tracking skills, and by the time he recovers, the path will be too hard to follow."

Melissa added, "So even if we had the canoe, he can't be moved, and so we're spared the choice of leaving him here."

Adam shook his head. "Wouldn't have been much of a choice for me."

Hawks snickered. "But then you haven't seen Camila's big brothers."

As they were mulling this over, Medi stepped out of the hut and grabbed Adam's arm, pointing to her hut. Apparently she needed to retrieve more ointments.

"Wait," Hawks said. He then turned to Melissa. "Ask her if Jo will recover."

Melissa communicated with Medi, who responded, although it took several back-and-forths. She turned to them. "She's says he will die from fever, two sun days, if she doesn't . . . breathe it out of him."

"What?"

"I think she burns some herbs and swats the smoke so that he inhales it, and it chases the bug away."

They all looked fairly skeptical. Melissa turned to Medi and asked if this were the only cure. There was another exchange, including her pantomiming digging a grave. They got the message.

"Ask how long it will take him to recover," Hawks said.

The reply was all fingers on both hands.

Medi turned to leave and looked to Adam to join her, but he pushed his hands in the direction of her hut, telling her to go without him. He wanted to be part of this next discussion. The group headed for Hawks's hut, but Melissa steered them to the common grounds. "I've been indoors too long. Need some fresh air."

They sat around on the tree stump chairs. Melissa turned to Hawks. "Why did you ask how long it will take for his recovery?"

"I was thinking that if we found a suitable big log. We could cut it out to make a canoe."

Adam looked interested. "How long would that take?"

"With only one machete and with only me skilled enough, besides Jo, to carve it out . . . too long."

"But after he's recovered," Adam added.

"Three months, but then the dry season will be nearly over. I think our best bet is to keep looking for where Ika hid the canoe."

Melissa shook her head. "I thought we had resigned ourselves to staying here during the dry season?"

"Yes, I agree, but we still need to make our way back after that."

They were quiet for a long moment. "If we're going to stay here for four months," Adam added. "We need to figure out what they do for protein in the dry season when they can't fish."

Hawks said, "Well, we have the double-sided axe, and we can make better spears. Deering and I can hunt for game," Hawks said rather unconvincingly.

Deering asked, "You have doubts?"

"Without a pistol and without Jo's help, it'll be . . . a challenge."

Deering turned to Adam. "Do you really think we can survive on plant protein alone?"

He thought about that for a long moment. "Our bodies would adapt, but it could take more than four months, I would imagine. After that, we will have lost a great deal of strength and be drained of the energy needed to make the return trip."

"Longer than I plan to stay. So that's settled," Hawks said.

Deering added, "What if we hiked back to the next flowing river furo and caught fish there?"

Hawks shook his head, "The waters will recede very quickly now, and we would have to get back to Arroyo River to fish. We would burn up more energy hiking than we would gain from the fish we could catch and we would be constantly exposed to the elements—further depleting what energy we had left."

It took nearly a week for Medi to free up time from her care of Jo and her other activities to deal with Adam's inquiry. With Melissa in tow, they talked with the medicine woman in her hut about sources of plant protein, which was, as with all communication with the women, including Ikagi, somewhat protracted. Medi did have a dried-out fish skeleton as a kind of animal adornment on her wall. After Melissa failed to explain their request, Adam picked up a plant used for food and put beside the fish skeleton, and then he pointed to his mouth and then his stomach.

Medi had an "aha" moment and put her hands up to indicate as much. Next Adam showed her a picture of the dark-purple olive-sized fruit from the Pataua palm tree that Hawks had brought back from his last trip to the Uni tribe, which helped sell the expedition to Connor Croft. Medi looked at the picture with both acknowledgment and excitement—these cross-cultural breakthroughs were seemingly as important to the Amazon women as to the exploratory group. She now picked up her plant-gathering bag and grabbed a long tree branch cleared of its lower stubs but with a thick bent leafless branch at its top.

As they tromped out of the hut, Melissa turned to Adam. "What's with the long stick?"

"I assume she uses it to pull down clusters of fruit hanging from the palms that you would otherwise have to shimmy up the trunk to reach."

They headed down the path that she had taken earlier with Adam in search of medicinal plants, but this time they walked farther and at some point, left the path to push their way through the jungle foliage. Eventually they came to a plot of a half-dozen palms together, all of which had clusters of the purple fruit. Medi was able to pull down several of the low-hanging fruit clusters, but was too short to reach some of those higher up. Melissa took the stick and was able to pull down a couple more clusters. This would be plenty for the time being.

When they arrived at the path, Medi turned to walk to the village. Adam took her arm to stop her. He now took out a cluster of fruit from the bag and pointed to other plants and trees in the area. It took a moment for her to realize that he was asking if there were any other trees or plants with fruits or nuts with a similar "fish" or high-protein content. She thought for a moment, and then she turned, and they walked farther down the path and then into the jungle again until they came to a grove of six-foot-tall plants with alternate, heart-shaped, serrated leaves up to four inches long. The unripe fruit was apparently green, while the ripened fruit, which she began to pick, was blackish brown in fruit capsules with four or five lobes. They watched how she harvested the ripe fruit and followed after her until the gathering bag was full with both fruits.

When they got back to the village, Medi pick up several empty water skins and indicated for Adam to walk down to the spring and gather water for her to process the palm oil. Adam shook off the water skins, went to their store of equipment, and took an empty fuel can, whose top they had cut off and whose interior had been thoroughly washed out, and used it to carry the water from the spring on the other side of the village. Meanwhile Medi and Melissa had laid out the palm fruit on a wooden preparation table and used what amounted to a wooden mallet to break open the fruit and remove the pulpy interior filled with its seeds. When Adam returned, Medi had him pour some water into a large wooden bowl in which they now soaked the palm fruit pulp. But before they started, Medi examined the container and indicated for Adam to start a fire and heat the remaining water.

Hawks and Deering were sitting in the common area sharpening their hunting spears, when Adam came over to fire area with the can of water. They put down their spears and the machete and came over.

"What's up Adam?" Hawks asked.

"We gathered up some of the Pataua palm fruit. Medi and Melissa are soaking the pulp to remove the seeds."

Hawks nodded his head. "I see. And you're heating the water to let the oil float to the surface to skim it out?"

"Yes. Matter of fact," Adam replied, the question hanging in the air.

"Remember, I'm the one who brought the palm fruit back for analysis, and I watched the natives extract the oil."

Adam now looked at the wide fire hole, which, unlike most fireplaces, didn't have a metal frame to hang a pot from or an elevated structure to sit one on. Hawks saw the problem, took the metal can from Adam and set it down in the middle of the hole.

"You don't want to boil the water, just heat it halfway to a boil," Hawks said. Adam nodded his head. "Are you sure they'll be ready for it? I mean, how long will it take to soak the seeds out of the pulp?"

"I better check." Adam hurried back to Medi's hut, and Melissa was able to explain the situation. Medi stepped outside and turned to Melissa, who translated what she indicated as, "When sun . . ." She now put her thumb and index finger two inches apart. "That high above trees."

Adam hurried back and gave them the time table. "That's about in three hours, and it should only take half an hour to heat it to the right temperature." Hawks now looked at his explorer's watch, which was still working, and told Adam, "We'll wait until three o'clock to start the fire. But let's prep it."

They now gathered the fire wood and stripped branches, placed them around the can with kindling, and then the two men went back to sharpening their spears.

At the appointed time, Adam checked with the women, who assured him that the pulp was almost ready. They lit the fire and soon the water was hot enough to submerge the fruit pulp. Hawks kicked a few embers away so as not to boil the water but left enough to keep it warm during the skimming process. Adam helped the two women bring out the pulp, which they now dumped into the hot water. Medi left and returned with clean wooden bowls and a skimming cloth. Soon a dark green-yellowish liquid started to float to the surface. Medi and Melissa skimmed the oil into the bowls. It took a few hours to complete the process, with Adam manning the fire. In the end it looked like they had about a quart of the oil.

Afterward Adam shook his head. "That's a lot of work for so little oil."

Hawks was standing nearby. "Welcome to the Amazon, old boy."

CHAPTER SEVENTEEN

The next morning Hawks rummaged through their camping supplies and found a medium-sized fishing net with its four-foot telescopic handle. He brought it out to the common area where Deering was sharpening another spear.

"Didn't think we were going fishing."

"I'm thinking we can use this net to snare birds and maybe a monkey."

"Wouldn't they be out of reach with that short of a handle?" Deering asked.

"That's why we need to affix it to a long-branch pole, which will add another ten feet to its length."

They took a stripped pole that they were going to use as a spear, tried to attach the handle of the fishing net to it, but discovered they would have to wrap vine around three feet of the handle and the pole for it to be stable enough not to break off. This required them finding a longer branch, cutting it down, stripping it, and then attaching the net. The extension was only about twelve feet or so.

"That's only going to reach the lowest branches, and from what I've seen, the birds, not to mention the monkeys, perch higher up in the trees," Deering said.

"We may have to develop a strategy." Hawks paused for a moment. "We could find a tree full of birds; I could go down a couple trees, climb up it a ways and out on a limb, and then you throw a rock to scatter the birds. Hopefully one will fly low enough in my direction for me to net it."

"Okay, that sounds reasonable, but I'll be on the ground, and how do I defend myself if an animal comes around?"

Hawks took out the axe, which he had been throwing against a tree yesterday to sharpen his skills. He now had Deering take a whack at it. It took the rest of the morning for him just to hit the tree, let alone stick the axe into it. "You could climb the tree instead," Hawks finally said.

"Yeah, I feel more comfortable doing that."

They headed out in the early afternoon and tried this strategy several times in different areas of the nearby jungle, but Deering was unable to snare a single bird. They broke it off early, and back at the village Hawks had Bennett work on his throwing skills with the axe for self-protection so that tomorrow he could climb the tree with the net. They headed out in the morning, but Hawks was just as unsuccessful. They did spear, or wound, a small rodent and clubbed it to death. Deering was satisfied with the kill, but Hawks wanted to use it for bait. They set it out, hid behind a nearby tree and waited. After a couple hours, some scavenger birds descended on the dead rodent, and Hawks was able to snare one of them with the net, while Deering hit it with the club.

They bagged their kill, moved the dead rodent to another area, but couldn't lure and kill another bird, or monkey for that matter. They came back to the camp rather dejected. Hawks plucked the bird and skinned the rodent and roasted both of them at the village fireplace, but only he was willing to eat the fare. The others in the group, used to rodents being disease-infected back home, didn't want to risk it, and the bird barely provided enough meat for one person. Hawks and Deering needed to strategize their hunting tactics. "Maybe we should build a snare and try to capture a small capybara."

"You've done this before?" Deering asked.

"Well, not really. I've seen natives in Africa use them, but the rope and spring snares take real skill to construct." Deering gave him a questioning look. "But a deadfall snare, which is much simpler, might work."

"Deadfall?"

"You find a much-traveled animal path next to a ledge; you place a large flat stone on the ledge or the edge of a shallow ravine held up by a stake; you tie a rope to it, and stretch it across the path, and tie it to another stake. The animal trips the cord, pulls the stake loose, and the stone falls on it."

Deering looked back at him in amazement. "And that works?"

"I've seen it work on small animals."

Deering could see that Hawks was getting desperate, and so he agreed to help him find the location, set the trap, and periodically check it with him. It took a few days to find the suitable site—a path to the lake with lots of animal droppings the size that would indicate capybara or coatis or even a pacca. They set their snare, which in itself took an afternoon of trial and error. Afterword Hawks took a gallon can of water from the lake to douse the site of their smell. They came back and checked it twice a day, but after three days they hadn't caught anything, or even had the snare triggered.

The night of the third day, while they sat around the common area and ate a meal prepared by Melissa and the women, Deering ventured to say, "This isn't panning out Hawks. Maybe we should come up with another idea."

"I've seen hunters spent weeks to snare small animals in the wild."

"You mean seasoned tribal hunters who've grown up in the jungle or forest, and are as much an animal as their prey?"

Hawks shook his head. "Okay, Deering. If you want to give up on it and eat this swill for another four months, be my guest, and I'll keep at it on my own, or until Jo recovers." He now tossed away his remaining bowl of food and headed down the path to the furo.

Deering figured he needed some time alone, that Hawks wasn't used to having his male skills questioned, or even worse, having them fail him. Melissa came over and asked what had upset Hawks. He told her about his problems on the hunting expeditions.

"Well, if you're done with it, I could use some help with this impossible language of theirs."

"Okay, brief me in the morning. I'm pretty exhausted by it all, and want to get to sleep early, or at least before Hawks returns.

Deering and Melissa met at the common area the next morning, since she needed a larger table to spread out her work. She quickly brought Deering up to date.

"At first, influenced by the Amazon legend, I assumed their language or their now colloquial version of it, was from the area around the Black Sea where this tribe of women were reported to be located in several historical accounts. That would make the language Proto-Indo-European like the Scythians."

"An offshoot of the Indo-Iranian languages."

"Exactly, which are Aryan, but the predominate use of consonants in preference to vowels suggest a Semitic language."

"Like the Sumerian/Akkadian cuneiform on the axe handle."

Melissa nodded her head and let out a sigh. "Yes, that should've been obvious to me, but I think I was hoping their language would locate them in the lands of the ancient Amazon women, or the eastern Mediterranean and their seafaring countries."

"To account for how they could've gotten here?"

"Yes, but that's putting the carriage before the horse," Melissa added.

"But western Iraq, previously Mesopotamia, is only a couple hundred miles from the sea."

"Desert miles, which is a big difference, especially back then."

"So, where has that gotten you?" Deering asked, a bit distracted by Hawks trudging across the village carrying his hunting gear and ignoring them.

Melissa paused. "Is it really safe for him to go out alone?"

"You mean without me, or someone else totally defenseless in the wild," Deering spit out.

"And you couldn't talk him out of it?"

"Didn't even try. He's so single-minded that he'd probably give your old man a run for his money."

"Yeah. They're cut from the same cloth." Melissa glanced at her paperwork, or her yellow-pad of notes, then looked up. "When the words themselves didn't sound familiar to any of the Semitic languages I knew—the branch of which is probably long extinct—I got Ikagi to give me a sentence, or a complete action like, 'Ikagi throws a stone at a wild boar.' This helped because, as best as I could determine, she used the SVO construction: subject, verb, object of ancient Akkadian, unlike the VSO alignment of classical Semitic languages like Arabic and Hebrew."

"Well that's interesting."

"Yes, and while I'm more familiar with the Babylonian or southern dialect of Akkadian, I think she's speaking in the northern or Assyrian dialect."

"Which would put them closer to the Black Sea and the old stomping grounds of the ancient Amazons."

"Of course, this is all conjecture, since the language has been so diluted, that I could be completely wrong."

"Well, at least you've established a grammatical order, and given a vocabulary of nouns and verbs, which you can gather by pointing out objects and suggesting various motions, that should allow you to communicate better."

"I know. But I've done some of that, and I'm still stuck at using words and not sentences to communicate."

Deering nodded his head. After a long moment, he said, "You know, I've been in foreign lands, especially in Africa, where you don't know the local language, but construct a kind of pidgin between theirs and yours, which is built from words, sounds, even body language, like Hawaiian Creole English."

Melissa's face lit up. "You're right. I've been trying to figure out their language, when it would be faster to create a common language between us. I've studied Hawaiian pidgin, and that's a great model." Her enthusiasm got the better of her. "Bennett, I could kiss you."

He laughed. "Well, let's not get carried away, my dear."

After they explored this approach a little more, and Deering gave her examples of how he had gone about creating English pidgin with East African natives, he left while Melissa went in search of Ikagi to begin this process.

Deering went back to his hut, changed into the shorts he used for taking a shower, and headed to the spring behind the village where they had set up a cloth-sluice shower. He poured a can of water into the sluice and stood under it while he washed up with a soap substitute that the women used. Unlike the tribal women, these Amazons, if he could still use that term, were hygienic. Somewhat cooled off, he went back to his hut and lay down in his hammock. Since the time they had left the tribal village in search of these women, he hadn't had much of chance to think things out for himself, and now with Hawks out and about, he took advantage of the opportunity.

He had learned from past experience that when confronted with an impasse—in this case, the lack of ready transport back to civilization—you didn't fight against the grain, like Hawk's under-qualified hunting trips—you adapted or even surrendered to the situation. But the stringent European mental straightjacket, which is what he hated most about living in England and dealing with his countrymen, forced every situation to conform to something that could be readily managed. This is what he liked so much about native populations around the world; they knew how to go with the flow, as it were, to take what nature provided and make the most of it, never pounding a square peg into a round hole. If bread and beans was all that was available, you ate it and were grateful for it.

But he had to admit, this was unlike any dilemma he had ever faced. Of course he been stranded in the wild, but when your car or transport broke down or was stolen, you could usually walk twenty miles to the nearest town to get help, or radio for it from there. But now there was no means of outside communication and no transports out if they didn't find their canoe. He assumed at some point Connor Croft would mount a rescue operation, but the best they could do was fly high overhead, not knowing where the Uni village was—not to mention that they weren't even there—and so they were left to their own devices. He had no problem with a protein-deficient diet—most indigenous populations of the world subsisted on rice alone, as he had when living with them. That didn't bother him. What was challenging was the total mystery surrounding these women: how they got here, how they had sustained themselves all these years, maybe for centuries, how they had evolved this matriarchal society of theirs, how they remained light-skinned after generations of mating with dark-skinned natives and why they had no male children. One would suspect that like their Amazon namesakes, they would be closed off to outside intrusion, but their group was readily accepted. Yes, they needed baby makers, but so far, after more than a month here, the men weren't being sought out.

Ika's death was part of this mystery. He sensed that getting to the bottom of it would reveal more answers. That he was killed by a jaguar, given the condition of his torn-apart body, was still suspect in his mind. Maybe there was a jungle beast out there, but if that were the case, why were the women immune to his attack? Could they somehow control this creature? The native tribesmen believed it killed the men who sought out the women for sex, but was that from jealousy? Why would an animal be jealous of men? What if the animal had been a native, a past consort of the women, and had been somehow afflicted and mutated or evolved into this beast? No, that was much too farfetched even for him in this weird situation. Evolutionary change didn't work that fast anyway—would any of this really matter if they didn't make it back?

Melissa, out of breath, unexpectedly stuck her head into his hut. "Come quick. Hawks has been wounded by something!"

Deering slipped on his safari shorts and headed outside.

"Medi is trying to fix it, but it's a pretty nasty cut or bite."

Outside Medi's hut, Hawks was sitting on a tree stump chair writhing in pain while Medi and Adam tried to staunch the flow of blood.

"Hey, Deering," said Hawks, trying to pretend he was still in charge of his surroundings, "The damn deadfall snare worked, but the stone wasn't big enough to kill the capybara. When I got there, he was squealing like a guinea pig, then he charged me and took a bite out of my leg. I poked him in the eye with my spear to get him off me, but he's still out there wounded. You ought go after him. He's a big one, maybe seventy kilograms."

Deering almost laughed. "Sterling. You've got to be kidding."

Hawks shook his head. "Then, Melissa, you could do it. Just needs a chop in the head with the axe, and we can feast on him."

Hawks now let out a shriek that quickly brought his focus back to reality, "Damn. Watch what you guys are doing!"

Deering knelt down to take a look at the wound himself. The capybara had bit deep into his calf muscle and it looked like he had cut into one of the tendons, but the bleeding was letting up. He turned to Adam. "We may need to stitch this up. Does she have any fine thread?"

Melissa asked the question of Medi and translated slowly as she spoke. "She says she take care of wounds like this—but man may not walk good again, but won't die."

"Shit," Hawks said to this prognosis. "Deering you must have some first aide experience from living in the wild. Can you stitch the tendon back together?"

He took a closer look at the wound. "It's not torn off and could heal itself, but I don't think you want me fooling around with it. When we get back to the States, a surgeon can probably repair it. For right now, you don't want to get the wound infected, and I think Medi can handle that by lashing the sides of the wound together and let it naturally close up."

Hawks just shook his head in frustration. Finally Melissa and Bennett stepped away to allow the medicine women to deal with the injury as best she could. "I was afraid something like this might happen," Melissa finally said.

"Well, don't blame me. If I had been there, we'd probably both would have been attacked."

"No. I wasn't blaming you, Bennett. I just had a sense of . . . darkness descending around us."

Bennett let out a sigh. "Well, that doesn't sound good."

CHAPTER EIGHTEEN

It took two weeks before Jo was up and about and eating dinner with them at the common area. He wasn't totally recovered, and his eyes still had a kind of yellowish jaundiced look, but he was definitely more himself. Hawks regaled him with stories of his hunting trips, and Jo pointed out what he could've done differently, but that killing animals without a bow and arrow was difficult. He explained that spears were used on group hunting trips, rarely as a single weapon, where the hunters would circle an animal, close in, and kill them with several spear blows. Hawks's wound was healing, or at least the surface abrasion. Medi's treatment worked well for that. He walked with a limp, and only a surgeon could repair the torn ligament in his calf muscle, so hunting even with Jo once the boy was fully recovered was not possible.

The headway Melissa was making with Ikagi, as she focused more on using a pidgin combination of her language and English to communicate, brought them closer together. As Melissa had noted earlier, Ikagi and the other women expressed their affection for each other in very sexual ways, but it didn't seem to create the kind of attachments that she was used to seeing between women, or for that matter, between men and women, in her society. Often, if one of their language sessions lasted into the early evening,

Ikagi would sleep with Melissa, and they would fondle each other, but never engaged in outright sexual congest. This was curious and made Melissa wonder how finger manipulation had been enough to sustain the Amazon women's sex lives all this time, but the fact that their lovemaking was again more affectionate than driven by orgasmic releases might account for that.

Several nights later Deering stuck his head into her hut, saw the two of them fondling each other in the hammock, and stepped back out. "Hate to . . . bother you, but Adam's missing, and Jo's going crazy saying the jungle beast got him."

"Give me a moment." Melissa told Ikagi to wait for her as she got dressed and stepped outside. Deering looked down, apparently embarrassed by what he had interrupted. "Come on, Bennett. This can't be a surprise to you."

He took her by the arm and walked her back to Hawks's hut. "Adam was last seen with Medi, the medicine woman, going into the woods after dinner. Too late to pick herbs."

"So they had sex, and Jo thinks that's what triggers the beast's appearance and murderous rampage?"

"That seems to be the legend," Bennet said.

They arrived and stepped into the hut. Jo was circling around the centerpiece table waving his hands. He saw Melissa and repeated the spiel he had been giving the men about Luison's jealous retribution.

Finally Melissa was able to sit him down on the edge of Deering's hammock. "Adam told us that he works in the jungle with Medi, and they take naps together, but no sex."

Jo waved his hand. "That during day. Luison, like jaguars, hunts night."

"But you have been with these women, and you haven't been attacked."

No response from Jo. There was no reasoning with him. Then the grass door parted, and Adam stepped into the hut.

"You guys having a party without me?"

Hawks was about to explain their predicament but stopped short. "Too many people. Let's do this outside." They stepped out of the hut, and Hawks and Deering pulled over a couple tree trunk chairs. Jo sat on the ground cross-legged, and Melissa sat next to him, rubbing his arm and trying to calm him down.

After the three men sat, Hawks explained the situation. "Jo saw you heading into the jungle after dinner with Medi, and when you didn't return, he feared that the jungle beast had gotten to you."

Adam nodded his head. "Oh, I see."

"So you made love to Medi?" Melissa asked without a hint of coyness.

Adam was hesitant to give the group details.

Hawks added, "Come on, old boy. That's nothing new to us, but we're still trying to figure out this whole beast legend and if it holds water."

"No one wants to admit this, but we may never get out of here," ventured Adam.

"You don't need an excuse here for what you do with your private life," said Melissa.

To which Deering commented, "It's true, we may never get out of here. It's also true that people do things in the dark that they would never do in the light of day."

"We're on a scientific exploration, we're not making a documentary on tribal culture—so tell us what happened," said Melissa.

"So what happens here stays here?" added Adam somewhat sheepishly.

"On a personal level, yes," said Deering confidently "I think we can all agree to that."

"Then let's just say it was a wild ride—more than one wild ride—something I can't remember happening anytime recently!" said Adam smugly.

Melissa smiled and said, "These women don't have our civilized sexual baggage to inhibit them and it seems to be fading with the rest of us, too" causing the others to cast their eyes downward.

"Without modern society's cultural sunshine, I think it's clear to all of us which culture's morals take over in the dark of night," Deering felt the need to add.

"Anyway," Adam said, "she rolled off of me afterward, quickly put on her skirt, and ran back to the village."

"Wham bam thank you ma'am kind of thing, with her being the man," Hawks said.

Jo was listening to him. "She afraid that beast attack and run away."

Adam nodded his head. "Maybe, but she didn't seem fearful, sad maybe and—"

"Or the opposite of what you would expect after an exciting romp in the jungle," Hawks added to lighten the mood.

Melissa looked over at Deering, "Do you think the hormones released during intercourse attracts whatever it is? I've read studies to that effect, that female animals secrete odors that attract males for mating, and it might be the trigger."

"Let's call it a night," Hawks said hurriedly, as if to quash this speculation. He now turned to Jo. "Are you going to be all right?"

He stood up. "I glad Adam good, but afraid for us."

Hawks walked Jo back to this hut and went inside with him. Deering turned to Melissa. "Those two have lots of history. Maybe he can talk him down."

"Well, you're right about my investigation, and this seems to fit into some kind of puzzle about their sexual behavior."

Deering sneered. "Well, I'll let you get back to your . . . study."

Melissa laughed. "Actually, it is more like a study than what I'm used to." She turned and sashayed back to her hut. Deering watched her walk away and wondered if she was flirting with him.

Deering and Hawks figured that the best way to understand this legend was to explore the tribe's mythos, or their history as far back as they could remember or would tell him. He knew that they had no paper records, but maybe there were artifacts that would reveal more about their origins. He talked to Melissa, who explained their interest to Ikagi, and she took the three of them to what they came to understand was the tribe's "old crone," or history keeper. The woman lived in her own hut at the end of the village and was partially blind and a little deaf, but Ikagi was able to communicate with her. To help prod her memory, Hawks took out the bronze axe and handed it to the woman. She practically caressed the instrument and said something to Ikagi, who translates it for Melissa.

"She say it old, very old, from before."

"From before what?" Hawks asked.

There was another go around between the three of them, and Melissa turned back to Hawks. "Apparently 'many, many moons ago,' they lived somewhere else and came here, and much was lost or couldn't be moved."

Hawks held up the axe. "Ask if what they couldn't bring was more weapons like this?"

Again after much discussion, Melissa translated it as, "Only part of what was left behind."

Hawks, knowing what he was about to say was purely speculation was still generally excited. "Which might account for a change in their behavior from warlike hunters to farmers living off the land. Ask her if there is anything she has from . . . before, that she can show us."

Melissa translated for Ikagi who talked with the woman, but she now put up her hands and waved them. Hawks got the message. Melissa was finally able to clarify.

"She's like the Sacred Daykeeper in the Mayan tradition, and doesn't seem willing to confide in us, or at least not yet."

"I understand." Hawks now removed his watch and showed it to the woman, who was fascinated by all the moving dials, and told Melissa to tell her that in his country, he is a Keeper of Time as well.

There was an exchange; the woman got the message, and they were told to come back another day, that she needed to consult the sky goddess, which they took to be the planet Venus whom they seemed to worship.

The three of them left, and Melissa said that she would prod Ikagi to set up another meeting with the Keeper. Hawks expressed his gratitude for her being the conduit for this exchange. As he walked away, Melissa realized that Sterling had been at loose ends after they got stranded here, but now there was something that drew his interest and his energy, and that could help him get through the next couple of months before they could leave for home.

So the group appeared to settle into the rhythm of the village's life. Adam continued to work with Medi identifying plants and their medicinal use, which he would then dry out and put samples into one of his specimen vials filled with alcohol. He was curious that, after their first sexual conjoining that, while they did continue, it was less frequent. It appeared as if she was following some kind of inner rhythm not solely dictated by desire. Or maybe it was Jo's presence that dampened the mood. Once he had fully recovered from his jungle fever, the boy began to accompany them on their trips into the jungle. Jo also seemed a little lost, and this gave him a focus. At one point, Adam was suspicious and asked him if he was their chaperon. He shook off the inquiry, but Adam also noticed that Jo had not picked up where he left off with his "girlfriends." This was strange behavior given his sexual philandering at the Uni village. Finally, wondering if there was more to his celibacy, Adam talked with Melissa about it.

She shared his concern and finally approached Jo weeks after he began working with them. "So Jo, you don't like village girls anymore?"

"They are good, but not want to get killed by jungle beast."

"But Adam . . . cavorts with Medi, and Luison hasn't come."

Jo shook his head. "Men who have . . . sex with village women die like Ika."

Melissa then asked, "And you are afraid for Adam. That the jungle beast will get him too, and that's why you . . . tag along?"

Jo wasn't sure how to answer this inquiry. "I want be Medicine Man some day. Good training."

Jo now pulled away and headed back to his hut. Deering had watched this exchange and stepped over. "What was that about?"

"Adam was wondering if Jo was chaperoning him and Medi, and the fact that he had not taken up with his . . . girlfriends."

Deering nodded his head. "He's afraid Luison will kill Adam if he continues to have sex with Medi, he thinks the same will happen to him, which is why he won't . . . take up with the girls anymore."

"I think that's it."

"Well, I would encourage him to stay vigilant. There seems to be a connection."

"But not a problem for you?" Melissa asked.

"I'm not inclined to 'take up' with any of them. I mean, I like sex, and I like the casual attitude the native women have about it, but the civilized side of me likes friendships, too, and how sex evolves from that."

"They do seem disinclined toward relationships, and even Ikagi who is very . . . affectionate, doesn't step over that line." Melissa thought for a moment. "You know, they are very sexual with lots of women, maybe it's the one-on-one thing." She now had a mischievous thought. "Well, Deering, you can communicate with Ikagi, she knows enough pidgin, maybe you could lure her away, or . . . join us" she said somewhat jokingly.

Deering grimaced and shook his head. "I think I'll see how Hawks is doing with the Keeper."

The woman was definitely showing signs of interest in him, but what was he to do about it? He was beginning to like Melissa, saw something of what Hawks had originally said about her, that she was made of stern stuff. But given the circumstances of what was happening in the village and the mystery of this jungle beast, it was best not to get distracted.

Several weeks, later Deering was in Hawks's hut listening to Hawks and Melissa telling a story the Keeper had related about the "before" time. She said, with Ikagi's translation, that they were living in the hills between the jungle and the white-capped mountains where the sun lived.

"The Andes," Deering said hesitantly.

"Maybe. And then she says their hunters came back and told of men with shining heads riding beasts with four legs that had come to the mountains and killed the natives.—Could the shiny heads be metal helmets and the beasts be horses—the Spanish conquest of the Incas in the early 1500s?" Melissa questioned.

"Possibly. But it will require something more concrete than the imperfect interpretation of the ramblings of an old woman to determine that issue. I asked her what happened after that, if they fought them, like the Francisco de Orellana legend, but she didn't know," Hawks said.

"Or wouldn't say," Deering said.

"No, I think she is telling us what she was told. She said other Keepers had remembered animal skins with pictures of these beasts, and the tales were passed down to them after the drawings faded or the skins were used."

"If the story does relate to the time of the Spanish conquest, that gives us a historical reference," Deering said. "They were together as a tribe of women some five hundred years ago."

"Which means they didn't arrive with them," Hawks added.

Deering shook his head. "Then how in the hell did they get here?"

At that moment Jo barged into the hut and appeared to be in some kind of a transfixed state. "I dead man!"

Hawks grabbed him by the arm and sat him down on an upturned water can. Melissa retrieved some water and gave it to him.

"Okay, Jo. Take it easy, and tell us what happened."

After a long while he finally gathered himself together. "I out in jungle. Want to find plant we drop on way back from harvest."

"With Adam and Medi?"

"Yes. We come to village; she say important plant fall out bag, and I go look for it."

Deering asked, "Did her asking you seem at all suspicious?"

Jo shook his head. "We have a full bag."

"Then what happened?" Hawks asked.

"I find plant, but feel sleepy or foggy, then all go dark. I wake up, find clothes off, and white stuff on . . . sex thing. I make babies with woman. Luison come for me."

Deering listened carefully. "So you were unconscious the whole time and don't remember who she was?"

"Not remember much, but like in dream, see images like on dream-medicine and feel . . . excited."

Deering turned to Adam. "Have you seen Medi pick any hallucinogenic plants?"

"Not that I know of, but she has all kinds of potions we haven't gotten to."

"Beast get me now. I dead man," Jo said.

"Look, beast kill Ika before he come back to village. You escaped. It go back to jungle, not come to village with night torches and light," Deering said.

This seemed to mollify him slightly. Melissa volunteered to take him back to his hut and stay with him for awhile. After they left, Hawks turned to Deering. "I'm sure that's the story he'll tell Camila, or how he got drugged and couldn't help himself."

"I wouldn't dismiss this story so readily."

"Come on, Deering. Women have been hearing that tale from drunks and addicts for God knows how long—'I wasn't my fault, something made me do it'—it's all rubbish," Hawks said.

"I guess, but it's his level of fright that concerns me." Hawks nodded his head.

"There is something . . . strange going on here."

"Yeah, sex with native women and a guilty conscience."

"So, you're not concerned for him?" Deering asked.

"There's no jealous beast and no jaguar is going to prance

into a village of humans—besides, how would either of them know which hut he was in? Now you have me thinking crazy like the rest of you."

An hour later, after both Hawks and Deering had settled into their hammocks, Melissa stuck her head into their hut. "He's sound asleep now. We'll talk about it in the morning.

The next day Adam worked with Medi, but they didn't go into the jungle, not that Jo would have joined them. He stayed in his hut all day, and finally Melissa had to take him something to eat and drink, but she couldn't coax him out.

Everybody else went about their business, Hawks and Deering with the Keeper, and Melissa continued her pidgin conversion with Ikagi. After dinner, which again Melissa had to deliver to Jo in his hut, with words of encouragement, they all retired early. It appeared that nothing would come of Jo's sexual exploit.

CHAPTER NINETEEN

The evening cacophony of howler monkeys was pierced by a terrified scream. When Melissa approached Jo's hut, the three men were already gathered around the front, Hawks kneeling down and examining what appeared to be drag marks, when Melissa saw what had happened. She stood back for a moment, somewhat in shock. "Something dragged Jo out of his hut!"

Deering turned to her. "It first attacked him inside. There's blood and torn tissue there."

"But how . . . how would it know which hut?" Melissa shook her head in consternation.

Hawks stood up, as if to arrest this line of inquiry. He now pulled everybody back from the track marks. "See the swiveling back-and-forth arc of his feet being dragged along."

"You mean, as if he was grasped by an animal's jaws and swung side to side during its retreat into the jungle," Deering said.

"That's my point. This was a jaguar attack, not some mystical jungle beast with hands."

"There's no missing limbs or anything," Adam added.

"Exactly." Hawks turned to Deering. "Grab a couple of our spears and . . . dammit, they're no flashlights left."

"You're not going after it?" Melissa asked.

Hawks assured her, "If he hears us tramping down the path, he might let go of Jo. Animals attack solitary figures, and run from groups."

"What about torches?" Adam asked.

"Okay, let's grab a couple, dip them in that vegetable oil they use, and light them. That'll scare it off even better."

It look the three men about ten minutes to replenish the evening's burnt-out torches. After Hawks and Deering headed down the path into the jungle, Adam looked around the common area. "Why didn't the women respond to his cries?"

"I know. That's strange. I was with Ikagi, and she wouldn't come with me."

"Well, we know it's not the sex-and-die legend we've been told, or it would've attacked Jo in the jungle last night."

"I guess so." Melissa headed back to her hut, but when she got there, Ikagi was gone. This was puzzling to her. The women generally seemed sympathetic to their group's plight and had been helpful during their long stay, but you would expect a little more concern about Jo's attack, unless it triggered their own frightful reaction.

Somewhat later, Deering stuck his head into Melissa's hut. She hadn't been able to fall asleep and sat up in her hammock. "Did you find any trace of him?"

"No, by the time we headed down the trail, his cries had stopped, and then we came to a spot where he was dragged off into the jungle, and we gave up at that point."

"My God. What's happening here?"

"Look, it's late, and Hawks is a bit concerned about you being alone at night, unprotected. Do you mind if I roll out our one sleeping bag here, just for the night, or until we can figure this out."

"Thanks, Bennett. I'd appreciate that."

"Okay, I'll grab it and the axe and be back. Try to sleep. Hawks wants the two of us to head out at first light to pick up the trail."

When Deering returned to their hut, he found Adam sitting up in his hammock shaking nervously and sipping water out of a wooden bowl. Hawks turned to him. "He's got a bad case of the shakes."

"He was fine earlier. Anything happen in between?"

"No, but I've seen this before. It's a delayed reaction to animal carnage in the wild. Happens to Whites in Africa all the time."

"Imagine Medi could help."

"Well, he tried going over there, but she wouldn't have anything to do with him for now."

Adam piped up. "I, I was talking to Melissa about it. How the women aren't . . . concerned, or . . ."

"Or they switch it off to hide their fear, which is what you see in African villages where there's been lots of animal attacks," Hawks added hurriedly.

Deering grabbed the sleeping bag. "Are you going somewhere?" Adam asked nervously.

"Yeah, I'm going to stay the night with Melissa . . . for the time being."

"Really? Why don't you bring her here instead?"

Hawks snickered. "Go ahead, Bennett. I'll babysit him."

As Deering walked back to Melissa's hut, he wondered about Hawks's somewhat blasé attitude about Jo⊠s attack and apparent death. Was this his own delayed shock reaction, or a way to hide his deeper concern? Despite his explanation for the drag marks, it seemed unlikely that a jaguar had the jaw-strength to drag a 160-pound man hundreds of yards down a path and then into the thick foliage. There may indeed be a beast loose in this jungle, he thought.

A little after dawn, the three men headed down the trail into the jungle. Adam had refused to stay in the hut alone, still afraid for his life. Hawks handed him the roll of canvass for the remains. "If the jaguar attacks, throw it over him and run."

"Very funny, Hawks. I think I'll throw it over you and run," Adam shot back.

"That's the spirit."

While the sun had risen, it was still low on the horizon, and the jungle was beginning to lighten up just a bit, but not like midday. They soon found where Jo had been dragged off the path into the jungle. Hawks used the machete to swat their way through the thick bush until they came to his ravaged body.

Adam turned away and threw up.

"Okay, we've seen this before; let's just gather his remains and leave."

"No, let me take a closer look, Sterling," Deering said. He now knelt down and examined what remained of the body and how it had been pulled apart with great force. This seemed to confirm his earlier suspicion that this was not a jaguar attack. He didn't want to start a fight with Hawks, and so he kept his suspicions to himself.

"Let's do it."

Adam unfurled and laid out the canvass nearby, and Hawks and Deering gathered up the pulled-apart bits and pieces of their guide and dropped them on it. While his stomach was still queasy, he was a scientist and used to assessing the pure facts of a situation. "Look, Hawks, seeing the remains, this doesn't look like any jaguar attack to me."

"And you've seen plenty of them, I take it?" Hawks replied sarcastically.

"No, but this body wasn't mauled, it was torn apart with great force."

"Thanks for your opinion, but let's get the remains before it attracts more . . . predators."

Adam started to reply, but Deering shook him off. They wrapped the canvass around the remains, and it took all three of them to walk the tube to where they decided to dig a hole as best they could on nearby soft, wet ground, and they buried him there.

When the men returned from burying Jo's remains, Hawks waved Melissa over to his hut. She made her excuses with the women preparing the dough to be baked into loaves of bread. Since the women were using the tree trunk chairs, and it was too hot to gather inside the hut, the group formed a circle in the shade of a nearby tree.

Before Hawks could establish his agenda, Melissa asked Deering, "So the body was torn apart like Ika's?"

"Yes, and it doesn't look at all like a Jaguar attack to me."

Adam added, "I agree, despite Hawks's claims to the contrary."

Sterling tried to laugh off their speculation, but was met with cold glaring stares. "Okay, I'll admit that's looking less and less likely, but that begs the question: what the hell kind of animal is it?"

"Let's take another track," Adam said. "Let's assume there is such a creature, given the torn-apart remains. Why is he attacking men and not these women?"

"Why do animals attack humans in the wild? To protect their lair and for food," Hawks said.

"What if the women can communicate with it? What if they have some control over it? I've seen shamans on psychedelics communicate with animals," Deering added.

Adam shook his head. "These women are so peaceful and accepting; I can't imagine them being involved in any of this."

At that moment the unmistakable sound of a low-flying airplane could be heard. Everybody stood up and stepped out into the clearing of the common area and stared up at the sky.

"Maybe it's a rescue party that Connor mounted," Hawks said.

Melissa and Adam started to wave their hands. "Can you see it?" Melissa asked.

"No, and they won't see us because the tall tree canopy pretty much hides our small open location—unless they fly right over us."

"Maybe we should start a bonfire, and let them see the rising smoke," Adam said.

"Yes, hurry." They gathered branches used for the cooking fire as quickly as they could, but by the time they had it ready, the plane's engine sounds had begun to fade away.

"Shit, let's get this built so we can ignite it on a moment's notice; if it comes back this way we'll be ready," Hawks said.

The village women had put down what they were doing to look up in the sky. Ikagi now came over and asked Melissa about the strange sky sounds. She told her that it was the white man's flying machine looking for them.

"They come, take you away?" Ikagi asked in alarm, or that was Melissa's pidgin interpretation.

"If they spot us, they'll come with canoes but not for a long time."

This seemed to mollify Ikagi's concern, and she walked back to the women, who had resumed their activities.

After they gathered again under the tree, Hawks told Melissa, "You need to have some straight talk with Ikagi about these attacks."

"Okay, but it's not like I haven't tried already."

"Try harder. Our lives are at stake here." He now turned to Adam. "For now, I wouldn't go prancing off into the jungle with Medi at night."

"Okay, but I'm going to continue my work with her and won't erect any barriers between us."

"Well, some in our community would look askance at us having sex with native women we work with," Hawks said.

Adam bristled at this suggestion. Hawks quickly added, "Well, at least probe her about psychedelic plants and see if she has any." He now turned to Deering. "I'm going to take our double-sided axe apart, and we'll embed each side into a three-foot-long branch handle for a regular-size axe for each of our protection at night."

"So you think this . . . whatever it is, will attack again?" Melissa asked.

"That's why they put down dogs who attack or viciously bite humans, even in self-defense. They'll do it again."

That night, their communal dinner with the women was a bit strained. Deering figured that while they might not have overheard their earlier discussion, or for that matter understood it, those who live close to nature had a sixth sense about people and animals and could sense their unease. It still amazed everyone that none of these women inquired about last night's attack and their finding

Jo's remains in the jungle.

After dinner and cleanup, Melissa invited Ikagi back to her hut. The woman smiled assuming that this wasn't a language session. But upon their arrival there, Melissa sat on one of the grass mats that she had woven and indicated for Ikagi to sit on the other.

"You mad me?" Ikagi asked right off.

"No. I not know why you and others act like nothing happened last night."

After Melissa rephrased this another way, the woman answered, "We sad for boy lost, but we can do nothing."

"Why beast attack men who . . . with women?" she asked.

She stood up. "Not talk about jungle beast."

Melissa stood up and touched her arm. "Know you not like talk about, but it kill two of us, and we scared."

Ikagi looked back at Melissa with sadness. Melissa now wrapped her arms around Ikagi to comfort her. They stepped over to the hammock and lay down. Soon Ikagi asleep, as if the stress of the earlier questioning had created such a conflict that she sought sleep rather than pleasure.

Later that night Deering stuck his head into the hut, but seeing the two of them in the hammock, he started to back out.

"Bennett, give us a minute. I'll have her go back to her hut."

After Ikagi was awakened and had gotten dressed and had left, Bennett stepped back inside, carrying the axe on its three-foot handle, which looked rather formidable.

"Maybe you should just stand outside the hut like a gargoyle holding that thing."

"Yeah, well, unlike them, I do need my sleep." Deering laid out his sleeping bag and slipped inside fully clothed. "Did you talk with Ikagi?"

"I tried, but any mention of the beast is just shattering for her, probably for the others as well. It's like some kind of collective shock, like you see after natural disasters."

"You sure that's not just some defense mechanism to hide

behind?" Deering asked.

"No, she was generally conflicted and fearful, like what Hawks described of African women after animal attacks."

"Did she mention the sky sound?'

"No, we never got around to that, but I think my earlier explanation of them taking a long time to find us assuaged her concerns."

"Concerns about you leaving her, or something else?" Deering asked.

"Again, while we're affectionate, it's not like we have a . . . love relationship. So, something else."

"Would be good to know what that is."

"I'll continue to probe her, but this is a very gray area for her and probably the others as well."

"Maybe Adam can pry something out of Medi."

Deering reached over and snubbed out the flame, and the two of them tried to get some sleep, but given the circumstances and the now evident sexual tension between them, neither slept very well.

CHAPTER TWENTY

The strain of the story's recollection was having a deleterious effect on Melissa, and she began to cough up phlegm. Mattie pressed the caller device, and Dr. Marcum opened the door and hurried inside. He rushed up to the bed, reached behind Melissa, and leaned her forward while he collected the mucus discharge on a medical napkin. He now handed his patient her water bottle. Melissa took several sips from the straw and leaned back. Joel raised the bed to a sitting position.

He turned to Mattie. "I'm afraid that does it. I must insist that you stop . . . whatever it is you're doing."

"We're almost done here, Joel. Just a few more minutes," Melissa said, her voice strained.

"But Melissa—"

"But nothing. If I die telling this story, so be it. Go, and let me finish."

Marcum gave Mattie a withering look, then turned and left the room, shutting the door behind him.

"Mother, maybe Joel's right. This is a little much for you."

"Oh, now you're concerned. A little late my dear, don't you think?" She paused and seemed confused. "Where were we now?"

"Your guide had been killed, and, as a group, you realized that these were no Jaguar attacks." Melissa nodded her head and closed her eyes. "But what in God's name could it be? Certainly not some mythical creature in the Amazon jungle."

Melissa opened her eyes and added rather cryptically, "It was a creature, for sure, but as to its nature, we were uncertain."

"What were your options?"

"As Ika had told us on the way to their village, there are long-standing myths of jungle spirits, like El Tunchi, that could have a basis in fact."

Mattie snorted in disbelief. "Really, mother. Some evil spirit materialized and tore these people to death?"

"Well, something real was there, but our concern at this point was the women's involvement, or how much we could trust them."

"Or whether they had some control over it?"

"Yes, that was being suggested."

"But you're not going to tell me?"

"Oh, I'm going to be completely forthright, but as the story calls for it."

"Jesus, mother. Just get on with it, would you," Mattie spit out.

*****

A few days later, after the group had settled back into the village life, Adam and Melissa approached Medi about her possible use of psychedelic mushrooms and plants. He was aware of the 1957 Life magazine article by Richard Schultes, "Seeking the Magic Mushroom," which introduced psilocybin to the researchers in America. This led to the Harvard Psilocybin Project conducted by Drs. Timothy Leary and Richard Alpert in the early 1960s. As he now recalled, and what seemed to be of particular interest here, was the Marsh Chapel Experiment in which Harvard divinity students took psilocybin to see if it could induce profound religious experiences. Nine of the ten participants reported such visions. Given the periodic ecstatic dance rituals in homage of their Venus deity, it made sense that these women could be taking some plant psychedelics to induce their trance states, which they had all witnessed. Medi was cautious when the two of them stepped into her hut days after Jo's death, possibly afraid that this would be the topic of their discussion or exploration. But while it took several back-

and-forth translations, even after Adam had updated Melissa on the subject, Medi finally got the gist of this inquiry.

She now drew them out of the hut and around back where she was drying out striking purple-colored mushrooms and another variety with an impressive brownish-white coiffure in a wooden shed. She asked if they wanted samples, and Adam said he would but could collect them later. They returned to the hut, and Adam asked her about their medicinal use.

What he gathered from the translation was its use was to relieve "sadness" in the women. This immediately grabbed Melissa's interest. She said village women seemed "content," and asked why they got "sad," which is what he had noticed in Ikagi recently. This seemed to make Medi leery or cautious, and picking up on that shift in tone, Adam asked if it allowed them to see their "goddess."

Once they translation was made, Medi was immediately enthusiastic and said it helped dancers to see the star goddess and talk with her and get her advice. After several more go-rounds, Medi affectionately touched Adam's arm, and Melissa got the message. She made her excuses and left the two of them alone.

Medi now gathered her collection bag, and she and Adam headed down the path into the jungle. At some point, they turned off the path and made their way down a secondary trail that was fairly overgrown but allowed their easy passage. Suddenly they came to a clearing amongst the undergrowth and tall trees of at least a twenty-yard square and filled with mushrooms of several varieties. Apparently some secretion from their roots kept the jungle at bay and allowed their unimpeded growth. Adam was amazed as much by the "clearing" effect as he was by all the different varieties, some of which grew on the trees that surrounded the clearing. Medi took her time to gather the ripe mushrooms for her use, and she instructed Adam as to how to pick them. Afterward they headed back to the main path, but on the trip back to the village, Medi waylaid them to another small clearing, where they lay down on the soft undergrowth and made love.

After leaving Medi's hut, Melissa sought out the old Keeper of history. Since she was unable to have a substantive talk with Ikagi about the jungle beast, she wondered if this old crone might be more forthcoming or less guarded. The test would be speaking to her without Ikagi's translation. The woman was alone as usual and was making an herbal tea with room-temperature water. She invited Melissa inside and prepared a cup for her. To start, she had a cordial exchange with simple questions and answers so as to pick up the rhythm of her talk and its verbal nuances. She was pleased that the communication was easier than she expected. Then Melissa asked her about their tribe's passage from the old world of "before" to here. The legend was of a long trip, far beyond areas that were known by them. Melissa asked how they were being guided.

The Keeper looked up at the roof and said, "Goddess tell us where to go."

She clarified this to mean, the one in the sky. Melissa asked about the danger of their passage. She said they arrived without harm.

"But you no longer fight or have weapons. What changed?"

After several go-rounds, the old crone got the gist of this inquiry. She finally answered rather ingeniously, "The Goddess keep us alive."

Melissa made several further attempts to clarify her statement, and could only elicit nods."

The old crone now claimed to be tired and in need of rest and dismissed her. As Melissa stepped out of the woman's hut, Ikagi approached her and asked why she didn't come to her to help with the "words." She told the woman that she wanted to delve into the "old language" of the tribe, or see if she could "navigate" it alone. That didn't answer her question, but Ikagi apparently dismissed her concern and drew Melissa into the women's meal preparation.

Earlier, Hawks and Deering had walked down to the mostly dried-out lake, but where, because of the open space, you could see a wider patch of the sky. In the distance they could see clouds forming, not dark yet, but the dry season was coming to an end.

"So this is what you wanted me to see?" Deering asked.

"Yeah, and that we need to resume our search for the canoe."

"I'm all for that." The men headed back to the village and gathered a day's supply of food and water and headed out in search of the canoe. The fact that Ika had been found on the path from the entrance furo to the village, and not from the lake path, seem to indicate that he might have hidden the canoe along the west side of the lake or even in the jungle next to this furo. Using the machete, they cut their way up this furo to the lake, but did not find the canoe. So they headed around the west side of the lake. On their earlier search they had not had a machete and had had to slither their way through the undergrowth, now they cut back the mid-growth plants and could search more thoroughly. They even began to follow some of the dried-out furos that drew water from the lake. This was a fairly large canoe, and Ika couldn't have dragged it too far off the lake or down one of these furos that were still flowing with water four months ago. By noon Hawks leg was acting up, and he couldn't go much farther, so they quit for the day and backtracked to the entry furo and then to the village. Deering had cut a tree branch that Hawks could use as a crutch of sorts, as much as it irritated him to use it. There was no way that the smaller Deering could walk him back, his arm draped over the anthropologist's shoulder.

That night, after they ate dinner, the group came back to Hawks's hut but gathered under a nearby tree, since it was still hot and very humid. Adam had talked Hawks into letting Medi treat his leg with some kind of salve and used a split of sorts to keep it straight. So he sat on the one tree stump chair that they were able to bring over from the common area, where the women were still gathered for dinner. Everybody was interested in hearing about Adam and Melissa's talk with Medi about psychedelic plants.

Adam gave a summary of their talk. "So they do use psychedelic plants, but mostly for the ecstatic religious ritual. This is not dissimilar to what Leary and Alpert reported in their Marsh Chapel Experiment."

"Before it was closed down, and they were given the boot," Hawks said derisively.

"Which does not discredit the results of drug-induced religious ecstasy reported, which aligns with similar episodes down through history all the way back to the Delphi."

Before Hawks could further discredit this rebuttal, Melissa added, "But what really interests me is that she uses it for medicinal purposes as well, to treat 'sadness' in the women."

"Which makes you wonder what they're sad about, since they seem pretty adjusted to their life here," Deering added

"When I tried to talk to Ikagi about the jungle beast, I got what I could only call an upsurge of sadness, and so I backed off."

"Sadness or remorse?" Deering asked.

Adam quickly added, "There's no way they have anything to do with these . . . incidents. They're just sad for our loss, as they were of Ika's, that's all."

Melissa said, "I snuck in to see the 'Keeper' without Ikagi. She told me the legend of their migration from the land 'before.'"

Hawks added impatiently, "We have covered that already."

"Exactly, and so I asked if anything had changed. Well, she took a few minutes to compose her reply. Finally, she said that they were kept alive by the goddess."

"I'm sure she meant Venus," Deering said.

"I made that connection, but she was emphatic. It was a goddess.'"

Hawks snickered. "I feel like I'm in an Oxford lecture hall watching two dons trying to figure out how many angels fit on the head of a pin."

Melissa leveled Hawks with a ferocious look. "Don't you dare try to minimize what we're attempting to figure out. Our lives may depend on it."

Hawks picked up his cane and walked out of the hut without saying another word.

Deering turned to Melissa. "About time someone put him in his place."

It took a week for Hawks's leg to mend—Medi's treatment worked wonders. In the interim, the village and the surrounding jungle had received its first light rainfall. Several days later, Adam did not return from his day's search for medicinal plants. After night fell, the three of them tried to question Medi, but she only shrugged and walked away.

Despite the awkwardness of the situation, they all felt afterward that Medi was withholding something she knew about Adam's wherabouts. Interestingly enough, they had become unplugged enough from the Western world and its distractions to reclaim more of their innate intuitive sense of things.

The next morning, Hawks and Deering headed down the path into the jungle that Adam and Medi usually took on their plant expeditions. They went slowly and carefully checked any ingress points along the path where Adam might've gone off into the jungle. They did find the path that led to the magic mushroom patch, or how Adam had identified it. Hawks had them carefully circle the clearing, staying in the jungle's undergrowth to check for fresh footprints in the dirt. The first rain had been light, and enough of it had been caught by the overhanging branches that it wouldn't have washed them away, but they didn't find any.

"So you were thinking he might've ingested some mushroom and is tripping out?" Deering asked.

"The thought did cross my mind."

"Well, they had already collected a batch of them, and maybe he kept some for himself," Deering said.

"No. He's not that adventurous. Let's head back to the path

and follow it farther down."

They spent the rest of the day traveling down this path and taking any possible offshoots, but came up empty-handed. That night they gathered together after dinner.

Hawks started off, "This isn't looking good. Adam is not one to stay out on his own, especially after what happened to Ika and Jo."

"So you think he's been killed, too, and we just haven't found the remains?" Deering asked.

"That's the only thing that makes sense."

"Makes sense!" Melissa shouted. "Does any of this make any damn sense?"

Deering put a hand on her arm. "Calm down. We need to keep even-keeled." He now turned to Hawks. "Tomorrow, whether we find Adam or not, we start searching for that canoe until we find it so we can get out of here."

"So you think the coming wet season and our possible departure plays into Adam's killing, if that's what has happened?" Melissa asked.

Deering replied excitedly, "Maybe, but we can't think our way out of this. It's pure survival instinct now, and it tells me to get the hell out of here."

Hawks nodded. "I agree." He now turned to Melissa. "Take Adam's hammock tonight. I want us all staying together until we're out of here."

The next morning Melissa packed provisions for an all-day expedition, and they left the village at first light. The idea was, since they had already checked most of the dried-up perimeter of the lake, to fan out ten yards into the jungle along this perimeter, which was as far as they figured one person could've dragged the canoe in high water. By midday they had made very little progress around the eastside of the lake, but they ate lunch and resume their search. An hour later, Hawks tripped over a vine and wrenched his knee and strained his calf tendons.

"Well, let's call it a day," Deering said.

Hawks shook his head. "No, you two keep going. The path is clear enough back to the village; I'll find another branch cane."

"But I thought we weren't going to get separated," Melissa said.

"I'm figuring that applies to nighttime, which is when this animal seems to prowl."

Against his better judgment, Deering finally agreed, but first he cut off a branch and fashioned it as cane for Hawks. They watched him hobble down the lake path they had cleared, and then they resumed their search. By late afternoon, they had found no trace of the canoe. They decided to head back, but when they arrived in the village at nightfall, Hawks was not in his hut and the women claimed they had not seen him return.

They checked the nearby spring and its shower, but he was nowhere to be found.

"Jesus, Bennett. I know we're desperate to get out of here, but we shouldn't have let him go off alone in his condition. Maybe he stumbled off the trail and is lying there. Or—God no—is he another victim?" Melissa asked, her hands shaking.

Deering just shook his head. "If he was okay, he would've been back before nightfall, but if he had trouble walking, it may take him a bit longer. Don't give up on him yet—he's one tough cookie—let's wait a bit and see."

They grabbed one of the axes and went back to the spring to shower off the jungle grime. When they returned, Ikagi had saved them dinner—three plates of it, which was a hopeful sign. Then, an hour later, Hawks stumbled back into the village, wide-eyed and terrified. He was muttering incoherently, and it took a while for Melissa's ministration to bring him around. He drank several bowls of water.

"What the hell happened, Sterling?" Deering was finally able to ask.

"I don't believe it. I was halfway to the village, when my vision started to blur and I felt dizzy, and then my mind was fogged over, just like poor Jo reported. Serves me right I guess for criticizing his story. Well, one of the women—I couldn't discern her features—appeared and I had a sudden irresistible urge to have sex with her. It was so primal that it felt animalistic and at the same time it seemed to be happening to someone else—I was just an observer. It seemed to go on . . . forever." He caught his breath, as if the recall made him pant. "When I regained full consciousness, she had gone, and it was getting dark, and so I put on my clothes and stumbled back here."

They both took this account seriously. "But when could you have been drugged?" Melissa asked. "And how could it override your mental inhibitions but not your primal urges?"

"To answer your second question, there are drugs that can do that," Deering said, and then added, "especially psychedelics. But what is alarming, Hawks, since you and I have maintained a professional distance with these women, is that they are now resorting to drugging us to have sex—just like they did to Jo when he resisted"

"Apparently that's why we were welcomed into the village, since they couldn't imagine men resisting their allure, and that's also why it's taken so long for them to force the issue." Melissa said.

Hawks nodded his head. "And there can only be one purpose: to procreate."

"Then the beast kills us off when we're no longer of use to them," Deering added.

Everybody looked around at each other; Hawks said, "At the direction of the women."

Melissa looked indignant, "Even if they have that kind of control over a wild beast, you think they have the desire to kill men?"

Hawks replied, "In our world or theirs, women get rid of men when they are no longer of use to them—it just takes longer in our world." Melissa's jaw dropped and before she could speak Hawks stated something all could agree with, "We've got to get out of here now!"

"But first we need to protect you and us from," Deering paused a moment to collect his thoughts, "the beast."

CHAPTER TWENTY-ONE

They decided to construct more of a door for Hawks's hut, and while the two men headed over to Jo's hut to salvage some of its wooden braces, Melissa gathered up as much vine cord as she could find. They met back at the hut and began to fashion a real door made from the braces and the hanging reeds, and held together by the vine cord. As they worked, they continued their discussion.

"So the women have sex with Ika and Adam and drug the uncooperative Jo to procreate with them, but kill the men before any signs of pregnancy?" Deering asked.

Still a bit rattled, Hawks said, "Again, while they appear more civilized than the Uni tribesmen, they have the same primitive sensitivity and, maybe on an unconscious level, can sense within a day the change a fertilized egg would produce in their bodies."

"So, either Medi or Adam wasn't very fertile and that's why it took this long to impregnate Medi, or so we might assume?" Deering asked.

"That would be my assumption," Hawks said.

Melissa looked askance at him. "No. There's no plan here; this isn't part of some scheme."

Deering stopped wrapping one of the braces and looked over at Melissa. "They have to procreate to survive as a tribe and for that matter as a species. It's one of our most basic instincts."

"But why would they kill the men afterward? Given the scarcity of men coming here."

Before either of the men could answer this question, Ikagi wandered over and asked what they were doing. When the question was translated, both men gave Melissa cautious looks.

She stood up.

"We build door to make hut . . . stronger."

"You no come back to hut for us, and no spend night with man there?"

"No, I'll stay here until . . . Adam returns."

She looked sad and said her goodbyes and walked away. Deering quickly added, "Don't you think it odd for her not to mention Hawks's return?" The others nodded their heads. "They have an amazing lack of what psychologists would call emotional 'affect.'"

"That's what I've pointed out in my relationship with her. Endearing and a bit sexual, but not deeply emotionally connected."

"But they're connected to this beast somehow?" Deeriing seemed to ask himself.

Melissa shook her head.

Deering and Hawks exchanged doubtful looks.

They were able to attach the door, but given the limited timeframe and the lack of metal hinges, it was not as sturdy as they would have liked. It was dark now, and while Melissa lay down in Adam's hammock to rest, Hawks and Deering sat back from the door on makeshift stools holding their axes. They had taken down both of their hammocks to give them more room to maneuver inside the hut if attacked by this jungle beast. After a short while, Melissa fell off to sleep.

"How can she sleep under these circumstances?" Hawks asked.

Deering shook his head. They sat down to guard the door, but after a while, Bennett was beginning to feel drowsy. "Hawks, are you feeling okay?"

The archeologist closed his eyes. "No, I'm feeling a bit woozy." He opened his eyes. "Dammit. We ate Ikagi's dinners. They must've had drugs in them." He stood and scooped up a bowl of water from the container and handed it to Deering, while he took another for himself. Hawks now took out his pocketknife and sliced his arm a couple times before handing it to Deering. "The cut will pump some adrenalin into our systems to keep us more alert."

Deering did the same. "Staying awake is the least of our problem."

"Stand and walk around holding your axe, and be ready to jump into action."

About fifteen minutes later, they heard an animal howl close to the village, then the unmistakable sound of clawed feet scraping across the hardened common's ground.

"Shit. That must be . . ."

Suddenly, the makeshift door was pulled off its jambs, and the silhouette of an eight-foot-tall, two-legged hairy beast with huge fangs for teeth stood in the doorway. It had shining red eyes that seemed to project light directly in Hawk's direction. Melissa woke up and screamed from her hammock. All were paralyzed for what seemed like an eternity, but it was just a few seconds. Then both men began to swing their axes at it, Deering thought he had hit it, but the beast stepped inside and easily swatted Deering onto his back. It then grabbed Hawks by the neck, which seemed to immediately make his body go limp, and he dropped the axe. The beast backed away with its red eyes still shining brightly in the night and quickly dragged Hawks off into the dark.

Deering picked up his axe and followed them out of the door with Melissa behind him. The roar of the beast had awakened the women, who stuck their heads out of the grass doors. Ikagi stepped out of her hut. Melissa, looking for help, spotted her and ran over and shrieked, "Make it stop."

Ikagi didn't answer. Melissa shook her and yelled louder, "Make it stop!"

"We can no stop." Ikagi said in a calm, low tone of voice.

The beast had now dragged Hawks out of sight. In the throes of a fear-induced adrenalin rush, Deering chased after them, then stopped right before the threshold of the jungle. Melissa ran to Deering and seemed willing to chase the beast down into the jungle.

Deering put a hand on her arm. "We'll never catch it, and even if we did, without a gun or rifle, we can't stop it."

Melissa started to collapse. Bennett dropped his axe and took the woman into his arms and carried her back to the hut. The women watched him and the spectacle with looks of trepidation. Ikagi remained fixed in the center of the commons.

Deering lay Melissa back into the hammock, retrieved a bowl of water for her, then turned to go back outside. "Bennett, please don't leave me."

"I'm just going to retrieve the axe; we may need them both tomorrow."

Outside, it was starting to rain. He had to grab the axe and wash it off before he returned to the hut as it appeared in the dim light that there was a dark stain on it. After Bennett brought the axe inside and set it upright to dry off, he sat in Hawks's hammock. "Bennett, please sleep with me, hold me, or I'm going to go nuts."

Deering stepped out, grabbed the makeshift door, and set it in place. He then slipped off his shoes and wet outer shirt, and slipped into the hammock with Melissa. She let him put an arm under her, and she wrapped her arms and legs around him and cried for the loss of her friend and their bleak plight.

Deering gently stroked her arm but said nothing, not knowing what would sooth anybody in such a desperate situation. After a while, Melissa fell asleep, her body completely relaxed against the sturdy muscular frame that she now entwined.

The next morning, Melissa went back to her hut to retrieve her belongings and move them back to Deering's hut. Ikagi interrupted her.

"You not leave?" she asked.

Melissa continued to gather up and stuff clothes into her large backpack as the anger built up in her. "I move to man's hut." Finally she stood up and turned around. "Why did you not help us last night?"

Ikagi now looked up, her face twisted with the sadness Melissa had seen earlier, but she seemed at a loss as to how to answer her. She bowed her head, unable to clarify their situation with the beast. Melissa turned back to her packing, as Ikagi picked up a few loose things and helped her move them to Deering's hut.

He had filled his backpack with a day's worth of food and water. When the two of them arrived, Deering handed Melissa Hawks's axe. "You ready?"

"Just let me dump this in the hut."

Ikagi now turned to him. "You go away?"

"We are going to look for our friend," he said rather coldly.

She bowed and backed away from him and his hostile glare and returned to the group of women working in the common area. Melissa stepped out holding the axe. "Let's go."

"Did you get anything out of her?"

"She wouldn't or couldn't answer me."

Deering gave her a skeptical look.

As they walked out of the village, they noticed one of the women limping and slipping into Medi's hut, but neither made mention of it. Once they were headed down the jungle path, Melissa asked, "So, are we really going to look for Hawks's remains?"

"I wish we had time for such niceties, but we're going to circle around to the lake and continue to look for the canoe."

"Yes, of course. I must be a little shell-shocked."

Deering reached over and patted her on the arm. "It's all right. You're holding up pretty well."

"You mean for a woman?" Melissa said with an edge to her voice.

"For anybody."

"Do we hold hands now?" Melissa said with a smirk. Deering tried to raise a smile and walked ahead of her down the narrow path.

The path was blood-stained, the tree limb canopy still protecting the undergrowth from the rain, and they saw where the beast had dragged Hawks off into the jungle foliage. This was a bit sobering, and they walked on without comment. At one point, the path turned east away from the lake, and Deering used the machete and at times the axe to cut a path back to it. It took some time to get to the lake. They stood on the perimeter and marveled at how quickly it was filling up.

"A couple more days of heavy rainfall, and it might be navigable if we can find the canoe," Deering said.

They resumed their search where they had left off on the eastside of the lake. Here the blowing rain from across the lake had penetrated into the surrounding undergrowth, and after slipping through it to search for the canoe, they were soon soaked to the bone. It was hot and humid, but their wet clothes didn't impede their search, although near the lake they would occasionally slip in the mud. While Hawks and Deering, along with the others, had earlier searched the perimeter of the lake and walked down the west-side furos, they had not gone very deep into the jungle on either side. An hour later Melissa slipped and fell backwards and, looking up, spotted a piece of ribbon tied to an upper branch that wasn't noticeable from a standing position.

"Bennett, come here and take a look."

He stepped over, knelt down, and looked up into the tree. "That's definitely one of our ribbon markers. Ika must've slipped it off one of the furo branches when we weren't looking."

"So he planned this from the start?" Melissa asked.

"He's the one who was drawn by the sexual allure of the women."

Deering helped Melissa to her feet. They were now inches apart. She reached up and flicked some leaves off his hair. He now reached over, pulled her to him, and kissed her on the lips. She pressed her body against his and held the lip lock until he broke it.

She smiled and rubbed her face. "It's been a while since I've gotten chafed by a stubby beard." He looked at her questioningly. "I like it." She now turned and headed into the wet undergrowth. They could see where the brush would provide a perfect spot to conceal the canoe in high water, and if she hadn't seen the ribbon, they might not have gone far enough into the brush to find it. They had to almost stumble upon it to see it.

There it was sitting with low hanging branches concealing almost every inch of it. They removed the branches; the paddles and the extra can of gasoline were still there. Deering now did an inspection of the exterior and saw that it was intact and ready to be paddled out of here when the water level allowed it.

"Should we leave it here, or drag it closer to the lake?" Melissa asked.

"Let's keep the branch camouflage, but move it a bit closer in case I have to come back myself and quickly pull it into the lake."

The two of them pulled it closer, left the ribbon marker, but made their own mark on the tree trunk to identify the spot, and then pushed back the growth as they slipped out of the jungle so no one else would spot their ingress point.

As they walked into the village, first cutting back over to the jungle path, they saw the woman who had been limping earlier but was now walking around easily, doing her daily chores.

"What do you make of that?" Deering asked.

"I don't know; they all work pretty hard," Melissa said, not really wanting to speculate further.

The plan was for them to fill their backpacks with food and water and what they would need to survive the long canoe trip and leave most of their clothes and other items here. They just needed to get back to the deeper furos where they could use the motor and then onto Rio Arrojo River, where they would be a day or so from civilization. Melissa assured Deering that her father wouldn't give up the search until they found dead bodies, and so they just needed to get out in the open so they could be spotted from overhead.

Of course, the main problem for them was how to keep Deering from becoming the last male fatality in this deadly mating game. "You know we can only eat from a common pot," Deering said, once they had gotten back to the village, washed up, and were lying in the hammock. "We can't let them drug us with separate meals."

"Again, you think this is some kind of conspiracy. Maybe it's just one of the women wanting to have sex with Hawks or you."

Deering sat back in the hammock, Melissa by his side, and gave this some thought. "Either way, we need to be careful of what we eat and drink."

Melissa nodded her head. "You know, Hawks did have his metal canteen, while we carried plastic bottles of water."

"That's it, of course. So before we got back today, they . . . she may have drugged the water container. Let's dump the water, thoroughly wash it out, and go to the spring to refill it."

"But someone could always slip in here while we're eating at the common area," Deering added.

"Okay. Let's leave it out, but only drink from the smaller plastic containers that we'll hide among our things."

Later, Ikagi came to their hut and asked if they had found Hawks. They said they had, and had buried him. She said she was sorry and seemed genuinely sad. She now invited them to a dinner celebration for Venus, who had brought them the rains of life that were now coming every day. Melissa said to go ahead and that they would come shortly.

"Look, Bennett, we need to be very careful what we eat and drink, and especially decline any plant liquor, which would make us less cautious."

"Agreed.

They ate dinner with them, carefully eating and drinking out of the common pots and dishes. Afterward the dancing ritual and homage to their star deity was more ecstatic than usual, and the young women danced totally naked and made a display of themselves to Deering, or so Melissa thought. Several times individual wooden cups of liquor were passed to them, but they declined and after a while could sense an edge to one or two of the women trying to foist the drinks on them.

That night, back at their hut and charged from all of the sexual display, Deering was a little more cuddly, but Melissa was still too rattled to respond and turned on her side away from him. They both fell into a light, if disturbed, sleep.

CHAPTER TWENTY-TWO

It rained hard that night, and the clouds blocked out the early-morning light, so the two of them woke up later than usual. Bennett told Melissa to continue packing food and water for their trip, that they were going to leave today. Melissa thought they should eat with the others to gain some strength for their long canoe trip, but should be as cautious as the previous night and only eat from common pots. The women welcomed them to their first meal, which they were just finishing up. They ate rice and vegetables with bread, and there were some left-over bird eggs. Deering showed Melissa how to crack the large eggs and swallow the yolk and its white albumin.

"Great protein," Deering insisted.

While Melissa helped clean the common area and wash the plates, Deering headed back to the lake to move the canoe in the low light down to the entrance furo for easier and quicker access. The overnight rainfall had helped fill the lake, and there was only a few feet of muddy border now. He pushed the canoe out into water, his boots and pants covered with the slushy mud, but was able to wash himself off with a dip in the lake. When he reached the furo, the passageway was much narrower, but still navigable.

He paddled the canoe down to the furo path, but wasn't sure if he should just tie the boat to an overhanging branch, or whether he needed to hide it here as well. On several occasions Ikagi's recent concern about them leaving the village was troubling and made him much more cautious in their dealings with her. If found, would the women move or destroy the canoe and block their escape? Deering found a good hiding place twenty yards up from path, pulled the canoe up and under the foliage and lay a cover of branches over it.

As he walked back up the path, Bennett became a bit woozy and figured it was due to this early-morning exertion, but then his mind became fogged over like what Jo and Hawks had described. His last thought before his mind and body were taken over by the powerful potion, was how did they drug him? Suddenly, one of the Amazon women appeared in the shadows of the overhanging trees, and she forcefully grabbed Deering by the arm and dragged him into the jungle. He tried to fight off the sexual impulse rising in him but it was too overwhelming. Even if his mind wanted to resist, his body wouldn't let him. His mind went blank, but some part of him could feel the erotic sensations of this animalistic conjoining, and he ravaged the woman, who repeatedly clawed him on the back and chest. Afterward Deering lay on the wet undergrowth for some time before he fully recovered his senses. The woman had gone, but he knew that the jungle beast would kill him like it had killed the other men.

Deering slipped into his wet clothes and hurried back to the village, circling around in the jungle to the back of his hut so as not to alert the women in the commons area. He called to Melissa from there and told her to bring him a change of clothing and his backpack. They had decided that Deering would carry the heavier water containers and Melissa the food items. She was puzzled by this request, but gathered up Deering's clothes and grabbed his backpack. She stuffed Adam's journal and some keepsakes she had gathered into the backpack. Melissa looked outside, and when it was clear, she hurried around to the back of the hut.

She was alarmed by what she found. "Bennett. What the hell happened?"

"They drugged me somehow, and on the way back from the furo where I left the canoe, one of the women attacked me, and we had sex." Melissa looked astonished. "I couldn't help it, really. It was overpowering."

She nodded her head. "Jesus. But we were careful with what we ate and drank."

"Look, we don't have time to talk about it. Go back into the hut, get me a drying cloth, and meet me at the spring. Act casual, as if nothing has happened and that you're just getting washed up."

Melissa was able to walk across the commons without much notice. With the heavy rains the last two days, most of the women were in the fields working together to plant and irrigate their next crop. She did see Ikagi stick her head out of the hut as she passed, but Melissa didn't engage her in conversation. At the spring, which was on the other side of the village from fields, Bennett had already washed himself but hid behind the tree until he could get dressed. He didn't want her to see all the scratch marks on his chest and back.

"Really, Bennett. We are sleeping together."

Nevertheless, she handed him the drying cloth and turned her back as he got dressed. "So, how did they drug you?" Melissa asked.

"I've been thinking about that," Deering said, "and, since you're not affected and we pretty much ate out of the same pots, they must've laced the entire meal with a drug that only affects men."

"Is that even possible?"

"It could be a herbal testosterone enhancer mixed with some kind of psychedelic, which the enhancer offsets in the women, and it only affects men."

"But . . . ?" Melissa questioned.

"We don't have time to debate this; I'm on a death-watch, and I've got to get us out of here now."

"Of course. Sorry, Bennett," Melissa said and hugged him.

"You head back to the hut across the commons, and I'll pick up the water pack and take the jungle route back to the lake path, and then at the lake head down to the furo where

I'm going to bring the canoe." He explained to Melissa exactly where he would be with the canoe, asked her if she could find it, and she nodded her head. "You carry the food pack but strap it to your back, and I'll be waiting for you at the canoe."

"Ikagi was watching me earlier. What do I tell her if she asks where I'm going with the backpack?"

"Tell her that we're camping out and looking for the canoe."

"Okay. Luckily, she and the old Keeper seem to be the only women in the village right now."

"Good. Let's take advantage of that, but don't let her follow you. Give me enough time to cut back through to where I hid the canoe and to bring it to where I said I'd meet you." Bennett gave her a half-hug and then hurried back into the jungle.

Melissa hid her dry clothes and Deering's wet ones in the drying cloth and headed back to the hut. As she walked across the commons, Ikagi again stuck her head out of the grass door, but Melissa kept going and slipped into their hut. She shoved two sets of clean clothes for them in her backpack, but they would leave everything else behind.

She waited for nearly an hour, which would've been plenty of time for Deering to cut back and bring the canoe around, and, hopefully, Ikagi had given up her surveillance of them. When Melissa stepped out of the hut, her pack strapped to her back, she turned to head down the furo path. Before she took two steps, Ikagi ran over to her.

"Where you go with things?" she asked rather suspiciously.

"Just food. We camp out by lake to look for canoe," Melissa said.

Ikagi gave her a cold penetrating look. "Where man?"

"He down by lake. I meet him there, and we build camp. You come visit later."

"I not believe," Ikagi said in a deepening voice. "You leave for white man's world."

Melissa finally said in all confidence. "I not want lie, Ikagi, but man have sex with woman, and we afraid beast kill him."

Ikagi grabbed Melissa by the arm. "You leave, but man must stay."

Melissa furiously shook her head and pulled her arm away. "I need him!"

Ikagi's voice deepened further and a dark shadow seemed to pass over her features, she yelled, "I need man too."

Suddenly, Ikagi's face started to grow a ridge that bulged out from behind her eyebrows; her face began to expand and become hairy, with large teeth sprouting from her enlarged mouth.

Melissa looked on in disbelief. For a few seconds she couldn't speak or move. Then she screamed. Adrenaline surged through her body as she dropped everything and ran down the path. Her mind seemed separated from the world around her, but she thought she could hear something chasing after her. Her shoes came untied and she ran out of them and race barefooted across the jungle path. The nicks from rough roots and thorns bloodied her feet but also added to her adrenalin rush. Melissa knew that she couldn't fall or falter now. If she did, she would be dead.

In the distance, she could see Deering and the canoe at the end of the path. He used one of the paddles to push the canoe through the mud and closer to shore. Seeing Melissa running for her life and sensing that she was in immediate danger, he stepped onto the path wielding one of their makeshift axes. Melissa could hear the animal growling and getting closer. At the furo she practically launched herself into Deering's arms as he stood in the mud three feet away. He caught Melissa, hurriedly placed her and the axe in the canoe, then pushed it out of the mud into the water and hopped aboard.

Deering pulled the starter cord several times but the outboard motor wouldn't catch. The beast had now reached the edge of the path, only separated from them by twenty feet or so. Deering desperately tried to start the motor, afraid the beast might enter the water and swim after them, but it stopped at the edge of the muddy furo border, and then the jungle beast ROARED, and ROARED again. The sound vibrations practically knocked him backward. This set off Melissa, scared out of her mind, to screaming in reply. The beast crouched down in preparation to launch itself toward the canoe just as the motor came to life. Deering, with shaking hands, was able to turn the motor's throttle to full speed allowing both of them to escape the prospect of imminent death.

As Deering looked back to make sure they were out of reach, he could see the beast slowly transforming back into a human shape. In a few moments he could recognize who the beast was turning into. It was Ikagi—an astonishing sight he could barely believe.

Deering reached over. "Melissa, stop. Look back."

Mellisa turned toward the beast to find Akagi almost fully back to herself standing there at the path's end. Instead of seeing the terrifying face of the beast, in its place she saw Ikagi's face again torn by the sadness she had seen earlier. However, this time it drew no sympathy from her. Melissa shouted, "She killed them; she killed all of them!" She now fainted and fell back onto the floor of the canoe. As Ikagi stood statue-like, Deering continued to maneuver the canoe to the other end of the lake until they reached the next furo. It appeared to be shallower than the other furo and after several hundred yards, the engine sputtered to a stop. Deering now paddled over to the other side of the furo and moored the canoe to an overhanging limb to attend to Melissa. He lifted her up and braced her against the front of the canoe, then dipped a cloth into one of the water jugs and patted her face. She came around, blinking her eyes and trying to focus on him.

"It's all right, Melissa. We made it out of there, and they can't reach us now."

"Water."

Deering hurriedly poured water into their cup-bowl and she sipped it dry, and he kept refilling it until she had had enough.

"Oh my God, Bennett. It was her all along. How did we miss

that?"

"Melissa, dear. Don't think about it, just rest. We'll talk later, but now I have to take advantage of the light to spot the ribbons and get us out of here."

"Oh, God, the ribbons. I hope the rain hasn't washed them away."

Bennett patted her arm. "Don't worry. We just need to head west into the setting sun, the reverse of Ika's inbound direction."

"But the outboard, it shut down," she added.

Deering now slipped over the edge of the canoe into the rivulet and stepped over to the outboard. He reached down and pulled the vines and plant stems that clung to the rotor. He held them up for Melissa to see. "It's not the outboard; it's the river plants—why we paddled into here earlier."

"Oh, Bennett. Can you really paddle us out of here?" Melissa asked in a plaintive voice.

"As I recall, there's only a mile or so of furos too shallow to motor through. We'll be all right."

Deering now slid back into the canoe. He put the water pack behind her back for more of a cushion, and returned to the back of the canoe and started to paddle from one side to the other heading down the furo west toward the sun, now lower in the sky but still clouded over. He crossed over and stuck to the south side of the furos where Hawks had strung the ribbons as Ika directed them east into the jungle. An hour later, he spotted one of the ribbons on a low branch at the intersection of two furos and took the one bearing in a westward direction. In the next couple of hours, he found two more and kept heading toward the now-setting sun. Before they lost the light of day, Deering paddled over to a clearing.

Melissa looked over at him. "Why are we stopping? We still have another hour of light."

"Yes, but I'm exhausted, and we've lost the food pack and need to scrounge around in the jungle for something to eat before we camp for the night."

Melissa nodded her head. "Sorry. All I could think of was getting away as fast as I could."

Deering carefully crawled to the back of the canoe. "I wasn't complaining, my dear. Just starting a fact."

"Well, tomorrow I can help you paddle."

"I think the next furo will be deep enough for me to start the outboard."

"Let's hope it was the clogged rotor and not the engine itself," Melissa said.

"Courtesy of Connor Croft, this is a fairly new outboard, one of the two that Hawks had wired money ahead for Jo to buy. It'll work just fine."

The mere mention of the boy's name brought tears to Melissa's eyes. Deering now started to slip out of the canoe, and Melissa followed after him. "Whoo. I think you need to stay here; you're still weak," said Deering.

"Yes, but you don't know the local fruits and berries like I do, and you might just poison us," Melissa joked.

Deering smiled. "Good point." He now helped Melissa out of the canoe into the shallow water, and they stepped up to the small clearing. Deering had grabbed a canvass bag, and it only took them twenty minutes to pick enough fruits and berries to sustain them for another day.

They sat in the canoe—they decided they'd sleep there, since the jungle was filled with predators and they didn't have the numbers to keep them at bay.

"So what's the plan, Bennett?" Melissa asked while they were munching away on their yellow passion fruit.

"Well, once we can use the outboard, I think it's only a half day back to the Rio Arroyo, and then it's not too far, or only hours, to the Rio Pardo, and then up the Curuca River."

"So we're not going to stop at the Uni tribe village?" Melissa asked.

Deering shook his head. "Not after losing Ika and even Hawks, who they had an attachment to."

"You don't think they'll sympathize with our plight?"

"That's just it. We can't tell how they'll react. Again, they're Stone Age tribesmen held together by kinship ties, and we just got one of their brothers killed."

"But how long can we last eating fruits and berries?" Melissa asked.

"Well, I figure once we get out from under this jungle overhang, on the Rio Arroyo, or at least the Rio Pardo River, you're father's scouts might spot us."

"I think he'd have boats in the water as well," Melissa said. Deering nodded. She went on, "So we just need to last a few days, and we might just get rescued while we are still in relatively good shape, or so we hope."

"We can't plan on getting swooped up by a rescue party. Fortunately, we have enough fuel with only the two of us to make it back to Benjamin Constant."

Melissa sighed. "Yes, only the two of us. Are we ready to talk about this?"

"Wish we had filled one of the jugs with their plant liquor, but, yes, it's playing on our minds, and we need to talk it out before we get to sleep."

"Okay, let me begin," Melissa said.

CHAPTER TWENTY-THREE

"What really gets me is that I trusted Ikagi, felt a bond with her and her tribe of women, and thought they were gentle souls like the bonobos, who your friend said released their aggression through continual sexual contact."

"I failed to mention that my friend said he believed the bonobos's gentle nature may have more to do with their ample food supply than their release of aggression through sexual sharing."

"But she lied to me. She said she couldn't stop the beast, and it was her all along."

Deering shook his head. "It wasn't only her. I think it was all of them. When you yelled at her to stop the beast, she said 'We can't stop.' And while the beast was dragging Hawks to his death, you were imploring Ikagi to stop him. She couldn't be in two places at the same time—there had to be more than one of them that could change into that beast."

Melissa paused for a moment. "So you think they all had this beast within them?"

"Well, remember the morning after Hawks was killed, and the woman who had a gash on her right leg?"

"Of course, where you had struck the beast with the axe."

"And later that day when we came back from the lake, she was walking around fully healed."

"Well, we've seen the effects of Medi's potions; look how fast Hawks's torn ligament partially healed."

"I think it was that and also her . . . metamorphosis."

"An animal's accelerated healing ability?" Melissa asked. Deering nodded his head. "But why kill the men?"

"Well, they couldn't kill them when they first arrived; they needed to procreate with them for the tribe to survive, so something triggers the beast to emerge and kill them."

"Maybe the conception, like we figured with Luison, is what triggers the metamorphosis."

"That would explain how Adam had sex with Medi early on without any . . . consequences," Deering said.

"Okay, but Ika was killed nearly four months ago and none of the women have shown."

"Some women, especially those who are very fit like these women, don't show much in their first few months of pregnancy."

"But why kill them at all?" Melissa asked.

"I know. I've been trying to figure that out, and then I thought that like us, most of the tribesmen would approach the village during the wet season, maybe toward its end, when the rivers and furos were still navigable."

"So, they're getting pregnant during a dry period with low protein content in their diet," Melissa said thinking to herself. "Oh my God. Could it be the pregnancy triggers the metamorphosis because of the need to eat meat for protein to sustain the fetus's early spurt of growth?"

"Yes, it could, and it could also be that the metamorphosis allows them to distance themselves from the natural revulsion of eating human flesh."

"But why didn't they just keep hunting game?" Melissa asked.

"It's like Jo said about tribes moving about after they had depleted an area of its game, but to stay undetected, the Amazon women couldn't move, and evolution, or some other process, provided them with an alternative."

Melissa leaned back against the water pack. "But, it started to rain again, and they could go fish in the lake, so why kill you?"

"Like Ikagi said, they can't stop it; it's inbred at this point. I think if a man showed up with a cooler filled with steaks, they'd still be compelled to mate with and kill him."

"Jesus. We need to warn the other tribes!"

"The tribes already know they are in danger from their own belief in their jealous beast myth and they have survived for hundreds, if not thousands, of years interacting with these women. Nothing we can tell them will keep them from seeking out these beautiful women. And without tribesmen fathering more children, the women can't survive as a tribe."

Melissa looked back at him in frustration. "What if we made this a small-game reserve? Maybe they could see their way back to hunting again and just mate with these men and not kill them. We could bring them into the civilized world."

"But this metamorphosis is an adaptation ingrained in their being. Trying to change it or to bring them into the civilized world may produce unintended consequences not just for them, but for the outside world as well."

"So, we don't tell anyone about this—it remains our secret?" Melissa asked.

Deering shrugged his shoulders. "We'll figure that out later, and really, that's the least of our worries right now. We need to find our way out of here and then we need to come up with a plausible story to explain the deaths of the others; I mean, there will be inquiries by the Brazilian government."

"Oh shit, what are we going to say?"

"Look, we're really tired. Let's get some sleep, if we can, and talk about it on our trip out."

Deering now started to make room to sleep at the other end of the canoe. "Hey, buddy. You sleep down here." Melissa leveled the pack out to make a pillow, lay back with her legs spread for Bennett to sleep with his head on her stomach.

He smiled. "Yes, a much better accommodation."

They had moored both ends of the canoe to overhead hanging branches, so it was more stable and less likely to tip over with them moving about inside. They both quickly fell asleep, despite the light rainfall, but it was a restless sleep. Melissa dreamt about her confrontation with Ikagi in the village and how she began to transform into this jungle beast. She relived her race down the furo path and her rescue by Deering, but then she watched the jungle beast slowly turning back into her friend Ikagi. She saw the tears welling up in her eyes as Melissa cried as well, and they had a moment of eye contact before the dream ended. Melissa was left with a deeper understanding of the dilemma faced by the Amazon women.

Melissa woke up alone in the canoe. She rubbed her eyes clear, and then heard Deering tramping back through the jungle to the canoe. "I didn't want to wake you, and I thought I'd gather some breakfast for us while you were sleeping."

He handed her the canvass bag with the fruits and berries, and slipped back into the canoe. Melissa examined them carefully. "I watched where you picked last night's meal. Should be the same things."

"Okay, but if I get food poisoning, I'll feed you to the crocs."

Deering puts up his hands. "Fair enough."

They began to eat their breakfast while sipping water from their one wooden bowl-cup. Melissa's eyes seemed to lose their focus and after a short while she said, "I think I know why they give up their male babies."

"I silently thought about that question while we were with them and could never really come to a convincing answer" replied Deering.

Melissa added, "You know, despite the metamorphosis they go through, compelled by something we don't understand, they're still mothers and we've seen how well they nurture their female offspring. Even the bonobo mothers, as your friend reported, keep close bonds with their male offspring."

"Many primitive tribes kill female infants but honor their male offspring because they grow up to be hunters of game and future tribal protectors. So giving up a male is a puzzling turnabout."

Melissa eyes were now clearly focused, "They know what will eventually happen to these boys once they come of age—they would rather give them away than see them face what's in store for them."

Deering nodded. "You're right, and I guess that's a benign instinct."

"Bennett. It's terrible what they did and how we lost the others, but as you said, they are driven to perpetuate their species."

Bennett reached over and took her hand. "Let's not talk about it. We've got a couple long days ahead of us and we need our strength—unless we're really lucky and get rescued by dear old dad."

Melissa laughed. "Connor is going to have a fit when he finds us."

"So you think he's out here with the hired help?"

"Most definitely. He's always been one to lead the charge."

"Well, his checkbook could come in handy when dealing with the Brazilian authorities; they are fairly corrupt and open to bribes," Deering added.

"Yeah, we do need to come up with our . . . cover story."

"First, let's get going while it's still fairly cool." Deering collected the scooped-out fruit and berry vines and tossed them overboard. "Reach up and untie your end of cord, and I'll do the back end." After they had pushed away from shore and Deering had paddled to the middle of the furo, he started the engine with just one pull. "Hopefully, it's deep enough here to motor our way out."

Deering steered down the middle of the furo, but when they came to some forking furos, he glided closer to the south side looking for Hawks' colored strings to get directions. Finding more markers and heading west each time, they had finally reached the Rio Arroyo River by early afternoon. Deering pulled over under the overhang of branches. "I think this is our story: the next day after visiting the Marubo tribe and after a heavy rainfall and with difficult river currents, the second canoe tripped over with Paulo, Adam, and you. And while I was able to rescue you, we lost Paulo and Adam. The Marubo tribe will probably have found Paulo's chewed up remains in the river south of their village and pieces of the canoe, and its believable that Adam's body was never found. But, given that you were in charge, you thought it was best we continue on to Hawks's tribe. After staying there for several weeks, we heard of another uncontacted tribe deeper in the jungle, and one of their young men agreed to take us there. We found them, but were attacked by another tribe, and we lost Hawks and the native boy in the battle. The rivers had receded during this period and we were forced to stay with the uncontacted tribe during the dry season. With the return of the rains, you and I made our way back to where we were rescued, or if not, to Benjamin Constants."

"Won't they want us to take them back to the second uncontacted tribe?" Melissa asked.

"We'll say we've been traveling for days, ran out of food, and were near delirious by the time we were rescued, and wouldn't be able to retrace our route."

"It's a good thing you collected the color ribbon markers," Melissa added.

"Yeah, we better get rid of them where no one will ever find them." Deering slipped out of the canoe, stepped into the jungle, dug a hole and buried the ribbons, and disguised his trail back to the boat.

"You want to rest or try to find some more fruit?"

Melissa shook her head. "In fact, after our last two meals, I need to use the ladies room."

Deering pointed to the jungle. "Be my guest, but turn off the overhead light when you're finished."

Once they headed up the Rio Arrojo, which was filling up with the recent rains, it was only an hour or so—given that they were traveling lighter and faster—until they came to the turnoff for the Rio Pardo, which was a much wider river. While they were motoring up the Pardo, a high-flying plane spotted them and flew down to get a better look. Melissa crouched in the canoe and waved to them. It was a small two-engine Cessna, which slowed down, came around, and flew over them at two hundred feet. Someone with a bullhorn yelled out, "If you're Dr. Croft, stop waving your hands."

Melissa pulled them down, and they circled around and made another pass. "Keep heading up the Rio Pardo to the Curuca." The plane now flew off and gained altitude, no doubt heading back to an airfield near Benjamin Constants. An hour later, as they were turning onto the Rio Curuca, they came upon a large double-decker river boat. It stopped in the middle of the river, and they were directed to pull the canoe alongside of it. Melissa was lifted up onto the boat and then they reached out for Deering. Before Deering attempted to come aboard he inconspicuously slipped the remaining bronze axe into the river where it sank to the bottom.

After a doctor had checked them over and had taken blood samples, a Brazilian police officer stepped over holding a clipboard with photos of their expedition members. He checked off their photos. "And what happened to Sterling Hawks and Dr. Caruthers, and your guides Paulo Sousa and Joao Silva?"

Deering spoke up. "They were killed, two in a canoe tip-over, and two by hostile Indians, but we're still pretty much in shock, so can you wait for the details."

The man nodded his head. "Yes, of course. But we will conduct an official investigation. The guides were citizens of Brazil."

"We understand, and we'll be completely forthright with you."

Someone now escorted them to a bedroom with a bath where they could wash up, and that person then brought them something to eat.

Melissa asked. "Is my father, Connor Croft, onboard?"

"No, ma'am. But we've alerted him about your rescue, and he will be waiting back at the county seat in Benjamin Constants."

"Can I talk to him by radio phone?"

"Yes. I will arrange that."

After the aide left, Melissa turned to Deering. "Let's take a shower together, so we can talk." As the hot water poured over them and they began to soap up, Melissa said, "You and Dad handle the police; I'm going to play the role of the wilting female in shock."

Deering laughed, "This I've got to see."

Back in Benjamin Constants, Melissa had her reunion with Connor, who upon hearing some of her doctored story, was more inclined to cut Deering some slack for allowing this expedition to "get out of hand." He was even more pleased when he discovered that the two of them had coupled up and had plans to stay together. They were required by the government to stay in Brazil for another week before they could fly home. The government pressed Deering to do a flyover in a scout plane with one of their jungle officials to spot the second village, but he begged off and told them that he didn't follow the guide's direction into the jungle and coming back they were delirious and just headed west or into the setting sun. They were not satisfied, but Connor was able to forestall their inquiry with a series of bribes going all the way up to the regional governor. He also agreed to compensate the families of the two guides for their loss, which further helped resolve the situation and freed Deering and Melissa to return home. Melissa urged her father to consider a grant to create an indigenous zone in the area they had visited that would be off-limits to the outside world. It would be designed to protect the few remaining uncontacted tribes in this region from any detrimental unintended consequences the outside world might inflict upon it, and he started a conversation with the appropriate government officials.

Finally, on the flight back to the States in the Croft Pharmaceuticals' private plane, Connor sat across from the two of them. "Okay, cut the crap, what really happened?"

"Are you sure you want to hear this?" Melissa asked as she began to shiver just from the thought of retelling the story.

He took one look at the fear and terror in his daughter's

eyes and Deering's equally shattered look, and reconsidered his request. "You know, maybe it's better I don't know. I'm just glad to have you back, and as Conrad said, the jungle is "The Heart of Darkness," and so let's leave it at that." Melissa sighed in relief. "But, my dear, you're going into therapy, and you can work it all out with your doctor."

She started to resist, but Deering grabbed her hand. "I think your father is right, Melissa. It was quite an ordeal, and we both need to put this behind us and go forward with our lives . . . together."

Connors smiled. "Excellent. When's the wedding?"

*****

Mattie sat back in her chair in total astonishment. "Not your typical 'boy meets girl, boy beds girl, and they live happily ever after romance.'"

"Which was not the case with us."

"Tell me, mother. If you recall, I lived through it."

Melissa now leaned forward and coughed up several dark wads of phlegm. Mattie reached for the caller.

"No. I don't want to be interrupted."

"Mother, seems like we've come to the end of your story. Let's let Joel tend to you now."

"You believe me, don't you?" Melissa said. She could see the doubt in her daughter's eyes. "You must promise me not to reveal this story to anyone and to keep the area we had set aside as off-limits to any intrusion from the outside world."

Mattie paused to control any unseemly reaction given her mother's condition. "Well, yes, I will do the best I can."

"Don't patronize me, dear. You must believe what I've told you and carry out my request."

"Well, carrying out your request would be a first," Mattie said.

Melissa laughed, which caused another paroxysm of coughing. "Your father wanted to tell you earlier." She now struggled to sit up in bed. "But I insisted that we wait. He may have even written a letter to you, but I never saw it."

This peaked Mattie's interest. "A letter confirming your story?"

"Yes, and maybe more. Your father was a very complex man with deep feelings."

They both let this sentiment settle. "Did either of you ever return to Brazil?"

"No. Not even for the ceremony initiating the indigenous zone that Connor arranged to have set aside."

"Connor never mentioned it."

"He refused to go back himself and was one of the last pharmaceutical companies to explore that region for plant cures."

"That's surprising."

"Well, he may have talked with my psychiatrist and gotten a hint of the trauma I endured and felt an abhorrence for the region."

Melissa felt very tired and had Mattie lower her bed to a reclining position. She gave her a moment to rest. "Mother, why are you telling me this now?"

"Your father and I want the tribal people's lives to remain as they are. We believe both the women's tribe and the outside world are better off without knowledge of each other. But on a personal level, this was a terrible ordeal. It shocked me and made me reassess my life of privilege. It changed forever my relationship with men and with your father. It deepened my feeling response, not just toward myself, but to others and to life itself." Melissa's voice became whisper soft and Mattie had to lean in very close to hear her next words, "I'm hoping this might start you on a similar journey."

Melissa now closed her eyes, took a deep breath, and began to slip away.

"Mother. Mother! Are you all right?" When Mattie didn't get a response, she pushed the caller button and Dr. Marcum hurried into the room. Mattie stepped back as he called his medical entourage in for assistance. Melissa never woke up again and died peacefully in her sleep later that night. Mattie stayed the whole time, haunted by her mother's tale and her deathbed entreaty to her, and determined to discover if there was any truth to her mother's changeling story.

EPILOGUE

Mattie suffered through her mother's funeral at the Catholic Kermit in Key Biscayne, a large affair attended by local dignitaries, including the Cuban-born mayor and the current CEO of Croft Pharmaceuticals, Brent Howell. CROFT PHARMA was now a public company conglomerate listed on the New York stock exchange. Mattie owned a controlling 51 percent share from her inheritance. She held the after-funeral gathering at the family home, following her mother's expressed wishes. Mattie would have had it at the Ritz Carlton to accommodate everybody who attended the funeral, but her mother wanted this to be of a more personal nature. Mattie's ex-husband, Everett Foster, had called and offered to accompany her to both events, especially now that she was one of the wealthiest women in the world, but she told him to panhandle somewhere else. She was escorted by her mother's elderly black assistant, Edward Balsam. Mattie stood in the condolence line for an hour and afterward let Brent act as the host while everyone stuffed their mouths with food.

The next day Mattie couldn't wait to start looking through her family's archives for that letter her father may have written her, or any other evidence to support her mother's outrageous story. Balsam had helped her find and gather the albums and memorabilia earlier in the week. She had also checked the family's safe deposit box at Chase bank in Miami, but there was nothing of interest there pertaining to her search.

Mattie turned the family's huge redwood dining table into her work station, and looked through the last photo album first, where her mother had pasted such things as her college diploma and the publishing announcements for her two books, along with the many newspaper clippings about her grandfather and her father's deaths. She then went back and quickly scanned through the albums devoted to her grandparents' life and her mother's childhood. Mattie only looked in earnest at those albums starting in the mid-1960s when her mother had first planned this expedition to the Amazon. She was discouraged to find several pages where photos or clippings had been removed, but there was still enough left behind to tell the story of her mother's rescue from the Amazon, her wedding to Bennett Deering, and Mattie's birth several years later. But there was nothing about the actual expedition or any photos of it. She remembered the photo of two of the explorers— Sterling Hawks and the native guide Joao, taken at a boatshed in Tabatinga, Brazil—but her mother had taken that from her as a child and ripped it up.

What she did review and kept turning the pages to read was the story of their lives after their return from South America. Her mother accompanied her father on every archeological dig after that to the detriment of her own career—although these expeditions sometimes brought them to ancient sites where Melissa could continue to study the area's ancient languages. What was interesting was that after the Amazon Basin expedition, her father didn't go traipsing off to the Middle East or to the ancient Mesopotamian sites of Assyria in northern Iraq, the questionable home of Hawks's axe and its supposed connection to these Amazon women, despite the worldwide archeological interest in the area in the 1970s and 80s. If there had been any truth to Melissa's story, you would have thought they would have followed up on it, but after South America, he focused on India, Indonesian, and China. The photos also verified what she had long suspected: her parent's relationship flourished on these expeditions but floundered when they were stuck at home in Miami and were required to do the civilized dance with their family and friends. As a school girl, she had been to some of the later digs in India and China on vacations from school, but by then there was something missing in their relationship, or something continued to bother them and split them further apart. Images from her mother's story kept tugging at her. She would need to talk with Dr. Marcum to put them to rest.

They met at Marcum's Mount Sinai Key Biscayne Physician offices. He figured this was just a routine follow-up about her mother's last illness and death, but once he heard the subject of the inquiry, he stood up and closed his office door and motioned Mattie over to the couch setting.

"First of all, Madeline, your mother did not have Alzheimer's disease or a severe form of dementia."

"Yes, I realized that, but what concerns me is the story she told me in the last hours of her death about . . ."

Marcum held up his hand. "Please, don't share the contents with me. I respect your mother's request to keep this conversation with you private."

"Okay, I wasn't going to go into specific details anyway, but then tell me, from your experience with deathbed patients and maybe research into the matter, if any near- death patients suddenly go bonkers and tell the most bizarre tales."

Marcum consider this for a moment. "Actually, it's usually contrary to that, in what is now officially called Terminal Lucidity, mentally impaired patients, even those with sever Alzheimer's, suddenly have moments or even hours of complete lucidity. They recall names, their histories together, and surroundings usually just prior to dying."

Mattie considered this phenomenon and noted that her mother was more lucid than on her last visit several weeks earlier.

The doctor asked, "Does this story, without giving me any details, refer to your mother's expedition to the Amazon in which four people were killed?"

Mattie nodded. "Yes."

"May I venture a . . . diagnosis of sorts, based on my talk with your mother's psychiatrist?"

"She was still seeing him?" Mattie asked.

"Yes, after your father's death, Melissa suffered from bouts of depression, but this . . . confession—or I assume it was—could be a case of survivor's guilt. And not just 'what I could've done' or 'should've done' to prevent it, but as Carl Jung says about dreams, how they often compensate the conscious mind's attitude, Melissa could have imagined a scenario with great discoveries that justified their loss, and with great clarity in the end, I might add, as you may have noticed."

Mattie sighed in relief. "Of course. This explains it." She paused. "Carl Jung. I would never have suspected an interest there."

"Well, Madeline, dealing with your family over the years did stretch my normal resources."

Mattie laughed as they both stood. She shook the doctor's hand. "Thank you, Joel. You've set my mind to rest."

Mattie now turned and walked out of the doctor's office, heading back to the university to finally finish proofing that article for the Journal of Evolutionary Biology.

That night at the mansion, Mattie packed the albums into a box for safe keeping—maybe, if she ever got married, her children would want to see them. But as she was handling one of the larger albums, it slipped out of her hand and fell onto the hardwood floor. Its binding split, and a small notebook that had been sewn into the inside back cover of the album spilled out. Mattie picked it up off the floor and sat down.

She was astonished by what she found. A journal entitled Miracle Cures from an Expedition to the Western Amazon Basin by Dr. Adam Caruthers."

As she scanned through the hand-written twenty-page journal, she saw drawings of rare plants and herbs with a description of how they were used by a local medicine man named Alem and his apprentice, Eno, which must have been from Hawks's tribe. Some of the miraculous claims were startling, but it was troubling that several pages at the end of the journal appeared to have been ripped out of the book. Why didn't her parents share this journal with her grandfather, who had paid for this expedition in search of medicinal plants? She immediately thought of Brent Howell, who had convinced the board years earlier to mount an expedition into the eastern Amazon basin, which had been fruitful, to see if they could next venture into this indigenous zone. One of the stipulations of her grandfather's ongoing grant to keep the area protected had been that, while the tribes would be protected, at some point the medicinal plant cures of this region would be exploited by their company with a percentage of the profits going back to the tribes. Mattie wondered if now, after the area's indigenous tribes and plants had been protected for fifty years, the time was ripe to retrieve these miracle cures.

BIBLIOGRAPHY

Chagnon, Napoleon A. Noble Savages. New York: Simon & Schuster, 2013.

Lamb, F. Bruce. Wizard of the Upper Amazon. Berkeley, CA: North Atlantic Books, 1986.

Mayor, Adrienne. The Amazons. Princeton, NJ: Princeton University Press, 2014.

Plotkin, Mark. Tales of a Shaman's Apprentice. New York: Penguin Books, 1993.

Wallace, Scott. The Unconquered. New York: Broadway Books, 2012.

Weisberger, Jonathan Miller. Rainforest Medicine. Berkeley, CA: North Atlantic Books, 2013.

AUTHOR

John Minichielli is an outdoorsman and adventurer who spent many years of his life traveling to the most remote places on the planet. His love of sport fishing and exploring new areas continues to motivate him to seek out new experiences on the edge of civilization.

Website: LegendOfTheAmazons.com